Praise for *Coincidence* and David Ambrose

'The joy of this intelligent, arresting and chilling text
isn't just the not knowing, for Ambrose has pulled off the
stickiest of tricks: a mystery that grows ever more
satisfying as the pieces are put in order' *The Times*

'The suspense is so good it's almost painful . . . the ideal
book for fans of fast-forward thrillers' *Sunday Express*

'A chilling tale that gets the old grey matter ticking'
Mirror

'Impossible to put down!' *B Magazine*

'Highly ingenious storytelling' Douglas Adams

'David Ambrose has a unique approach to the thriller'
Clare Francis

'No one monkeys around with your mind quite like
David Ambrose' Paul Davies, *Mirror*

'He just gets better and better' Anne Robinson, *Guardian*

'Ambrose writes with verve and lucidity, carrying the
reader with him every step of the way' *The Times*

'Disturbing but also exhilarating'
John Bayley, *Evening Standard*

Also by David Ambrose

The Man Who Turned into Himself
Mother of God
Hollywood Lies
Superstition
The Discrete Charm of Charlie Monk
A Memory of Demons

David Ambrose

COINCIDENCE

POCKET
BOOKS

LONDON • SYDNEY • NEW YORK • TOKYO • SINGAPORE • TORONTO

First published in Great Britain by Simon & Schuster UK Ltd, 2001
This edition published by Pocket Books, 2003
An imprint of Simon & Schuster UK Ltd
A Viacom company

A CIP catalogue record for this book is available from the British
Library

ISBN 0-7434-1573-6

Typeset by SX Composing DTP, Rayleigh, Essex
Printed and bound in Great Britain by
Cox & Wyman Ltd, Reading, Berkshire

'The unexamined life is not worth living.'

Socrates

'Philosophy. . . leaves everything as it is.'

Wittgenstein

GEORGE

CHAPTER 1

It started with my father's death. At least, that was how it seemed at the time. Now, looking back, I realize how impossible it is to be sure where anything really begins; or, for that matter, where, or even whether, it has ended.

I was alone at our apartment in Manhattan for the weekend. My wife, Sara, was in Chicago checking out a couple of young artists who were exhibiting there. She had her own gallery downtown in TriBeCa and a reputation for bringing new talent to the attention of a sophisticated market at just the right time. It was Sunday evening and I'd spent the day alone, trying to work up an idea for a new book. I write non-fiction books that occupy a kind of no-man's-land between real science and fantastical speculation. I've dealt with poltergeists, ESP of various kinds, stone circles, ley lines, the Pyramids. You get the idea. I have a good time and never knowingly write junk. I mean I don't just invent stuff or make claims I can't support without at least a respectable amount of evidence. They're not best-sellers, but at least they do well enough to keep my publishers coming back for more, so I suppose I can't complain. But I didn't have the vaguest notion what my next subject was going to be. I felt I was in a dead end, written out. Nothing would come together no matter how long I cudgelled my brain in search of a theme or framework that had some spark of novelty.

Around six thirty I poured myself a Scotch and took it out on the terrace where I watched the lights coming up across the park. It was the time of year when the trees were turning into a rich blend of copper, gold and red. Looking at them made me think of New England and that whole east coast, and of the small town where my father lived in a retirement home. I'd spoken to him on the phone earlier in the day, as I did most weekends. I went up to see him every couple of months or so, and I was about due for another visit. Maybe I'd go up at the end of the week, I told myself; or at the very latest the week after.

It was at that moment, when the image of my father and his sad frustrated life were at the forefront of my mind, that the phone rang. I went inside to answer it. It was Abigail Tucker, the superintendent of the home. I knew at once from the tone of her voice that he was dead. A heart attack, she said, less than an hour ago.

I thanked her for letting me know so quickly and said I'd take a train up in the morning. She agreed that there was no point in my rushing up immediately. She herself would make arrangements with the funeral home if I wished. I said I would be grateful for that and thanked her again.

When I hung up I didn't move for some time, just stood there looking at my reflection in the window, watching it grow clearer moment by moment as the light outside faded. What were you supposed to feel, I asked myself, on learning of your father's death? Was there something specific, something deep-rooted in the psyche, a special sense of loss? Or growth perhaps? And how remarkable that I should have been thinking of him at that very moment when the call came.

Except, of course, it wasn't at all remarkable. The association of trees, New England, the fact of having spoken to him that morning, and of feeling slightly guilty about putting off my next visit to him as long as I could explained the coincidence. But I felt no rush of remorse, no sense of unfinished business as a result of having missed that last chance to see him, no lack of 'closure', as your local corner therapist would call it. I felt nothing that I hadn't been feeling half an hour earlier. The only difference was that my father had been alive then and was dead now. A simple fact.

But, although I didn't consciously know it then, I had found both the subject and the title of my next book.

Coincidence.

The sky was overcast when I stepped off the train and crossed the footbridge to where a taxi waited to take me the last three miles to the home. As we wound up the hill I looked out at the familiar sights passing by, seeing them for the last time – and feeling, to be honest, little apart from relief that I would not have to make this journey again.

At least, I told myself, he had been well looked after. The place hadn't been cheap and had eaten up my father's modest capital as well as his pension, and had still required several thousand a year from my own pocket. But it was money I'd been happy to pay. Somehow it made up for the lack of warmth between us, allowing me to feel that I at least had done everything I possibly could, and that it was my father who had resented me and kept me at arm's length all my life, not I who had in any way let down, betrayed or walked away from him.

Sara, to her credit, had been as anxious as I was to ensure that he was given the best possible care when it became obvious five years ago that he was no longer fit to live alone. Two falls and a growing drink habit had done that.

He wasn't an alcoholic; it was just something to do. He was bored. My father had been bored, and bitter, almost all of his adult life. He had continued to drink in the home, though far less; it wasn't one of those regimented places that regarded old people as an inconvenience to be drugged senseless and kept out of the way as far as possible. They had their own rooms and, within reason, their own routines.

Mrs Tucker appeared at the door of the handsome old house as I got out of my taxi. She was a pleasant-looking woman around forty, dressed casually for the country and looking more like a favourite aunt than some matronly superintendent. She took me into her office, which looked on to a broad sweep of tree-covered countryside. I was impressed by the efficiency with which she had assembled all the necessary paperwork, but then reflected that this was not exactly a routine she was unaccustomed to in her line of work. Tea was brought in as we took care of everything, after which she drove me to the chapel of rest where my father's body had been taken the previous night. He was lying in a 'temporary casket'; I almost embarrassed myself by laughing out loud when I heard it called that.

We had already decided that the funeral was to be the following morning, Tuesday. There were no far-flung relatives to be informed and who would need time to make travel arrangements, therefore no sense in waiting. I had spoken to Sara, who said she would be back in New York that night and would either take a train or drive up early Tuesday. I told her it wasn't essential she be there and I would understand if she was too busy, but she wouldn't hear of not coming.

It only remained for me to pick the casket in which he would be buried. I chose the one I thought he would have chosen himself: simple to the point of being ascetic, but in the best materials and workmanship available. My father appreciated quality but dismissed with scorn anything that he felt could be described as chichi. Design for him was governed by function, all unnecessary ornamentation being regarded as the worst form of original sin.

I spent the afternoon going through the things in his room. It was bare and anonymous compared with some of the other rooms I glimpsed through open doors as I made my way along the corridor to his. Most people had pictures of their family, treasured possessions accumulated over a lifetime, gifts sent by friends and relatives. My father had nothing of that kind. A few books, mostly thrillers and adventure stories; a couple of suits, some sweaters and casual clothes; four pairs of shoes. The only things in his drawers, most of which were empty, were socks, shirts and underwear. I found his wallet in a bedside drawer. It contained a few dollars in cash, his driver's permit that he hung on to though he hadn't driven in years, and a few yellowing business cards. In the same drawer was a key ring with two small keys that looked as though they might fit a briefcase or a piece of luggage. I had found nothing of that kind in the room, but, as I double-checked, a young woman called Shirley who was on duty that afternoon put her head around the door. She had a round face and a bright smile, and I knew that she had made repeated efforts to draw my father out of his shell, all to no avail. She asked if I needed any help or whether I might like a cup of coffee or anything else. I thanked her and said I was fine, then gave her one half-empty and one unopened bottle of whisky from my father's drinks cabinet and suggested she pass them to one of the gardeners or keep them herself, whatever she chose. I also asked if she could arrange to give away his clothes if they were of use to anyone, otherwise perhaps send them to some local charity shop. She said she would see to it.

'By the way,' she said, 'would you like someone to bring up your father's chest from the store room, or will you deal with it down there?'

'Chest?' I said, surprised, because I had no memory of his having had any such thing when I helped him move in. 'How big?'

'Fairly large,' she said, using her hands to make a shape in the air that suggested a substantial piece of luggage.

'Is it locked?'

'I don't know.'

I looked at the keys that I still held in my hand.

'I'll come down,' I said, 'if you'll show me where it is.'

CHAPTER 2

The storeroom, which had been a four-car garage when the house had been privately owned, was a windowless cavern with two long strips of overhead lighting. One of the gardeners hauled a battered ribbed travelling trunk down from a shelf and dragged it into the middle of the concrete floor. He was delighted when Shirley presented him with the bottles of whisky I had given her, then they both tactfully withdrew to let me go through my father's things in private.

Both locks snapped open like mousetraps, but I hesitated a moment before lifting the lid. My first thought was that a trunk this size must almost certainly contain some of my father's paintings. My father, I should explain, was an unsuccessful artist who had given up in despair and bitterness and finished his working life behind the counter in a gentlemen's haberdashery. After he had been doing that for about a year my mother died – of an accidental overdose, according to the coroner's verdict. I, however, was convinced and still am that it was suicide. My father took his sense of failure out on her, not in any brutish physical way, but with a thousand little mental cruelties. All my life (I was twenty when she died) I had heard his peevish references to the way in which domestic chains were death to an artist's soul. Looking back now, it was almost as though he was preparing himself for a failure that in his heart he knew was unavoidable, and making sure that the blame could be laid elsewhere than on himself. Whether he really had talent or none at all I never knew. When he finally faced up to the fact that the success he yearned for had eluded him, he destroyed all his paintings in one frenzied afternoon and forbade any mention of them in his presence ever again.

So it was with mixed feelings that I finally opened the battered old trunk in that dark bunker of a place. My father's paintings, though I had lived with them for so many years, had left only the dimmest of memories in me: vague, abstract landscapes, a sparing use of colour, nothing that sprang to the eye any more than now sprang to mind. As I pushed back the lid I didn't know whether to expect a painful confirmation of my father's mediocrity, or to prepare myself for the even more painful discovery that he had been a true though neglected talent. Would it not be a bitter irony, I mused, if I could persuade Sara of his work's value and have her establish some small posthumous reputation for him?

But of course, and perhaps not for the first time, I found I had misjudged him. The trunk contained only bric-a-brac, the detritus of life that he had never found time or made the effort to throw away. Or perhaps this trunk was the place where he'd thrown it away and then forgotten about it. I rummaged through old cameras, a broken radio, a box of cheap cufflinks that had never been opened, books, letters, a scattering of old photographs and a couple of albums into which several more photographs had been fixed.

There was also a stack of yellowing old newspapers. They were intact, not cuttings, though most of them had been folded open at some particular page. Glancing through, I saw that several carried reviews of exhibitions my father had held over the years at various obscure galleries in out-of-the-way places. Their tone ranged from the dismissive to the patronizing, and I felt a sudden pang of sympathy for the poor man faced with this response to the work into which I knew he had poured everything he had to offer. It just hadn't been enough, that was all. There is a theory that provided you know you've done your best, then failure isn't so hard to bear. I don't think that's true. I think the worst thing of all must be to do your best, to work and slave and wring the last drop of talent you can find out of yourself, then to be told you've wasted your time, that you were never up to the endeavour in the first place.

I knelt there for some moments with a terrible sense of heartbreak for my father's wasted life, as well as for the undeserved misery into which his failure had dragged my poor, unassuming, unambitious mother. Tears stung my eyes. As I wiped them away, I realized that this was the moment of mourning I had not allowed myself so far: which, indeed, I had persuaded myself I had no need of. I had wept for my mother long ago, but never thought I would for him. I had been wrong again. He was my father, and whatever his faults I couldn't help but cherish him in some corner of my heart, and champion his heroism in attempting the dauntingly impossible task in life that he had set himself.

There is an odd and poignant fascination in old photographs. I picked up a handful that lay there in the trunk and started looking through them. They were mostly of holidays on various stretches of New England coastline, some taken before I was born and showing my parents as a handsome and happy young couple whom I could barely recognize as the same people I had grown up with. There

were several of me as a child during one long and
wonderful summer when we'd been lent a small house on
Cape Cod. I remember my father painting happily all day
while my mother and I went sailing with our neighbours,
who had two boys about my own age. That summer was the
best time of my childhood. Looking back, I think it was the
last good time my parents had together; it was certainly
the last good time we had together as a family.

I picked up one of the albums, wondering what
memories my parents (most likely, I thought, my mother)
had found worthy of preserving in this special way. The
pictures stuck on to the plain grey pages all dated from
before my birth, though only just. In a couple of them my
mother was heavily pregnant. These too were happy
pictures, most of them featuring another couple about the
same age as my parents and whom I'd never seen in my life.
Some of the pictures had obviously been taken in a private
garden, which I also didn't recognize, and which fairly
obviously belonged to the other couple, not my parents. In
several of them the man – good-looking with thick dark
hair and a winning smile – was turning steaks and sausages
on a barbecue, and in others pouring wine and serving
lunch to my parents. His wife, assuming that she was his
wife, was blonde and pretty. There were several pictures of
them with their arms around each other, clowning for the
camera. By comparison with them my parents were shy-
looking and reserved. All the same, I sensed a bond there
and a real warmth between the four of them. I was curious
to know who they were, and why they had disappeared
from my parents' life before I had ever known them.

I turned a page, and what I saw drew a small gasp of
surprise from me. As though in answer to my question
'Why didn't I know them?' was a picture that said,
unambiguously, 'You did'. It was a picture of me, aged
about ten I should think, sitting on a wall, a kind of stone
balustrade at the edge of a terrace or balcony, with the

unknown couple flanking me on either side. There seemed to be a garden behind us, with a big ornamental urn visible over my shoulder. They both wore evening clothes, he white tie and tails, she a glamorous ball gown. I wore just an ordinary shirt and short pants, but I had my arms around them and they around me. We were hugging each other and grinning at the camera like a happy family group. I found it hard to believe my eyes. I had absolutely no memory of the occasion.

I set the album down, still open at the puzzling photograph, and began racking my brain in an effort to recall where and when it had been taken. But my mind remained a complete blank. I thought back to my life at that age and started running through the months and years. Could there be some piece of my childhood, I asked myself, that I had for some reason forgotten? There were no gaps in my memory so far as I could see. But maybe that was how amnesia worked, disguising itself from its sufferer by hiding the fact that anything was missing.

Yet I couldn't believe that. From what little I knew of memory loss it was something of which the victim was intensely aware. Either that photograph was a fake – but why would anyone conceivably do that? – or the boy in that picture wasn't me.

If he wasn't me, the resemblance was remarkable. I compared it with the pictures of myself I'd been looking at only minutes earlier, all of which I remembered being taken. There was no doubt that the similarity was overwhelming.

It made no sense. There were no names or dates or information of any kind written alongside the pictures in the album. I pulled a few loose, including the one of myself with the unknown couple. There was nothing on the back of it either.

As I continued to puzzle, my gaze drifted from a corner of the album and on to one of the yellowing old newspapers

lying in the trunk. It was one I hadn't looked at yet, and I
saw now that it was an old copy of *Variety*, the show
business weekly. Curious to know what its connection
with my very non-show-business parents could be, I
picked it up.

Nothing on the front page caught my attention, so I
flipped through in search of whatever might be there that
could have caused my father to keep it in this little cache
of memorabilia.

On page four I found a quarter-page photograph of the
same couple, being showered with rice. The story was
headed: 'Jeffrey Hart marries his "Larry"'.

Rising British stage and film heart-throb Jeffrey Hart
yesterday married his dance and comedy partner Lauren
Paige ('Larry' to her many friends in the business). After
a short honeymoon the pair will embark on a nationwide
tour of 'The Reluctant Debutante' before returning to the
UK to fulfill film commitments there.'

So that's who my parents' friends were: actors. I had a
feeling they might have been fun, which made me regret
even more that I couldn't remember them. It also made me
feel the sadness of my parents' later years all the more
keenly. How much had changed within a few short years.

Why couldn't I remember those people?

CHAPTER 3

I had booked an executive suite at the Traveller's Rest. It was far larger than I needed for one night, but it would serve as a place for Sara to change clothes or get some rest if she wanted to. After an early and mercifully brief dinner in the Antler Room, where the service was prompt but the food awful, I went through my father's trunk once again in my room. Aside from the photographs and the copy of *Variety*, there was nothing in it that I felt inclined to keep for sentimental or any other reasons. I went down to the desk and asked for a large, strong envelope. I put the photo albums and the old showbiz paper in it, plus my father's unfortunate reviews, then tipped a porter to get rid of the trunk.

My phone rang. It was Sara on her way in from JFK to Manhattan. She would spend the night at the apartment, then come up first thing in the morning as planned. But there was something else she had to tell me. She would be coming up with our usual driver, Raoul, but instead of

returning to the city she was having him take her on up to
Boston, where she needed to spend a couple of days with
some gallery people she had met in Chicago. She asked if I
would like to go with her, but wasn't surprised when I said
no thanks: she knew how lost I was in the art world, and
how lost on me was most of the art she dealt in. She gave a
tolerant laugh, then asked if I were all right, not too
depressed by everything. I assured her I was fine, and said
I looked forward to seeing her in the morning.

Sara and I had been married a little over seven years ('the
seven-year hitch', as one of my heartier friends calls it) and
had no children. I had been married once before, too
young, when I was still teaching in college and before I
started writing full time. The marriage didn't last long, just
over three years; I'm glad to say we parted friends. Sara was
just over thirty when we met and had never been married
herself. One reason for this was that she'd put so much time
and energy into making a success of the gallery that she'd
had little of either left over for the more mundane business
of living. The other reason was that, amongst a handful of
less serious affairs, she'd had one long relationship that
had shown every sign of ending in marriage, but (for
reasons I never fully understood) had finally broken up.
The man in question had been a 'thrusting young lawyer'
(is there any other sort?) with political ambitions. I'd never
met him and had no idea what had become of him. The fact
is we didn't talk about our pasts all that much. We both felt,
I suppose, that it was a kind of adolescent thing to insist on
full disclosure of all previous sexual and romantic
attachments. We were too old for that: old enough to realize
how much more important it was to look forward than
back.

It was true that we were very different in many ways, but
then I suppose there is some truth in the adage that
opposites attract. For example, I, being a word person, have
little talent for the visual arts, though I realize the two

things are not mutually exclusive. Some people can do both as easily as walk and chew gum at the same time; but not me. The world of the art critic and the dealer, the process by which art was given value, either abstractly or financially, remained arcane to me. I'd learned a lot from my wife, but not enough to understand why some things I liked were unfashionable or just plain bad enough to be embarrassing, while some things I loathed were considered as the standard by which all else was judged. But we never argued or fell out over the issue. One of the reasons we got along so well was that neither of us had any hesitation in yielding to the other's expertise in their own field, while holding on to our own personal opinions, but knowing that's what they were: personal.

Sara got to the Traveller's Rest just after eleven next morning. In fact I need not have booked a suite at all because she needed neither to change nor to rest. She looked wonderful in a slim-fitting black suit and coat and a small black hat fixed at an almost jaunty angle on her long auburn hair. One of the things I had always loved about her (in truth was daunted by when I first met her) was an innate elegance that she had in her. Every movement, every gesture, was always carried out with casual grace and poise. There was nothing studied about her, no self-consciousness, none of the brittle look-at-me elegance of so many woman I saw in the circles she moved in. She also had a warmth and directness of manner that made people take to her immediately, to want to know her better and become her friend.

She folded me in her arms as she might have a lonely child. 'Has it been awful, darling? You sounded so down when I called you last night.'

'I'm all right. It's just, you know, memories.'

'I know. I do know.'

Sara knew because she had lost her parents in a freak hotel fire in the south of France when she was a teenager

and away at school. She was an only child, and the painful
shock of that bereavement had never entirely left her. It was
responsible, I always thought, for an appealing hint of
vulnerability that she carried with her alongside the image
of the astute and successful businesswoman that the world
saw. When I stepped back to look at her, both of us standing
in the middle of that dreary executive suite sitting room, I
saw that a tear had formed in the corner of her eye. As I
wiped it away with the tip of my finger she smiled
apologetically and dug in her purse for a tissue.

'I'm so sorry I was away . . .'

'It doesn't matter, really.'

'And now I can't even go back home with you.'

'Don't worry. I'm fine. I'm grateful you're here at all.
Thank you.'

She smiled again and planted a kiss lightly at the corner
of my mouth. I looked at my watch. 'Better be on our way,'
I said.

The funeral was at a small Presbyterian church on the
edge of town. Aside from the two of us and the minister, the
only people at the graveside were Abigail Tucker, Shirley,
and another member of staff from the home, and one of its
residents, a retired schoolmaster with whom my father had
played chess from time to time. It wasn't much of a farewell,
though it didn't surprise me, and it was probably more than
my father would have wanted if he'd had the choice.

Sara and I had lunch in a little place we found in the
restaurant guide that we had in the car. It was rustic-
pretentious and the chairs were like a whole booth to
yourself, but the food was surprisingly good. I had the best
coq au vin since we'd been in France the previous year, Sara
had the best grilled tuna steak she'd tasted in even longer.
We had a bottle of burgundy which was excellent, and we
drank a toast to my dad. Poor lost miserable son-of-a-bitch.
A loser. Big time. Sara reached across the table and squeezed
my hand. She knew what I was thinking and feeling.

'Fuck him,' I said, 'he made his choices and he got mad if I even tried to talk to him about them. I'd have liked him to know that I admired him in a way. Not in the same way that I despised him. Whatever that means.'

She reached for the bottle and topped up my glass.

'I'm getting a little drunk,' I said.

'Why not? As a matter of fact, so am I.'

I looked at her. I sometimes asked myself what a woman like that was doing with me. Not that I'm too embarrassing to be seen with, at least so I like to think. Hair beginning to streak with a little grey, but plenty of it still hanging in there, thank God. Moustache comes and goes, but at least that's a matter of choice. I suppose I look like what I am, or was, or maybe still am at heart: a kind of absent-minded college professor. Except I dress a little better than I used to.

It all started for me the night that the college president (I was teaching law in those days) called me in as a replacement dinner guest for someone who had the flu. The dinner was for a group of people who had contributed serious bucks to the library extension. Sara was among them. Her father was the establishment's most luminous alumnus, an engineer who came up with some small mechanical refinement of something no one had heard of that made him the darling of the military, and ultimately one of its biggest suppliers. I had been dazzled by her, and a little afraid. I hadn't even thought of falling in love with her. It was obviously impossible. She was beautiful, clever, and rich. Out of my class.

Yet – you know how it is – I'd fantasized that I could give her something she needed, something her life was lacking: something unconditional. We talked, she was staying over with the president and his wife, and we had dinner the following night. When the semester ended a week later I went to New York. We were married three months later.

It's a truism I've always accepted that in any relationship one partner loves more than the other. Not that the other doesn't love at all, just that one would be more destroyed than the other if the relationship were to end. The irony is that it's often the 'unconditional' lover who's the happier – as long as that love is accepted, of course. I felt lucky and privileged that mine had been.

'You know,' I said, 'the strangest thing happened yesterday. I was going through some stuff my father had left in an old trunk. There were a lot of old photographs, holidays and so on, all of which I remember. But there was one of me about age ten with a couple of people I don't ever remember meeting.'

'That's happened to me. You don't even know the picture's been taken, and someone you've just said a casual word to while you're crossing the room looks like your oldest friend.'

'But this one's posed, everyone smiling at the camera. And they're in evening dress.'

'And you?'

'Short pants and a sports shirt. But they were actors.'

'How d'you know?'

'Because there's a piece about their marriage in an old copy of *Variety* that was also in the trunk. It's really strange.'

'D'you have the picture with you?'

'It's back at the hotel. I'll show you later.'

I never did. By the time she dropped me off at the hotel we'd moved on to other topics of conversation. Besides, it was getting late and she had to start for Boston.

'I'll only be two days, three at the most. I'll send Raoul back to New York with the car and take the shuttle.'

It was starting to rain as we kissed goodbye under the log-built portico of the hotel. I watched, waving, till the car disappeared down the drive. Then I walked into the lobby and booked a cab to take me to the station in an hour.

CHAPTER 4

I've never been a big movie fan. Sara was somewhat more
so than I, but neither of us owned any reference books in
which I could check out the film careers of my mysterious
childhood friends. However, I had noticed a specialist
movie shop a few blocks from where we lived, and I walked
over to it the next morning.

The only Harts I could find any trace of in all the books
on the shelves were Dolores Hart, Harvey Hart, Moss Hart,
and William S. Hart. There had been a Mary Hart in B-
pictures in the thirties, who had later changed her name to
Lynne Roberts. Of course there was Lorenz Hart, the song
lyricist, who died in 1943. He had been popularly known
as 'Larry', just as Lauren Paige had been nicknamed 'Larry',
so that after her marriage she would presumably have been
known as 'Larry' Hart. But that was a pretty tenuous
connection. In fact not a connection at all, just a vague
coincidence. As to the careers of either Jeffrey Hart or
Lauren Paige, there was nothing.

I asked the man in charge if there were other sources I might consult. He produced a couple of tomes that specialized in obscure cult movies, but we drew a blank there too. He himself had never heard of Jeffrey Hart or Lauren Paige, or any variations thereof. Refusing to be defeated, he withdrew to the computer behind his desk and began a search of the Web. A few minutes later he handed me a printout listing five movies starring Jeffrey Hart, four of which co-starred Lauren Paige.

The information on the sheet of paper that he'd given me was minimal to say the least. Titles, stars, director, and in one case the writer. No plot descriptions, no critical comments or biographical information. *Spring In Piccadilly* was dated 1953 and starred both of them, as did *Whistling Through* in 1958. They appeared in support of a pop star trying to break into acting in *Girl Scout Patrol* in 1963, then in *There's A Spy In My Soup* in 1967. Jeffrey alone played a small role in *The Silver Spoon* in 1973.

Little though I knew or cared about the cinema, I formed the impression that this amounted to a less-than-glittering career. The 'rising heart-throb' written about in *Variety* had risen, it seemed, not very far. Whether he and Ms Paige were still alive I had no idea, though I imagined that if they were it would not be impossible to track them down. But just to find out when and where I had been photographed with them? It hardly seemed worth it.

It was a bright clear morning when I left the movie shop, not long after eleven. I was crossing Amsterdam at 87th, going east when, as I reached the far side, my attention fell, quite by chance, on something lying in the gutter. It was a playing card: the ace of hearts.

It wasn't the word-play, the pun of 'Harts' and 'hearts', that drew my attention to it. What made me stop and pick the card up was a memory that it triggered which had lain dormant for many years. It was a memory of a literary agent I'd once known who'd since moved out to Los Angeles. Her name was Vanessa White. She had never been my agent but she represented a couple of other writers I knew well. Maybe it was the association of Los Angeles and Hollywood and the movie bookshop I'd just stepped out of that made the connection, I don't know. All I know is I saw that playing card and thought of Vanessa White.

She was an attractive and sophisticated young woman who delighted in telling the filthiest jokes I'd ever heard. I never figured out whether she was trying to shock people, or whether gross-out was the only thing she found genuinely funny. It was an odd contrast with her svelte appearance and normally rather delicate manner. She was a thoughtful, reflective woman. I remember her telling me once that she used to collect odd little things that struck her as signs pointing in a certain direction. She showed me a pocket at the back of her organizer where she kept small items cut out of newspapers and magazines, a stranger's scribble on some hotel phone pad, a pressed flower, and a playing card she'd found under a restaurant table. These things, she said, tended to lead her on to other things, to guide her life along a certain course that was for some reason the right way for her to go.

I never pretended to understand what she was talking about, nor did she explain it very clearly. But there had been something fascinating and oddly compelling about the way she talked about the phenomenon and it obviously held some deep personal significance for her. And there I was, finding a playing card in the street and thinking about her for the first time in years. Vanessa, of course, would have picked the card up and kept it, convinced that it would in some way lead her on to something else.

Impulsively, and I still don't know why I did this, I bent down, picked the card up and slipped it into my wallet. As I did so I felt a self-conscious, slightly sceptical smile spread across my face as I imagined the odds against running into Vanessa herself in a couple of blocks, or maybe just into one of those friends of mine that she used to represent. That would have been a coincidence worth, as the saying goes, writing home about. Or at least, perhaps, writing about.

But nothing happened. No familiar faces, nobody I even vaguely knew.

I walked on for several blocks.

Then something happened.

I think the image had reached my brain and my body had responded before I was fully conscious of what was in front of me. All I remember is finding that I'd stopped and was gazing into the window of one of those specialist cake shops that will make any kind of cake in any design of your choice. There, right in the middle of the window, was an ornate and sugary creation in the shape of a playing card. It was the ace of hearts.

As I've mentioned, it was early fall, a long way from Valentine's Day. If it had been February 14th, it would hardly have qualified as a coincidence. New York would have been wall-to-wall hearts. But what was a cake like that doing in the middle of a shop window in the fall? And how did I happen to chance on it just a few minutes after picking up that playing card?

My first instinct was to find a rational explanation. Suppose, for example, that whoever had ordered the cake had used a playing card to show people in the shop exactly what they wanted. It was conceivable, although unlikely: after all, who in the world doesn't know what the ace of hearts looks like anyway? But supposing that was what had happened. Then whoever it was had walked a couple of blocks north and either dropped the card or thrown it away. It was a reasonable explanation.

But then most people would think that coincidence was a reasonable explanation. The point where things got interesting, it occurred to me, would be where coincidence was *not* a reasonable explanation but something remarkable.

I walked on. Although the subject had been buzzing around at the back of my mind for the last few days, it was only then, I think, that I made the conscious decision to make coincidence the subject of my next book.

CHAPTER 5

I wasn't starting on the subject from absolute zero. I'd been briefly interested in the strangeness of coincidence years earlier. The first time I really wondered about it was in school, when I came across a list of remarkable similarities between the assassinations of presidents Lincoln and Kennedy. It went like this:

Lincoln was elected to Congress in 1847, Kennedy in 1947. The names Lincoln and Kennedy both contain seven letters. The wife of each president lost a son while she was first lady. Both presidents were shot in the head from behind on a Friday while sitting beside their wives; both were succeeded by a southerner named Johnson, and the two Johnsons were born a hundred years apart. Both their killers were themselves killed before they could be brought to justice. The names John Wilkes Booth and Lee Harvey Oswald both contain fifteen letters. Booth was born in 1839, Oswald in 1939. Lincoln had a secretary called Kennedy; Kennedy a secretary called Lincoln. Lincoln was killed in the Ford Theatre; Kennedy was killed in a Ford Lincoln.

Since then I've seen many variations of the same list, often longer and embellished with obsessive and borderline-insane detail. People have made careers out of investigating this single aspect of the Kennedy myth.

But then you'd expect a thing like that to attract the cranks.

I don't suppose anybody can remember the first coincidence that ever happened to them. I know I can't. By the time you become aware of coincidence it's already a fact of life, something you've always taken for granted because it's just been there, like the weather. A friend telephones as you're about to call them. You bump into some stranger who knows your cousin on the far side of the world. You have an amazing run of luck – which, after all, is just a chain of coincidences – at some game of chance.

There is no explanation for such things, and most people would probably say no need for one. A coincidence can be trivial, in fact usually is; or it can change your life – like the woman who picked up a phone and got a crossed line, and found herself listening to her husband calling his mistress from the office.

One man I know was given a coded flight reservation that was the same number as the licence plate of his car, which he'd totalled the previous week. (He took the flight: nothing happened.)

When Sara and I first met she had two cats named Daisy and Alice, which also happened to be the names of my two nieces. We laughed about the coincidence, but didn't regard it as an omen or anything like that.

But what is coincidence? Is it anything more than fluke? Blind chance, indifferent and unconscious of the human fates that may hinge on it?

Or is there more to it, something behind it?

A while after coming across the Kennedy–Lincoln connection, I discovered there was a fancy word for unlikely coincidence. The word was 'synchronicity', and it was coined by the psychologist C. G. Jung who, with the physicist Wolfgang Pauli, published a treatise called *Synchronicity: An Acausal Connecting Principle*. That was in 1952.

Surprisingly, there is still no mention in the *Encyclopædia Britannica* that these two remarkable men, despite being treated at length individually, ever knew each other. You will search the index in vain for any mention of synchronicity. In fact you will search pretty much the whole of scientific literature without success. It is an unsung collaboration between one man who created some of the most fundamental terms in which we think (including 'introvert' and 'extrovert', as well as the 'collective unconscious'), and another who made a vital contribution to quantum physics which won him the Nobel Prize.

Not exactly people in whose company you need feel embarrassed to be seen, I would have thought. Which makes the omission all the more curious.

Twenty years ago the *Concise Oxford Dictionary* didn't list the word either. Now it does, defining it as: 'The simultaneous occurrence of events which appear significantly related but have no discernible connection'.

One reason for the word's cautious emergence from the intellectual closet to which it had been consigned was Arthur Koestler's book, *The Roots of Coincidence*, published in 1972. In it he linked the idea to developments in modern physics such as quantum indeterminacy and probability theory, and traced it back to work done on 'seriality' around the turn of the century. Seriality means things happening in clusters. The Chinese wrote about that centuries ago, and most people have experienced this in one form or another. Why, for example, do so many people believe that things happen in threes? (And even if they do, does it mean anything?)

The following day I made a date to have lunch with my agent downtown. It was another pleasant fall day, so I decided to walk – at least part of the way. Somewhere on Madison and a little way below 57th I began to feel like a cup of coffee. Glancing at my watch, I saw that I had plenty of time, so I stopped at a small cafe that I didn't remember ever having been in before, or for that matter ever having noticed.

I slid into the first empty booth I came across. Someone had left a newspaper in the corner and I moved it out of my way. As I did so, I saw that it was folded open at a partially completed crossword. I don't normally have much interest in crosswords, but for some reason this one caught my attention, and I thought I'd try finishing it off as I drank my coffee.

Six across, I noticed, was filled in 'Heartfelt'.

More hearts. The card, the cake, now this. My interest moved up a notch.

By the time I finished my coffee I'd finished the puzzle too. (It was no great intellectual feat; the paper was just one of the tabloids.) One clue had 'Playwright Shaw's first name', which was George, which was also my own name. Another was 'No star without one', in five letters, which I worked out was 'Agent'.

I had read somewhere that crossword puzzles (as I say, I have never been a crossword addict) are well-known sources of synchronicity. Addicts say that they frequently find something they've been thinking about for days cropping up in one of the clues or as one of the answers. That was what seemed to be happening to me. I was on my way to see my agent, and this whole chain of 'false' or 'genuine' or simply 'marginal' synchronicity had started when I saw a playing card, the ace of hearts, that reminded me of yet another agent. And here I was finding my name, George, in a crossword puzzle that also contained the words 'heartfelt' and 'agent'.

A man laughed loudly in another booth across the room. I turned and saw that he was sitting with his back to me and was talking on a mobile phone. It was obvious that he was as unaware of my presence as I had been until then of his.

'Wow,' he said to whoever he was talking to and with absolutely no reference to me, 'that's quite a coincidence!'

When I left the cafe, I realized I'd been sitting there longer than I thought; if I didn't hurry, I'd be late for my lunch. I took a cab, giving the address in Little Italy where I was meeting my agent. As I rode I continued turning the morning's events over in my mind.

What I had was a string of coincidences which, so far as I could see, meant nothing, yet formed a pattern. But do patterns have to mean something? Or, to put it another way, can order arise from disorder without there being any significance attached to the process? Could so intricate a little sequence of coincidences, such as I'd just experienced, be pure fluke?

Or did such things, I asked myself, using Wordsworth's phrase of which I'm sure Jung would have approved, point to 'something far more deeply interfused'?

It was a while before I registered the fact that my cab wasn't moving and hadn't been for some time. I was staring at the same stalled vehicles all around me and a stretch of wall with a faded banner saying 'Liquidation Sale'. Traffic had been running smoothly till we reached a point just north of Penn Station, where we hit a gridlock so dense that it seemed as though all the vehicles in it had been welded together into a sprawling, immovable mass. There was the usual amount of honking, arm-waving and insult-calling, all to no avail. I decided my best bet was to take the subway, so I paid off the cab and started to walk briskly towards the nearest entrance.

At the top of the steps my mobile phone rang. I'd finally given in to progress a few months earlier and bought one. As far as I was concerned, it was just one more thing to lose; all the same I had to admit that, when I didn't lose it, it was sometimes useful.

'Hello,' I said, backing up a couple of steps and moving clear of the two-way torrent of people entering and exiting the subway.

A man's voice said, 'Larry, how's it going?'

'I'm sorry,' I said, 'you've got a wrong number. This isn't Larry.'

The man laughed and said, 'Come on, Larry, stop kidding around.'

'My name isn't Larry,' I repeated. 'You need to dial again.'

'You sure sound like him.'

'Listen,' I said, growing a touch exasperated by his insistence, 'I don't have time for this. I have to hang up now.'

I did so and carried on down the steps. I had some tokens in my pocket, so I went straight through and followed the signs for my platform.

Another small coincidence happened on the journey. The 'heart' image cropped up again. Across from my seat in the subway was an advertisement for the American Heart Association. I began to wonder – more whimsically than anxiously – if fate was trying to tell me something. Was I about to have some kind of romantic adventure, or a myocardial infarction? But I checked myself with a smile, marvelling at how fast we react to the slightest element of strangeness: at how the tiniest dislocation in the fabric of our everyday reality can throw us into the arms of fantasy. All it takes is an all but imperceptible change in the rhythm of things. A coincidence or two.

When I reached my destination and emerged into daylight, I still had a five-minute walk to the restaurant. I was already ten minutes late, but that wasn't a disaster; my agent would be contentedly sipping his first martini and leafing through a copy of the *Times*. Nonetheless, I hurried on as fast as I could.

I was vaguely aware that I was walking in the direction of an old movie theatre, beautifully kept in its near-pristine thirties design. I knew it well because it had recently presented an Orson Welles season. Sara was more of a film fan than me, but I'd gone along with her to see *Kane*, *Ambersons* and *Touch of Evil*, all in what the publicity boasted as 'sparkling new prints'.

The marquee reached out over the sidewalk, all red and white glass with silver and black trimmings. I glanced up at it, not really interested in what was showing, but what I saw stopped me in my tracks.

Facing me on the side of the marquee were two words, arranged as follows:

LARRY

HART

People pushed past me in both directions as I stood there. Patterns kept racing through my brain, but refused to make sense. All morning I had been seeing images of 'heart' as well as the printed word itself. Now here it was once again spelled as a surname, the name of my parents' mysterious friends, Jeffrey and 'Larry' Hart. And 'Larry' was who the man on the phone had wanted to talk to. Now this.

As I stared up at the name, I became aware of a man on a ladder that brought him level with it. I continued to watch in fascination as he reached for the 'T' of 'HART', then the 'R', and handed them down to a colleague on the ground.

In a moment all the letters had been removed and that side of the marquee was blank; obviously there was a change of programme that day.

I walked on underneath the canopy and out the far side. There I stopped to look back to see if the name 'Larry Hart' was repeated on that side.

What I saw was this:

LARRY PARKS
GINGER ROGERS   in 'THE JOLSON STORY'
        in 'ROXIE HART'

As I watched, the two men dragged their ladder over from the far side and began dismantling these words too, starting on the outside and working in.

I was, frankly, beginning to feel just a little bit odd. I went on my way quickly, anxious suddenly – and irrationally – to reach the comforting familiarity of the restaurant that I knew so well, and the reassuring company of my agent and old friend.

But my mind was buzzing with questions and possible answers. The first one was whether somebody could be playing a joke on me. But I didn't see how that was possible.

So what was going on?

Was something going on?

I remembered reading somewhere a theory that just by thinking about synchronicity you can make strange coincidences start happening around you. I suppose I could believe it up to a point, but only in the sense that you might be more aware than usual of things that could be interpreted as coincidences.

But even if the theory was true in a literal sense, it didn't explain anything. Attracting coincidences just by thinking about them was perhaps even more extraordinary than simply having them come at you out of the blue.

Anyway, there was no escaping the fact that since I had started thinking even half-seriously about coincidence and the theory of synchronicity, odd little coincidences had started happening to me.

At the very least I could enjoy the comfortable thought that my next book was taking shape with gratifying ease and speed.

Maybe (the eternally optimistic dream of every writer) this one would write itself.

CHAPTER 6

My agent, Lou Bennett, was getting on in years and set in his ways. He'd always kept his office in Little Italy, indifferent to the tides of fashion that came in and went out around him, and protected by a tenancy agreement that he said he'd be a fool to give up just to move to a grander address, even though he was one of the most respected elder statesmen of his profession. His habits included eating lunch in the same family-run Italian restaurant every day. If any of his clients wanted to see him, or if a publisher felt like worrying out the small print of a deal in a more leisurely fashion than by phone, then it was up to them to make the trek to Dino's near Broome and Mott. Most of them were happy to do it, partly for the privilege as well as the pleasure of being in business with Lou, partly for the food, which was just about the best to be found anywhere outside of the tiny village in Tuscany where the family who owned the place came from.

'I talked with Mike this morning,' he said. 'He thinks it's too close to your last one.'

I had told Lou on the phone that I was thinking of writing about coincidence and suggested he run the idea by Mike Babcock, who was the managing editor of my publishers. I was surprised to hear he wasn't more enthusiastic.

'It's nothing like my last one,' I protested. My last book had been about superstition and how often it was rooted in scientific and historical fact. 'I can see why he might think there's a connection, but this is really about something else. Anyway, I'm writing this book whether Mike likes the idea or not. Let me just tell you what's happened to me over the last few days.'

Lou listened to my story with an air of indulgent scepticism. 'Sure,' he said, 'you're right, I know. Weird stuff happens.'

There was the hint of a smile at the corner of his eyes. I knew he didn't entirely believe me. 'Let's have a grappa,' he said, signalling the elderly maitre d'.

I started to protest, but he waved my objections aside. 'Listen,' he said, 'you're not going to work this afternoon, so what the hell – have a proper lunch.'

It was true: the afternoon, after lunch with Lou, was invariably shot so far as work was concerned. Lou beamed broadly as the old dust-covered bottle was produced. He had a double, but I drew the line at a single. I don't think I've ever known anyone who could drink as much as Lou and yet continue to function efficiently throughout a long day. He must have been almost seventy, but had a constitution of a toughness I'm not sure they make any more.

'The point is,' I said, sitting back and letting the warmth of the liquor spread agreeably through my being, 'there isn't anybody alive who hasn't had some kind of strange coincidence happen to them at some time, and maybe more than one. It's a universal experience. How about you, for instance? Surely some unlikely coincidence must have happened to you at least once in your life.'

His eyebrows twitched up a notch. 'To me? Jesus, nothing happens to me. I'm just an agent. A second grappa after lunch is as exciting as my life gets.'

'Come on, Lou,' I said, determined to drag some kind of confession out of him, 'don't tell me you're the one person in the world who's never experienced a peculiar coincidence, because I'm not going to believe you. Maybe you just don't bother to remember them, like most people – but I'll bet you can think of something if you try.'

Lou shrugged, like an old man who'd seen it all before: still on top of his game, a master player, no longer easy to impress or concerned about impressing other people. His attention was focused for the moment on getting his cigar out of its cellophane wrapper. He'd smoked the same brand as long as I'd known him, and seemed never to have quite mastered the trick of getting those wrappers off. Eventually he got it lit, then shook out his match and exhaled a cloud of rich blue smoke. (Another reason why I suspect Lou ate there every day was that Dino's made up its own rules about who could smoke what and where, and anybody who didn't like the arrangement could stay away.)

'Well, I suppose,' he said, 'there was a thing one time. A few years ago I was doing some business in LA, and as always when I'm out there I called up an old friend of mine, a producer. We met for lunch, and he told me about something that had happened about a month earlier. He'd been out at the Film Fair at Santa Monica, and he saw *me* there talking to some guy. So he goes over and says, 'Lou, how can you be in town and not call me?' I mean, he was really pissed. We were friends. I *always* called. But this guy just looked at him like he was crazy. It was some other guy, not me. But not some guy who looked a *little* like me. According to this friend of mine, the guy was *me*.'

Lou held out his hands, palms up, his cigar clamped between two thick but perfectly manicured fingers.

'What can I tell you?'

'There you are, you see,' I said triumphantly. 'Something *did* happen to you. I don't believe there's one person you'll ever meet who hasn't had some extraordinary coincidence happen to them.'

'To be exact,' he said, 'it didn't happen to me. It happened to this friend of mine who thought he saw me. In fact, when you think about it, it isn't really a coincidence at all. It was a mistake – this friend of mine mistaking somebody else for me. That's not a coincidence.'

'Two people looking alike is a coincidence,' I said.

Lou shrugged. 'They say everybody has a double.'

'Maybe. There certainly seem to be plenty of lookalikes. Think of movie stars and politicians. They all have lookalikes.'

We sat in reflective silence for a while. Lou finished his brandy and set down the glass with an air of finality. 'Well,' he said, 'if this is the book you want to do, just go ahead and do it. I think we'll hook Mike on a couple of chapters – and probably make a better deal.'

With that, he signalled for the check, which I tried to pay, but Lou insisted it was his and scribbled his name across it. When we parted on the sidewalk, Lou shook my hand, grasping my elbow at the same time, as he always did.

'Let me know how you're getting on with the book,' he said. 'And give my love to Sara when you talk to her.'

He walked off towards his office, still puffing great clouds of smoke from what remained of his cigar. I set off in the opposite direction.

The actor Anthony Hopkins, asked to play a role in the film *The Girl from Petrovka*, wanted to read the novel by George Feifer on which it was to be based, but could not find a copy in any London bookshop. Waiting for an underground train at Leicester Square station, he came across a book left on a seat. It was a copy of the novel, with some scribbled notes in the margin. Meeting the

author later, Hopkins learned that a friend had lost
Feifer's annotated copy of the book. It was the copy
Hopkins had found.

I was standing in a second-hand bookshop that I'd strolled
up to in the Village. There is something called 'the library
angel' with which all writers and students are familiar. It
refers to the way in which, whenever you start researching
some particular subject, relevant books and pieces of
information start falling into your lap as though by magic.
It's a little like those times, which everyone has
experienced, not just writers, when you come across some
new and rather obscure word, then for the next few days
find it being so widely and frequently used that you can't
believe you hadn't been aware of it before.

Anyway, there I was trawling the shelves in search of
anything on coincidence or synchronicity. This 1990 book
by Brian Inglis was the first I pulled down, and the page at
which I opened it carried the story about Anthony Hopkins
and *The Girl from Petrovka*.

The extra little bit of weird spin on all this was that *The
Girl from Petrovka* was directed by Robert Ellis Miller from
a screenplay by Allan Scott and Chris Bryant – all three of
whom were friends of mine.

Well? Odd or not? At least I felt oddly encouraged in
some pleasantly post-prandial way. I bought a dozen or so
books on the subject that I hadn't come across before, and
took a cab back to the apartment. The traffic was still as
dense and slow-moving as it had been in the morning.

That was when I saw her – Sara. My cab was turning off
Third when it got caught in one of those gridlocks that fan
out in all directions. I was looking wearily around and
thinking how much I would prefer to walk if it wasn't for
the parcel of books I had to carry, when I saw her
unmistakable profile in the back of another cab two rows
over in the stalled traffic. At least I thought it was

unmistakable. It was just a glimpse before she turned away, talking to somebody in the cab with her who I couldn't see. I was on the point of throwing a bill at my driver and getting out when whoever it was with Sara obviously had the same idea. The far door of the cab opened and a tall well-built man with thick blonde hair got out, bent down to say something or maybe to plant a brief parting kiss – I couldn't see from where I was – then shut the door and strode briskly up the sidewalk, disappearing quickly in the crowd. My hand was on the door handle to run over and find out what was going on, when the line of traffic that Sara was in lurched forward and was siphoned off in a fluid movement that made catching up with her on foot impossible.

If, of course, it was Sara. I could have been mistaken. I'd caught only a glimpse. And of course I'd just been having that conversation with Lou about people having doubles. I was unquestionably primed, as a psychologist would say, for some fleeting misperception of this kind to happen.

Besides, Sara was in Boston. It was inconceivable she could be back in Manhattan without my knowing.

My taxi also began moving, though hers had by now long disappeared from view. I had an idea. Taking out my mobile phone I auto-dialled her mobile number. She replied at once.

'Hi,' I said, 'how are you? I miss you?'

'I miss you too. What are you doing?'

'I'm sitting in a cab between Lex and Park. Just had lunch with Lou.'

'How is he?'

'Fine. How are you?'

'Busy. I'll be back tomorrow, mid-afternoon.'

'Where are you? Is that traffic I can hear in the background?'

'Yes. I'm in a cab too.'

'A cab where?'

'In Boston, of course.'

'Where in Boston?'

'Between . . . I'm not sure, let me see . . . just coming up to the Hancock Building. Why?'

'Oh, nothing. A coincidence, both of us being in cabs.'

'Yes, I suppose it is rather.'

'I love you, Sara.'

'I'll see you tomorrow.'

CHAPTER 7

I spent the rest of the afternoon reading in the sleepy post-prandial haze that lunch with Lou always left me in. The more I read, drifting into a doze occasionally and waking with a start, the more I realized how elusive and unreliable the notion of coincidence was. I had long been aware that if you were really determined to believe in something, whether mysteries, conspiracies, or deep significance of any kind, then by and large you would always find evidence for it. When I thought about it, for example, I realized that I could make up a dozen coincidences right there and then, just looking around my own office in the apartment. Two identical pens lay at exactly the same angle on opposite sides of my desk. The colour of a rug on my floor was reflected in the colour of a car I could see out of my window. A plane crossed the sky immediately after I glimpsed the picture of a plane on the front page of my crumpled morning newspaper. But things like that didn't count. I was looking for them and I imposed the connection between them. A real coincidence has to sneak up on you and surprise you, like the punchline of a joke, except that there's no lead up to it, no structure. It doesn't make sense, yet it makes sense of an unexpected kind.

There didn't seem to be much new or startling in any of the books I'd bought. The examples presented were mostly of the 'Just Fancy That' variety:

A man lost his engraved fountain pen in Florence, South Carolina. Three years later he and his wife were in New York City. As they left their hotel, she spied a pen in the street. It was her husband's, his name clearly inscribed.

Some of them were so unlikely I almost had to laugh out loud:

When his station's phone number was changed, an English police constable accidentally gave a wrong version of the new number to a friend. A few days later, while checking over a factory in the middle of the night, he noticed that a door was open and a light on in the manager's office. He went to investigate. Nobody was in the office, but while he was there the telephone rang. He answered it. The caller was his friend, ringing the wrong number that the police constable had mistakenly given him – which turned out to be the ex-directory number of that particular office.

One or two were a little spooky:

In 1838 Edgar Allan Poe wrote a story called 'The Narrative of A. Gordon Pym', describing how three survivors of a shipwreck killed and ate the ship's cabin boy, whose name was Richard Parker. In 1884 *The Times* reported the trial of three survivors of a shipwreck on charges of murdering and eating the ship's cabin boy – whose name was Richard Parker.

This one was perhaps my favourite:

> In 1893 Henry Ziegland of Honey Grove, Texas, jilted his
> sweetheart, who killed herself. Her brother tried to
> avenge her by shooting Ziegland, but the bullet only
> grazed his face and buried itself in a tree. The brother,
> thinking he had killed Ziegland, committed suicide. In
> 1913 Ziegland was cutting down the tree that the bullet
> had hit. He had trouble getting the tree down, so in the
> end he used dynamite. The bullet was still lodged in the
> tree, and the explosion sent it through Ziegland's head –
> twenty years after it had been fired with intent to kill him.

Towards dusk I began to feel restless and decided to take a
walk. I'd already made up my mind to skip dinner, but
thought I might drop in a bar I liked over on Broadway and
have a couple of drinks. As I walked I turned over in my
mind an argument I had been reading about between Freud
and Jung. Freud regarded all talk of the paranormal –
including things like synchronicity – as nonsense. Jung, on
the other hand, always had an open mind, refusing, as he
put it, 'to commit the fashionable stupidity of regarding
everything I cannot explain as a fraud'. He grew
increasingly frustrated as he listened to Freud ranting on
against ESP, eventually feeling what he described as

> 'a curious sensation . . . as if my diaphragm was made of
> iron and was becoming red-hot . . . At that moment there
> was such a loud report in the bookcase, which stood right
> next to us, that we both started up in alarm, fearing the
> thing was going to topple over us.'

Freud refused to believe there was any connection between
this phenomenon and Jung's pent-up emotions. Jung
insisted that there was, and to prove his point he predicted
that in a moment it would happen again.

'Sure enough, no sooner had I said the words than the same detonation went off in the bookcase.'

At that moment I felt as though I'd jumped about a foot off the sidewalk – because just as I imagined that second 'detonation' in Jung's bookcase, a car backfired in front of me.

At least I think it was the car in front of me. It had stalled and the man behind the wheel appeared to be having some trouble getting it going. An older man with him was giving him advice, repeating a small and precise movement with his hand.

I didn't know that cars were still able to backfire. I thought that the well-timed backfire went out as a dramatic device with old black and white thrillers on late-night television. But then I asked myself, what did it matter if it weren't a backfire? What if it had nothing to do with that car at all? It was a noise, a loud noise, a detonation. It came from somewhere, and it happened just then, at the very moment I was thinking about one.

As I walked on, I replayed the incident in my head, recreating it as exactly as I could from the still-fresh memory. I realized there was something I'd overlooked in my anxiety, however unconscious, to find another coincidence. There had been other noises in the air – all kinds of noises, a rich tapestry of noises all happening at the same time. It just so happened that the one I'd heard was the nearest and loudest. Had it not occurred, I was quite sure when I thought back about it, I could have picked out any one of a number of other noises going on around me, and chosen to synchronize it with the story I was telling in my imagination. The whole incident was, on reflection, a clear example of how careful you have to be before claiming some perfectly normal phenomenon as a paranormal one. I went on my way, reassured in my scepticism.

It couldn't have been Sara I had seen that afternoon, I
told myself. It was out of the question. A near-double, that's
all. Like Lou and his friend in California. A coincidence.
Without significance.

I had a couple of drinks at the bar as planned, then a couple
more. As I was leaving I ran into some friends who insisted
I join them for dinner. It was still early and I had nothing
else to do, so I abandoned my decision not to eat and had
scrambled eggs and smoked salmon while they had steaks
and roast potatoes. I was in bed by eleven and dozing
fitfully as I watched the late-night talk shows. Before
finally switching off and going to sleep I made a last
desultory flip through the cable channels, and came across
an image that at once had me sitting bolt upright, not sure
at first whether I was awake or dreaming. An instant later I
was out of bed and flying across the room to shove a tape
into the VCR and hit the record button.

What I was looking at was a somewhat laboured comedy
scene – all dialogue and lots of theatrical arm-waving –
featuring the two people whose photographs I had found in
my father's trunk, and with whom I myself had been
photographed as a child sitting on an unknown terrace wall
at some equally unknown time or place.

Then something else hit me. I realized that the clothes
they were wearing were the same as in that photograph. Of
course, his white tie and tails were pretty much
anonymous; but it was her dress, the cut of the neckline
and the orchid at the shoulder, that convinced me.

On top of that, I then saw something else that took my
breath away. Exasperated by their argument, she flounced
up a short flight of steps. He followed her, protesting, and
they continued their quarrel on a terrace overlooking an
ornamental but obviously studio-bound garden. It was then
that I recognized the stone balustrade on which the three of
us had been photographed together. What clinched it was

the large ornamental urn visible behind me in the picture, and which, as I watched, they flounced past several times.

I didn't need to check it out later, though I did all the same when the credits rolled. I had been watching Jeffrey Hart and Lauren Paige in *There's A Spy In My Soup*.

CHAPTER 8

By three in the morning I had watched the video several times, fast-forwarding between the scenes involving either Jeffrey Hart or Lauren Paige or both. In particular I scrutinized the scene that featured the wall on which I had apparently at one time sat with them. Now, with the photograph in my hand and comparing it with stop-frame images, I was more than ever convinced that I was right. At some time in my childhood, a time of which I had no recollection, I had been photographed on that studio set with two people I had no memory of ever knowing, but who were clearly good friends of my parents.

I lay awake long into the night, turning things over in my mind, trying to make sense of what was going on. It seemed undeniable that *something* was going on; but then again, why should it 'make sense'? Nothing that I had ever read about synchronicity suggested that its meaning was accessible to logical analysis. The very essence of 'non-causal connection' amounted to a defiance of logic. If there were any overall pattern to these random subjective events, it would emerge of its own accord and in its own time. I felt a growing conviction that something had started and was taking its course. I had no idea what, but it was not over yet.

As I gazed up at the dim chiaroscuro patterns on the ceiling, the prospect of what might lie ahead, where I might be going on this journey, began to fill me with an apprehension that was not entirely pleasurable. In truth, I was beginning to be more than a little afraid. All right, maybe I was going to get a book out of this thing, but was it worth the risks that I felt lurked somewhere just beneath the surface? Was I unwittingly starting something that I would be unable to stop? Which was stronger, my writer's curiosity, or this sudden inexplicable unease? I would have to make my mind up soon. But how?

Then I remembered something I hadn't thought about in years. The I Ching, or Chinese Book of Changes. I'd come across it first of all in college, not long after first discovering synchronicity in school. At the time it was enjoying a certain fashion that was a hangover of the sixties. Kids consulted it over their love affairs, their careers, whether or not to major in this or that subject, where they should go on vacation. I remember even then thinking they were trivializing something that was more deeply rooted in the fabric of reality than they realized. In fact I became aware that if you asked it too often about trivial or irrelevant things the answers it gave would become increasingly meaningless and unhelpful. It seemed to have an in-built resistance to being misused. But I had taken it seriously for a while, and been startled more than once by the sharp pertinence of its answers to my questions.

The I Ching goes back to around 3000 BC, and its origins are inevitably shrouded in a certain amount of myth and mystery. Some authorities attribute the main body of its work to one Wen Wang as early as the 12th century BC. It has remained a profound influence on Chinese thought and philosophy, but did not reach the West until the nineteenth century. Jung seized on it as being central to his theories of synchronicity and the collective unconscious. It rests, like astrology, on the notion that all things in the universe are interrelated, and chance is the key to our understanding of our place as individuals in the great scheme of things.

The way the I Ching works is you throw three coins six times. (The Chinese originally used a more complicated system involving yarrow sticks; many still do.) Each throw, according to the distribution of heads and tails, gives you a line which will be either unbroken, broken, or changing. The pattern of the six lines (the hexagram) that you eventually assemble will correspond to one of sixty-four oracular pronouncements that have evolved over the long period of the book's use.

These pronouncements do not amount to direct answers to whatever questions or problems you may have on your mind. It is up to you, the reader, to divine the personal meaning of your hexagram from a close perusal of and reflection on the several pages of text that accompany each one of the sixty-four possible patterns.

To the more fundamentalist type of Western mind, with its dependence on strict logic, the whole thing smacks of empty superstition. To anyone with an element of mysticism in their being, however, it makes an interesting kind of sense, and its use frequently throws up startling insights and remarkable shafts of self-knowledge.

So it was that at almost four in the morning I pulled down my twenty-year-old copy of the I Ching from its shelf, picked out three nickels from my loose change on the dresser, and prepared to consider my fate.

Uppermost in my mind, when I thought about it, was not the question, 'What is this all about?' It was rather, 'Shall I go on with this thing or get out now?'

I felt sure that if I did go on, what it was about would be

made plain to me in time, perhaps painfully so. There was a passage of Koestler's that I'd come across a few days earlier. Describing a brush with synchronicity, he said:

'(It is) as if some mute power were tugging at your sleeve. It is then up to you to decipher the meaning of the inchoate message. If you ignore it, nothing at all will probably happen; but you may have missed a chance to remake your life, have passed a potential turning point without noticing it.'

Confident that I could 'ignore it' if I choose without fear of repercussions, I decided to let the I Ching guide my decision to stop now, or go on.

I shook my coins and threw them, six times in all. My hexagram was:

The interpretation of that was 'Revolution', for which the original Chinese character meant an animal's pelt, which was changed in the course of the year by 'moulting'. It spoke of the need for change everywhere in time, but urged extreme caution.

Because three of my lines were 'changing' lines, meaning I'd thrown three heads or three tails at the same time, I had an alternative hexagram to look up before I came to a conclusion. The 'changed' hexagram was:

——————————————————————
——————————————————————
——————————————————————
——————————   ——————————
——————————————————————
——————————————————————

This was 'Treading' – literally treading upon something, though it is also defined as the right way of conducting oneself. I read:

> Treading upon the tail of the tiger.
> It does not bite the man. Success.

I took the combination of the two hexagrams to mean that, although I was dealing with something dangerous, luck was on my side. Things would turn out for the best.

So I decided to go on.

Did I really believe that randomness, or chance, was some sort of key to the universe? I suppose that what I thought, more or less, was: why not? The idea made as much sense as anything else. I know Einstein refused to believe that God 'played dice with the universe', but he's been proved wrong about other things. For example, he believed that 'spooky' action at a distance (information travelling faster than light) was impossible. But since Bell's Theorem and the Aspect experiment in 1982, we've been able to demonstrate it routinely in the lab.

The physicist John Wheeler, who taught Richard Feynman, and who despises anything that smacks of superstition or the paranormal, once suggested that the reason all electrons behave alike is that there is only one electron in the whole universe, and that it zips back and forth painting reality as we know it like an image on a television screen.

He also came up with the idea that the Big Bang didn't happen until consciousness evolved many billions of years later and was able to look back through time and become aware of its own origin.

Go figure.

That was something I would try to do in the book.

CHAPTER 9

Sara got back on Wednesday afternoon as planned. Although I had intended telling her everything that had happened, including my having spotted her almost exact double while she was away, we didn't have a moment to talk before the evening, when we were due to go to a charity gala at the Lincoln Center. One of her wealthier clients had bought tickets and insisted we come along as his guests. It was hard to refuse, but even harder to keep my mind on the string of celebrities paraded before us doing their various party pieces.

There was a dinner afterwards, which I got through on automatic pilot as I always did with those affairs. It was when we were leaving that I saw Sara talking to some woman I didn't know, a statuesque blonde in an elaborate brocade dress and some ostentatious jewellery. Not someone with a gift for understatement. Sara waved me over and introduced me.

'This is my husband, George,' she said to the woman.

'George, this is Linda Coleman.' We shook hands and exchanged pleasantries. She was a good-looking woman, but behind the fixed smile she wore as a social mask I sensed an ice-cold nature and a will of steel. I wondered who and what Linda Coleman was. As we talked, her gaze wandered off to one side where she had seen someone. 'You must meet my husband,' she said.

I turned – and saw the tall blond man I'd seen with Sara, or her double, the previous day.

'Darling,' Linda Coleman said, 'come over and meet Sara's husband, George.'

Steve Coleman and I shook hands. The four of us chatted for a while. I didn't say anything about having seen him yesterday, and of course absolutely nothing about having seen him with Sara's double. I did, however, say that he seemed vaguely familiar. His wife seemed pleased by that and told me proudly that I might have seen his picture in the papers or on television. He was a lawyer who had been involved in a number of high-profile cases, and was now about to enter politics. He would be a candidate the following year for the state senate, and she managed to imply that this was only the beginning of what promised to be a glittering career. I sensed at once that her ambitious eye was already fixed on the ultimate prize: the White House, no less.

Sara and I didn't talk much in the car on the short ride home. She seemed a little tense, I thought, though trying not to show it. She was avoiding my eyes, looking out of the window, pretending to be preoccupied. At least that was how I read her mood. It was only when we stepped into the apartment and I closed the door behind me that I said, 'So that was the great love of your life. Steve Coleman. Right?'

She turned with a gasp. 'How did you . . . ?'

I smiled. 'We've been married a long time, Sara. I think I'm getting to know you a little by now.'

She relaxed and smiled back. 'It was a long time ago.'

'The thrusting young lawyer of legend.'

'That's the one.'

'So what happened? He ran off with the ice queen?'

She shrugged. 'It just petered out. The way these things do.'

'Lucky for me,' I said, and took her in my arms. 'I love you, Sara.'

'Careful, darling,' she said softly, 'you're getting make-up on your jacket.'

Next morning I checked the Yellow Pages for a detective agency. I found an advert that said 'Overseas Investigations Undertaken'. Their address was some way downtown between Broadway and Fifth. That was good, too. Less chance of being seen going in or out.

I felt quite strongly that I wanted to keep this whole thing to myself for the moment. I had decided against saying anything even to Sara, and in fact was quite relieved that she had never asked anything more about the strange photograph I had told her about of myself with Jeffrey Hart and Lauren Paige. Fortunately she seemed to have forgotten that whole conversation we'd had on the day of my father's funeral, and I was glad to leave things that way. Partly, of course, it was because I had made up my mind to write a book about coincidence, using my own experiences over the past few days as a way into the subject. Like most writers I had an almost superstitious fear of talking too soon about something I was working on. It's a fact that if you talk too much about it, you'll never write it. I've known very few writers who've felt otherwise.

But there was another element to my thinking. I felt that the fewer people I involved at this stage, the less likely I was to upset the delicate balance of what was going on. Something was taking its course, and I was now a willing part of the process. I wasn't sure how much baggage it could handle.

I called the agency; it sounded reassuring. I made an appointment. It looked reassuring. I suppose I'd half expected men who never took their hats off, lounged back with their feet on the desk, and tipped shots of whiskey into their coffee from bottles kept in a drawer. Instead I was greeted by a matronly receptionist with a pleasant smile who invited me to wait for a few minutes in a comfortable room with fresh flowers and a stack of current magazines and newspapers.

The associate I saw looked like a junior partner in a mid-size law firm. I explained I was tracing a family tree, but he didn't seem concerned about my motives. It was routine, he said. He asked one question: If these people were found, did I want them approached? I replied no, just tell me where they were, and I'd take it from there. He asked me to give what information I could to his assistant in another office, a Miss Shelley. Nadia Shelley, I remember. I saw the name on her desk and thought how striking it was. Striking girl too, as I recall, but businesslike and efficient. She assured me that everything would be passed on to their associates in London and the search would begin at once. A routine search of this kind, she said, was really very simple. I paid a surprisingly modest retainer which she told me they would not exceed without my written agreement. I should expect to hear from them within a couple of weeks.

I spent much of the next few days thinking about the law of large numbers. This is the paradox at the heart of probability theory as well as the foundation of all statistics. It is also, of course, central to the notion of coincidence. Yet, like so many of these things, the closer you examine it the harder it is to see and the more difficult to grasp.

The paradox is this. If I toss a coin in the air, there is a fifty per cent chance it will come down heads and fifty per cent it will come down tails. No matter how many times I toss it, the odds are fifty–fifty each time. But if I toss it a thousand times, it will come down more or less exactly five hundred times heads and five hundred times tails. Why this should be so is a mystery.

To many people, I confess, it doesn't seem like a mystery. It seems somehow – if obscurely – obvious. So try this.

Radioactive substances decay at an absolutely fixed rate, which is known as their 'half-life'. This is so precise that palaeontologists routinely measure the age of fossils using radio-carbon tests. Yet the decay of each individual atom comprising that radioactive substance is totally unpredictable and spontaneous. So what is the mechanism which causes large numbers of these unpredictable and spontaneous events to average out with a smoothness that allows the overall decay of the substance they constitute to be used as the most accurate historical clock we have yet discovered? The fact is that nobody knows.

The mathematician Warren Weaver once came up with another famous demonstration of the improbability of probability. He noted from the New York Department of Health records that between 1955 and 1959 the average number of people reportedly bitten by dogs each day in the city was 75.3 (1959), 73.6 (1956), 74.5 (1957), 74.5 (1958), and 72.4 (1959).

Even assuming (and it is only an assumption) that the human and dog populations of the city remained relatively stable throughout that four-year period, how did each dog know when it was his turn, or that when he'd had one bite, or maybe two, he was not to have a second or third?

There are many such intriguing examples. Most interesting to me was the idea that the law of large numbers seemed to be the only thing running seamlessly from the microscopic world and into the macroscopic. We are told that subatomic particles behave according to quantum indeterminacy: in other words, their behaviour is inherently unpredictable. However, when there are enough

of them, the law of large numbers causes them to average
out sufficiently to constitute the atoms and cells that make
up, say, a chair and table, a horizontally revolving wheel,
and a human being sitting at the table watching the wheel
spin as he plays roulette.

Why this should be so also remains obscure.

We are further told that by the time we get to the level of
the macroscopic world (the casino in which the game of
roulette is being played), the quantum fluctuations on the
microscopic level of reality are too small to be of
significance. And yet the game of roulette (like all games,
including the insurance business) is governed by the same
principle – the law of large numbers – that has assembled
the casino and the player out of their anarchic fundamental
elements in the first place.

All gambling is a quixotic joust against the odds, and the
odds are no more than another manifestation of the law of
large numbers. But the roulette ball does not know that, in
the long run, zero must come up once every thirty-seven
times if the casino is to stay in business. Yet, in reality, on
average, that is what it does.

Again, go figure.

CHAPTER 10

Sara was going to Philadelphia the following morning, which was a Saturday. I had been sleeping badly, and that night was no exception. I lay in the dark, watching her, listening to her breathe. I don't know why, but suddenly I knew she was awake. And I knew she knew that I was awake. Which meant that she was pretending to sleep to avoid talking to me. I knew in that moment that I knew a great deal, and had known it for some time. I just hadn't been willing to admit it to myself.

As though she read my thought, or perhaps she merely sensed my stillness and divined what lay behind it, she opened her eyes and turned to look at me. The words came from my mouth through no conscious decision on my part. It was as if they had spoken themselves.

'It's Steve, isn't it?' I heard myself say.

'Yes,' she said simply.

There was silence. I remember I lowered my head slightly. She may have taken it for, and perhaps it was, a

nod of acquiescence, a passive acceptance of the worst
blow that had ever been dealt me. My mouth was dry, I
swallowed hard. She began to speak. She was trying to
apologize, telling me how sorry she was. I cut her short. I
couldn't bear to hear it. I didn't want to think about it. I was
numb and I wanted to stay that way.

Then she said she thought we ought to separate. I looked
at her, still hardly able to believe that this was happening.
'I'll move out,' I said. 'While you're away I'll find somewhere. I'll arrange it.'

'Yes,' she said in a voice that was barely a whisper,
'perhaps that's best.'

I don't remember much else. I recall making some kind
of promise not to cause trouble, at the same time
wondering why I wasn't raging and breaking things and
threatening to kill them both. This sense of inner
dislocation between what I wanted to do and what I was
actually doing served only to heighten the unreality of the
moment. What was happening was impossible. And
perhaps because it was imposible I didn't believe that it
was happening. I moved through events as though they
were unreal, a dream from which I would awaken and
everything would once again be normal. I moved from our
bedroom into one of the guest rooms. I took a sleeping pill,
and then another one, because I wanted oblivion. More
than that, I *needed* it, because I feared that without it I
might go mad.

Next morning I woke abruptly just after seven. My head
was clear, in fact unusually so, and I remembered everything that had happened. I still felt strangely distanced
from it all, like a sleepwalker going through the motions
but not connecting with the world around me.

I shaved, dressed and made coffee. When Sara came ino
the kitchen I had breakfast ready. She looked at me
curiously, almost distrustfully, as though she feared some
hidden motive behind my calmness. I reassured her that

everything was going to be all right, that I was fine, although in fact I felt like I was bleeding to death inside.

She looked at her watch and said her cab would be arriving any second. Raoul had the weekends off unless we wanted him for something particularly important, and she had no wish to go by road to Philadelphia, so she was going by train and had ordered a cab to take her to the station. It was raining, so I went down with her, carrying an umbrella.

I stood there watching as her cab disappeared into the traffic. As she, Sara, disappeared. From my life. For ever. It was then that I felt for the first time a sense of panic. But it passed. I mastered it. I kept telling myself that I had to stay in control, that I couldn't afford not to. Because if I lost control, anything might happen.

The mailman was emerging as I went back into the lobby – the lobby of what had been *our* building, I remember thinking, but was now *her* building. I had my key ring so I opened the box. There were half a dozen letters for Sara, a couple of things for me. One of them was a long white envelope that bore the name of the detective agency I'd visited the previous week. I opened it right away and read it in the elevator. When I reached my floor, the doors had opened and closed again before I moved.

I didn't understand what had just happened to me. Not just that the elevator was moving again. It was what I read, and now read again, that had stunned me.

Dear Mr Daly,

    I write to inform you of the conclusion of the recent inquiry you commissioned this office to undertake on your behalf.

    Records in the United Kingdom show both Jeffrey Hart and Lauren Paige to be deceased, she in 1978, he in 1984. Further inquiry has established that their only living relative is a son, Laurence Jeffrey Hart. Mr. Hart is an author and journalist living in Manhattan. His address came to us as something of a surprise.

Perhaps you may be able to throw some light on this coincidence.

The address given for Larry Hart was my own.

CHAPTER 11

No matter how many times I re-read it, it didn't change. Nor did the phone number. They had written a letter to me at my address, telling me that the man I was looking for lived there.

But there was no man at my address apart from me. Nobody who, for example, could have been living under a false identity. It made no sense.

I became aware that the elevator had stopped again, and saw I was back on my floor. I stepped into the corridor and sleepwalked to the apartment, then stood looking out over the park, my head spinning.

Was it a joke of some kind? If so, whose?

Instinctively I picked up the phone to call the agency before remembering it was Saturday. I dialled all the same in case there was somebody there or an emergency number. I got an answering machine, with nothing to indicate when messages would be picked up. I asked that someone call me as soon as possible.

I looked at the envelope. The letter had been posted

yesterday, Friday. Why hadn't they called me? Didn't they foresee how great a shock this information would be to me? Didn't it occur to them that I might need to talk about it? Or did they think I was simply some kind of crackpot who should be kept at arm's length? They enclosed an account of their fees and expenses, which they said were covered by the retainer I'd paid. It wasn't a lot of money. At the same time they listed all the other services they could provide or advise on, including insurance and finance generally. Maybe they hoped to do more business. If so, they were going about it the wrong way. I intended to let them know that I was unhappy and angry about this.

At some point (I hadn't noticed when) my head had started throbbing painfully. Only now did I become aware of it and went to my bathroom in search of something to take for it. I discovered as I struggled with the child-proof cap on the bottle that my hands were shaking uncontrollably. I caught sight of my reflection in the mirror and for a surreal moment failed to recognize the hollow-eyed, drawn face that stared back at me. Then I thought it was little wonder I should look so terrible. In the space of only a few hours I had lost my wife and perhaps, if this letter was to be taken seriously, was now in the process of losing my sanity.

How could this be? How could any of it be? I knew only that I needed help, and it would have to come from someone who stood outside this whirlwind that was threatening to tear my life apart. But who was there? One or two friends at most I could call up and say my wife has left me and I'm falling apart. One or two only, but at least they were there – except when I came down to it I had to admit that I didn't really want to talk to them at all. I couldn't face any of it – the explaining, the sympathy, the empty words of reassurance. On top of which I wasn't even sure I could keep my mind on one thing long enough to talk coherently. Sara's announcement that she was in love with this man Steve had sent me reeling; on top of which the arrival of

this extraordinary letter, which appeared somehow to be
the culmination of a string of odd and often meaningless
coincidences, had scrambled my brains completely. I was
in no fit state to be with anyone.

So where was the help I still felt in need of to come from?
No sooner was the question framed than I knew the answer.
Somehow it seemed inevitable, the only thing that, in the
circumstances, offered some kind of lifeline. I took down
the I Ching once again, dug into my pocket for three coins,
and threw them six times. The base line was three tails,
therefore a changing line, giving first:

————— —————
————— —————
————— —————
———————————
———————————
———————————

This was 'T'ai', or 'Peace'. The judgement read:

> The small departs,
> The great approaches.
> Good fortune. Success.

'This hexagram,' I read, 'denotes a time in nature when
heaven seems to be on earth.'

Next, I looked up the alternative hexagram that was
created by the changing base line.

————— —————
————— —————
————— —————
———————————
———————————
—————————

This was 'Sheng', or 'Pushing Upward'. The judgement read:

> Pushing upward has supreme success.
> One must see the great man.
> Fear not.
> Departure toward the south
> Brings good fortune.

Between the two of them, I thought, I should feel reassured, even encouraged. The only possibly questionable note seemed to be 'departure toward the south', but I didn't suppose that in ancient China 'going south' had acquired the same negative connotation it has in our day.

I looked out of the window again. It had stopped raining. I knew it was impossible to concentrate, to keep my mind on either reading, writing or watching television for more than a few seconds at a time. And it was hardly the calm moment I'd been telling myself for months I needed to get back into meditation. I decided to take a walk in the park

The noise and movement all around me helped. Rollerblades, running-shoes, kids in strollers, ice-cream sellers, shrieks and laughter, deafening blasts of clashing music battling for air space – the whole cacophony created a welcome numbness in my brain. I looked without seeing and heard without listening. Somewhere at the back of my mind the worm of rationalization stirred and began whispering its poisonous balm into my inner ear. Sara didn't mean it. She would come to her senses. It was just a temporary fling, a renewal of an old passion that would burn itself out as it had last time. And as for that absurd letter, whoever typed it had simply made a mistake. It would all be sorted out on Monday with apologies and red faces all around.

I was walking north, and the Saturday morning crowds had thinned a little, the raucous music grown more distant. Back into the growing silence came the tantalizing doubts

and fears that I knew would drive me to distraction before
the weekend was through. Maybe the best thing I could do
was call a friend and get some Prozac, or whatever the
tranquillizer of choice was these days. Maybe I could just
sleep most of the weekend.

There was a bench in the corner of a winding, narrow
path around which rocks and overhanging branches had
created a kind of grotto. It was unoccupied and welcoming,
a secret oasis in a public place. I sat down, hunched
forward, elbows resting on my knees. I found myself
playing with the three coins I'd used earlier to cast that last
hexagram in the apartment. I realized I'd come out with no
other money, but it didn't matter; there was nothing I
needed to buy so urgently that I didn't have time to walk
back to the apartment and collect my wallet – which is
what I thought I probably would do, then go to a movie.
Anything to occupy my brain and get me through the day.

I continued to play with the coins, absently shaking,
turning and tipping them from hand to hand, until one
slipped through my fingers and hit the ground with a sharp
metallic clink. It landed on its edge and, before I could catch
it, started to roll down the path to my left, the path I had
climbed a few minutes earlier. Another man was coming up
now. He stopped the coin with his foot, then bent down to
pick it up. He wore a soft felt hat and sunglasses. I thought
there was something oddly familiar about his face when he
looked up at me. Then he removed his hat and sunglasses.

And I froze.

My first thought was that it was like looking in a mirror,
except the image wasn't reversed. Nor was it identical
except in the face and general build. He wore well-cut jeans
and a good jacket in contrast to my sweater, old cords and
scuffed loafers.

Gradually I became aware that our confrontation came as
no surprise to him. In fact he was watching my confusion
with amusement, even enjoying it. He took the last few

steps up the path and stood before me, holding out the coin I had dropped. I accepted it automatically without taking my eyes off his face.

'Who the hell are you?' I managed to demand, once I'd remembered to shut my mouth before trying to speak.

'I'm Larry Hart,' he said. 'Hadn't you guessed?'

I stared at him. I could think of nothing to say, yet everything I could think of was spinning through my mind.

'I know how you feel,' he said. 'I've been watching you for the past ten minutes. It's weird seeing yourself, isn't it?'

'Where the hell did you come from?'

He smiled. 'It's a long story.'

I felt a sudden suspicion, and asked him, 'Did you have anything to do with that letter I got this morning?'

He nodded with, I thought, a hint of apology. 'It was rather infantile, I agree. But any way I sprang this thing on you was going to be a shock. At least this way you had some warning.'

I toyed with a variety of non-conciliatory answers, but in the end let my indignation drop. It seemed a petty thing in the face of the discovery I found myself on the verge of making.

'Why don't you just tell me about this from wherever it starts?' I said.

CHAPTER 12

He put his hat and sunglasses back on. As we walked, no one gave us a second glance. Whether it was his intention to disguise himself I didn't know and didn't ask; I was, however, glad to be spared the idly curious stares that we might have otherwise attracted as such obvious twins.

'The day before yesterday,' he said, 'Thursday, I'm walking across town minding my own business, when suddenly I hear this woman's voice saying, "What a coincidence, Mr Daly. I was just about to call you." Naturally I don't pay any attention because I'm not Mr Daly and whoever the woman was couldn't possibly have been talking to me. Then I feel a hand on my arm, and I stop and turn. And I find myself looking at this very attractive young woman. Darkish blonde hair, smart business suit, kind of sparkly eyes, and this big mouth. I've always gone for women with big mouths. I'm not trying to be crude, but it's a fact. They turn me on.

'Anyway, I must have been looking kind of blank or something, because she says, like she's jogging my memory, "Nadia Shelley. From the agency. Last week. You remember me?"'

'Now, I have never seen this girl in my life before, but I am not about to let an opportunity like this go to waste. But I swear I only meant to play her along for a little while, then make some joke and let her off the hook. Naturally, I thought, who knows, maybe I'll get her phone number and we'll have a date some time. So we carry on walking, and she's saying, "I was going to call you and ask you to come to the office, but if you have time you could step up right now. As you know, we're just around the corner."'

'So now I'm wondering is this a pick-up, or some kind of a scam? Looking at her, it's hard to believe, so I look at my watch and say something vague about maybe having a couple of minutes. She gives a big smile. Oh, that mouth!

'I'm letting her lead the way. We turn a corner, catch a light and cross the street. As though just making conversation, but in reality trying to find out something of what's going on here, I say, "And what exactly was it you were going to call me about, Miss Shelley?"'

'She looks at me, kind of surprised, and says, "About that inquiry you hired us to undertake, Mr Daly. Tracing that English couple, those actors you were interested in – Jeffrey Hart and Lauren Paige."'

'I don't know what kind of expression was on my face at that moment, because she frowned and said, "You know, I believe you really *didn't* recognize me just now, did you? You were just being polite"'.

'"No, I recognized you," I said quickly. I didn't want to blow it now. "Of course I did. It's just that my mind was elsewhere, that's all."'

'She flashed me that big smile again. But this time it didn't do anything for me. Because suddenly my thoughts really *were* somewhere else.

'The two names she'd just mentioned – Jeffrey Hart and Lauren Paige – were my parents.'

The way Larry told the story, I knew I would have done the same thing he did at that point. I would have jettisoned all my good intentions about letting Nadia Shelley off the hook and telling her she had made a mistake. Just as Larry did, I would have followed her into the respectable-looking suite of offices, I would have met the same junior partner whom I, George, had spoken with the previous week, and I would have continued to let him labour under the misapprehension that he knew me. I would have wanted, just as Larry did, to learn everything I possibly could about this *Alice in Wonderland* situation that I seemed to have stumbled into.

Larry listened. He hoped that the other two in the room with him, Nadia Shelley and the junior partner, would take his stunned silence for interest and would not ask any questions or expect him to comment just yet. He was not ready to speak for the moment. He just checked every fact as it emerged against his memory. There was an absolute correspondence every time.

Why were these people telling him the story of his life? He listened to the familiar and painful story of how his parents' lives had gone from the glamour of their early success in the West End theatre, when they had briefly been stars and their future looked assured, to the dismal end they had both endured. The sixties had wiped out their style of acting, singing and dancing at a stroke. Everything they were and did was suddenly old hat. Overnight they were has-beens. They struggled on as long as they could, with provincial tours and summer seasons around the country, but they were relics of the past in the age of the Beatles and actors who looked and talked more like construction workers than matinee idols.

First they had gone bankrupt, then in 1974 they had divorced. Jeffrey had enjoyed a brief Indian summer hosting an afternoon game show on television, but Lauren ('Larry') was already in and out of clinics with a drinking problem that she seemed unable to master, and probably didn't want to. She had died in 1978.

Jeffrey, despite his brief popularity on television, had fared little better. By the mid-seventies he was terminally out of work, and in 1984, six years after his ex-wife's death, he took an overdose in the tiny apartment he was renting in south London.

Then Larry heard the words he had been waiting for, wondering if he was going to react. There had been a son. Laurence Jeffrey Hart. Larry.

He sat there listening to the junior partner speak of him as an abstraction, a name to which no face or physical reality was attached. He heard how he'd been born in 1957, a late child who must have seemed like the crowning happiness in the lives of his, at that time, still famous and successful parents.

Larry had seen photographs of his early childhood, though he remembered little of it. His parents had weathered Elvis and rock and roll by that time, which had instilled in them a false and very unfortunate confidence about the future; after all, there had still been an audience throughout the fifties for what they had to offer, so why wouldn't there always be one? They had lived to regret the money squandered on fashionable living, the rented house in Mayfair, the nanny and the cook, the Rolls-Royce and uniformed chauffeur. It had been a hard lesson, all the harder because too late.

The first surroundings of which the young Larry was really aware were a series of theatrical 'digs' that his parents lived in while touring old West End hits around the provinces. It was not a glamorous life, and his mother's drinking habit was beginning to make itself felt. She was still a lively and often flirtatious drunk, but the hangovers were getting worse.

Eventually Larry was sent away to school, paid for out of a trust left by grandparents. Holidays were a nightmare, shuttling between two desperately unhappy and now self-destructive parents. Perhaps out of a lack of imagination, at least that was how he felt about it, he became an actor and got a little work for a few years, mainly in fringe theatre. Then, as he heard the junior partner solemnly announcing, young Larry Hart had dropped out of sight. That was almost twenty years ago. The firm's associates in London had called Equity as well as his former agents, but nobody had any clue as to his whereabouts, or even whether he was alive or dead.

The junior partner closed the file he had been reading from and pushed it across his desk to the man he took to be his client. Did Mr Daly wish, he asked, to pursue further the search for Laurence Jeffrey Hart?

Larry took a deep breath. How tempting it was to tell them that the man they were discussing was sitting with them at that moment, but he had gone too far by now to be honest. There would be accusations of deception, all kinds of complications. Besides, his main concern was to find out why this man they took him for, George Daly, was so interested in him and his parents.

'I'd like to think about it,' he said. 'Over the weekend. I'll get back to you on Monday.'

With that they had shaken hands and he had stood up to leave. There was nothing to pay, Nadia Shelley informed him. Everything so far was covered by the retainer he'd paid on hiring them; he would find an itemized accounting in the folder.

He would also find, he knew because he had glimpsed it, the address and phone number of the client, George Daly. That was his prize.

And that was what had brought us, Larry Hart and me, to our Saturday morning encounter in the park.

CHAPTER 13

I have to say that if Larry's story did nothing else, it took my mind off the painful subject of my ailing marriage. Now and again, when my concentration faltered briefly, the memory of that softly spoken 'Yes' with which Sara had answered my question 'It's Steve, isn't it?' plunged again like a knife into my heart, and would have twisted there until I screamed for mercy had I not forced my attention back to Larry and the extraordinary coincidence of his meeting Nadia Shelley. It was tailor-made for the book I was planning to write. Work, I have always believed, is the best antidote to depression and despair, and here fate was handing me a more extraordinary story than I could ever have invented from my own imagination. I knew I must cling to it, stay focused, because in time this would be my way through and (I could only hope) eventually out the other side of the agony I now faced.

At my suggestion we walked back to the apartment together. Although Larry's 'disguise' would probably have

got him through the lobby without so much as a suspicious
glance from the doorman, I preferred not to take the risk.
Instead we went around the side of the building, where I
used my key to enter the garage, then we took the elevator
directly to my floor. Only when we had closed the front
door firmly behind us did he remove his hat and
sunglasses.

'Great view,' he said, looking around approvingly.

'Would you like some coffee? I can fix it in a minute.'

'Sure.'

He followed me into the kitchen, and while I made the
coffee filled me in on the 'missing' details of his life. When
he had realized that acting wasn't for him, he had got into
the music business more or less by accident: first of all as a
'roadie' on various UK tours by visiting American groups,
eventually returning to Los Angeles with one of them,
where he had lived for most of the last fifteen years – which
explained why no obvious trace of a British accent
remained. He had become a manager and record producer,
obviously with some success, because he had second
homes in Switzerland and Hawaii.

'OK,' I said as I handed him a mug of freshly brewed
coffee, 'I'm now going to tell you the whole story from my
side, and you will see why the key word in all of this is the
one you used in connection with your meeting Nadia
Shelley two days ago. That word is "coincidence". As a
matter of fact, I'm writing a book – I'm a writer, by the way
– about that very subject right now.'

'Hey, no kidding!'

I brought out the envelope filled with the things I had
found in my father's chest – the photographs, the old copy
of *Variety* – and gradually, throughout the afternoon,
pausing only to make a quick sandwich around two
o'clock, we put together a theory about what must have
happened, what accidents of fate (for want of a better word)
had brought us to this point.

What seemed inescapable was that we were twins. Of course we couldn't be absolutely sure without DNA tests, and we agreed we would both give blood samples on Monday. But the photographs and everything I knew about my parents pointed to one relatively simple though remarkable scenario. My mother, having become pregnant, was told that she was carrying twins. Bearing in mind my father's ambitions as an artist at that time, and my mother's slavish devotion to his career, they had decided that the financial burden of two children at once was too great. By some accident they had met and got to know two English actors touring a play around America in the late fifties. Jeffrey and 'Larry' Hart had been childless, perhaps unable for some medical reason to have children of their own, though they had wanted one. Perhaps they had been thinking about adopting already. Perhaps, for all I knew, 'theatricals' were not considered desirable parents by official adoption agencies. At any rate, it had suited both couples to make this private arrangement between themselves. My mother would have her twins, and give up one of them at birth to the Harts. They then, by whatever means (the details were unimportant, perhaps we would uncover them later) had somehow got their adopted baby into Britain and registered him – Larry – as their own by birth.

Larry leant back in the armchair he'd settled into and looked at the ceiling before letting the air out of his lungs with a whooshing sound. Then he looked at me and shook his head in wonderment.

'Who in the hell would believe this if we told them?' he asked.

'Pretty much everybody when I get this book written,' I said. 'We'll go on talk shows and do press interviews together – if you're agreeable, that is.'

'No problem.'

'There's a certain amount been written about synchronicity already, and some amazing coincidences recorded, but I've never come across anything as extraordinary as this.'

His face cracked into a grin. 'Tell you what,' he said, 'why don't we have a little fun with this while we can – you know, before everybody knows about it. It could make a whole extra chapter for the book.'

'Like what?' I asked him. 'What d'you have in mind?'

He shrugged. 'I dunno. That stuff that twins do when they're kids, I suppose. You know, swap roles, fool people into thinking that I'm you and you're me. The kind of stuff we'd have been doing if we *had* been kids together.'

For some reason I felt oddly dubious about this. Not just that I felt it was treating too frivolously something of potential importance: more a feeling that with all the other problems on my plate at that moment I wasn't really up to goofing around like some teenager. He must have read the reaction in my face, because he immediately tried to reassure me.

'Nothing serious. Just, you know, when your wife gets home, for example, you could be sitting right where you are now, and after a couple of minutes I could walk out of the bathroom. I don't know her, but I bet she's got a sense of humour. Can you imagine her reaction?'

He laughed at the thought of it, as though seeing the scene clearly in his head.

'I don't want to involve my wife in this,' I said quickly, and in a tone that wiped the smile from his face and left him once again anxiously reassuring me.

'You're right. That's kind of a dirty trick. Lousy idea. But there must be something we can do just to prove that we really are as identical as we think we are. I mean, if you called up a friend of yours to come over for a drink, then I opened the door pretending to be you, wouldn't that be great to see how long it took them to figure out something was wrong?'

I remained noncommittal, though I could see his point. The idea had some of appeal. He was right; it would make an amusing little episode for the book. Suddenly I thought of the perfect candidate to play the trick on. My agent, Lou Bennett. Lou hadn't been sure that he could sell my publishers on the idea of a book about synchronicity; but with this whole story attached, the discovery of my long-lost twin, I wouldn't have been surprised if we found ourselves in a bidding war.

Larry loved the idea of Lou. 'It's perfect,' he said, 'let's do it.'

I called Lou at home. He had a house on the east side in the seventies. It was already after four in the afternoon, and he said he had a couple of things to do and didn't have time to come over. However, he was dining at Smith and Wollensky's down on Third at eight o'clock and would be happy to meet somewhere for a drink around six thirty or seven. We settled on a bar we both knew.

'It's about the book,' I said, while Larry made signs at me not to say too much. 'Kind of a discovery I've made that I think you're going to really like. I'll tell you about it when we meet.'

I hung up and looked at Larry. We both began laughing. In a few moments we were cackling like idiots. I don't know about him, but I'm sure that my own hilarity came from a release of the pent-up tensions that I felt and still couldn't bring myself to talk about. It was a kind of hysteria, but I was grateful for it, and for the chain of events that had led up to it. I was grateful that I had something to distract me from the painful events and the unbearable truth that I was not yet ready to face up to.

'You'd better come and check out my wardrobe,' I said, wiping my eyes and getting my breath back, 'pick out what you're going to wear. I get the impression looking at you that you're a snappier dresser than me, so think of this as a character role.'

He laughed and followed me through the bedroom and into my walk-in closet. Half an hour later he was dressed in one of my casual tweed jackets, cords and a roll-neck sweater. I wore the jacket, designer jeans and handmade boots that he'd been wearing – everything a perfect fit. The boots were the most comfortable I'd ever worn, and I made up my mind to get some made for myself. I even tried on his hat and sunglasses. When we looked at each other, the transformation was complete.

'OK,' he said, 'here's the plan. Why don't I take a cab to meet your agent, then you follow on in about half an hour. When you walk in wearing my clothes, he's *really* not going to know which of us is which.'

'Wait a minute,' I said as an obstacle occurred to me, 'how will you recognize Lou? You've never seen him.'

Larry looked blank. 'Shit, I hadn't thought of that. Don't you have a photograph or something?'

Luckily I did have one, taken at some writers' dinner where Lou had been my guest. It was a good enough likeness for Larry to find him in a bar.

We took the elevator down to the garage again and exited the side of the building. After a couple of blocks Larry waved down a cab.

'This,' he said, getting in, 'is going to be fun.'

He pulled the cab door shut, and I watched it drive off into the gathering Manhattan dusk. He twisted around to look back at me through the rear window, and made an 'O' with his thumb and forefinger, grinning broadly with boyish pleasure.

I began walking in the same direction. After a couple of blocks – inevitably, I suppose – a certain melancholy descended on me again, but not with quite such a crippling heaviness as it had earlier. I still had the distraction of this strange new adventure. Something else to think about. Something that was by any standards remarkable. It had been both the saddest and the most astonishing day of my life. Such a coming together, a coincidence of opposites, must mean something in itself, I thought. A book, certainly. I had a book to write, of that there was no question. I would throw myself into it with all the energy I had.

Yet I sensed there was still something more to it all. The day was far from over, but by the time it was, I felt that I would know something more about the direction my life was going to take, was perhaps destined to take, from that point on.

It was a disturbing and at the same time an oddly liberating feeling.

LARRY

CHAPTER 14

It has always been a rule of thumb with me never to lie unless I have to, and even then to keep it to a minimum. I would never, for example, resort to an outright untruth where a simple exaggeration would suffice. Sometimes it is enough simply to leave some small detail out of the larger picture.

My encounter with Nadia Shelley happened exactly as I described it to George, though I confess to omitting any mention of the circumstances which led me to that point. When he did ask, later, I made up something bland about being in town on business and taking a walk.

The truth was that I had been attempting to enter a branch of the Chase Manhattan Bank at which I had set up an account under one of the various aliases I find it convenient to use from time to time, and into which I was expecting some urgently needed funds to be transferred. I had decided to approach the bank with caution. The possibility of a trap could not be ruled out. Therefore I

drove past in three different cabs before deciding whether
to risk an approach on foot. And sure enough, I saw them
waiting. There were two of them. One of them was black,
wearing sunglasses and a long tan leather coat. The other
was less tall but slightly broader, with chiselled Slavic
features and small deep-set eyes. Each time I passed they
were somewhere different, but they were always there.

As another old friend of mine, now deceased (while
resisting arrest) would have said, my sad ass was green,
green grass. It was going to take a miracle to get me out of
this.

Instead, things got worse. I saw him at the same time he
saw me. He was the third member of the team and cleverer
than the other two, which was why I'd missed him till then.
But he hadn't missed me.

He shouted something, and the three of them started
following my cab on foot. It took no more than a fast walk
with the heavy traffic at that time of day. I debated whether
to get out and run. Then, looking ahead, I saw a chance.

'Twenty if you get through before that light changes,' I
said, holding a bill over the driver's shoulder. He tried to
grab it, but I pulled it away. 'You've got to do it first,' I said.

He spoke with a guttural accent. 'If we see cop, you tell
him you having heart attack.'

He almost gave me one as he hit the gas, bounced off the
curb, and powered ahead with his fist on the horn,
provoking a screeching of brakes on all side. After the
intersection the traffic flowed better. My pursuers weren't
even clear of the snarl-up we'd created before we were out
of sight. I dropped my twenty into the front of the cab.

'Where to now?' he asked.

'I don't know,' I said, realizing I didn't. 'Just keep
driving.'

Where could I go? If they were staking out the bank it
meant they'd followed the money, which made it unlikely
they'd found my hotel. On the other hand, going back there

was a risk I didn't need to take. I had everything I needed with me, including my passport, my few remaining dollars, and a collection of plastic that hadn't worked for the past week.

'Pull over here,' I said, not wanting to spend any more money than I already had.

I got out and looked around, then started walking against a one-way system so that even if they came after me in a cab or another car, they couldn't follow me. It was after a few blocks of this zigzagging lose-a-tail strategy that I heard a voice behind me say, 'Mr Daly?', and then I felt a hand on my arm.

My first thought was I'd walked into another trap, but I quickly realized that this very attractive young woman was making a simple mistake, and if I let her go on making it she was going to take me to some place off the street, which was just what I needed at that moment.

Then came the rest. The coincidence. The realization that something very strange and interesting had happened.

I believe in coincidence. Doesn't everybody? If there is no such thing as coincidence, then everything must be planned or intended in some way, which makes no sense.

But I do not believe in synchronicity. I do not think there's anything more going on in coincidence, including repeated coincidence, than meets the eye. Coincidence is remarkable by definition, and the more it happens the more remarkable it is. But only idle minds find patterns in it and pretend it means something. People with nothing better to do.

People like George. Jerk-off George. What was I supposed to make of that story of his about finding playing cards and heart-shaped cakes, crossword puzzles and some name outside a movie theatre? Just more New Age crap as far as I was concerned.

As I said, I accept coincidence for what it is, and I accept that a remarkable coincidence happened to me. One

remarkable coincidence. That was running into Nadia
Shelley when I did. The fact that I was jerk-off George's
long-lost twin was not a coincidence, it was just a fact
waiting to be discovered. George found a clue to that
discovery when his father died, then he hired a detective
agency to follow it up. I happened to be where I was that
afternoon for no reason connected with George Daly or any
part of my family history. And then a woman who knew
George saw me and mistook me for George. It's not that big
a deal. But it is a coincidence, I grant you.

George, rubbing his hands with glee, said it was a classic
synchronicity.

Damn fool.

The first thing I had done after leaving Nadia Shelley's
office was take a cab across town to see where George lived.
It was an expensive address. The smallest apartments in a
building like that started at between two and three million,
and I saw from his file that he lived in the penthouse.

Anxious though I was to catch sight of him, I couldn't
hang around indefinitely without attracting attention
myself. I went around the corner and got a cup of coffee
while I thought this out. In the end I decided just to go
straight on in there and ring his bell. It was the most open
and honest way to handle this thing, the way that would
make the best impression on him. I was anxious to do that
because I wanted him to trust me. At that moment he
seemed like maybe my best chance.

Just as I got to the corner of the building a shiny black
chauffeur-driven town car surged out of the garage. Sitting
in the back was a dark-haired woman I'd never seen before,
and next to her was. . . myself.

It was truly the weirdest moment of my life, unreal and yet
happening, like the moment of shock people describe when
they're in some terrible accident. There was my identical
twin, my doppelganger, right there before my eyes.

Neither of them glanced my way, or I dare say they'd have had as big a shock. In a moment they were gone, heading downtown in the late afternoon traffic. I registered almost in retrospect the fact that they had both been wearing evening dress, which at this hour suggested they were headed for some gala performance at the Lincoln Center or somewhere similar. That meant it would be a late night, so there was little point in my hanging around.

That was when I had the idea of sending a letter – to 'myself' at his address. I looked at my watch. There was still time. I found a copy shop close by and quickly mocked up a sheet of plain paper with the detective agency's address. Then I did the same with an envelope. It took only a few moments to type and print the letter, then I caught the last post. It would be there in the morning.

There was one last thing I had to do that day, which was call my friend Skeeter up in Oregon. I made the call collect from a pay phone; Skeeter could afford it, with his ranch and the horses he'd bought after getting lucky that last time he and I did business. Skeeter owed me too much to refuse me the favour I was going to ask him. Also I knew too much about him, including where the bodies were buried – literally. I told him I was in Manhattan and needed – urgently – to get out. I had no money, people were looking for me, so I needed him to arrange a pick-up. He didn't hesitate, just asked when and where. I said the following day, somewhere in Manhattan. I didn't know exactly when or where, but I'd check back with him once he'd got everything set up and we'd do the details.

After that I had a drink in a bar and counted my dwindling reserve of dollars. There was just enough for a room in the cheapest hotel I could find. It was an uncomfortable and noisy night, as a result of which I was up early and on my way to George's apartment at about the time I expected the post to be delivered. It suddenly started to rain hard. I took cover under a bus shelter across from

the building's entrance, and to my surprise after a couple of
minutes saw George emerge with an umbrella, solicitously
shepherding his wife into a waiting cab. When he went
back in I saw him pick up his mail from one of the locked
brass boxes on the back wall of the lobby. I decided to give
him a while.

The rain stopped as abruptly as it had begun. I started
walking on the glistening wet sidewalk, intending to circle
a couple of blocks before giving him a call. I tried to
imagine him opening the letter and almost certainly re-
reading it several times in disbelief. Then he would try to
phone the agency, but I knew no one was there over the
weekend. Nadia Shelley had offered to give me an
emergency number when I'd asked about this, but I'd said
it wasn't necessary. The fact that she had offered it meant
almost certainly that George didn't have it, which was
useful to know.

After fifteen minutes I was ready to give him a call. I'd
noticed a pay phone near the bus shelter where I'd hidden
from the rain earlier. I imagined he'd be able to see it from
his balcony, which meant I could get him to look down and
I would wave to him – a suitably unthreatening way, I
thought, to break the ice.

When I got there, naturally enough, the pay phone was
busy. So I waited. But suddenly, in the background, I saw
George crossing towards the park. He was walking with his
shoulders hunched and his hands deep in his pockets, the
classic body language of tension and frustration.

I couldn't resist a faint smile of amusement as I set off
after him. Twenty minutes later we were talking.

CHAPTER 15

What did I want from him when we first looked at each other? I don't think I really knew. Whatever I could get, I suppose. A sympathetic ear, certainly, for the story I would tell him, and a little money to get me through the immediate future. I had only a few hours before I had to call Skeeter again. His team were probably in place by now, and I was certainly going to need money.

I was glad when he suggested we go back to his apartment to talk. I'd had more than enough of looking nervously over my shoulder, hoping he didn't notice. We spent the afternoon like a pair of teenagers hashing over their lives, comparing every little like and dislike, talking about our parents, figuring out their motives, and tracing the events which had, as it seemed to us, brought us to that point. At the end of it all we dreamed up this childish prank of switching roles and playing a joke on George's agent, Lou Bennett. I swear I hadn't planned it all. It was only as the day wore on and things started falling into place that I conceived of doing what I did. As I said, it's all about making the most of your chances.

After we'd tried on each other's clothes and were pretty sure that nobody would be able to tell which of us was which, I asked George if I could use his phone. He handed me a mobile, then went off to the kitchen for something, leaving me alone to talk in private. It wouldn't have mattered if he'd overheard what I had to say; it was innocuous enough. I simply called Skeeter and asked him if everything was in place. He confirmed that it was. I told him I would call him back in the next hour.

Dusk fell, and it was time for my rendezvous with Lou. I was anxious to get going, which made me careless. I should have been the one, not George, to point out that I needed some way of identifying Lou. It was a clumsy mistake on my part which, to a smarter man than George, might have suggested that I had no intention of keeping that appointment with his agent. Luckily, the moment passed without causing a problem.

We took the elevator to the garage and left the building as we had entered it, seeing no one. We walked a block or so, then I hailed a cab. As it drove off, I turned to grin back at George through the rear window, giving a little wave and a gesture of reassurance that everything was going to go just fine.

Then I took out his mobile phone that I'd brought with me, and called Skeeter again. I told him that in fifteen minutes' time I would be walking along Central Park South. I described the clothes – my clothes – that George would be wearing, though this was probably unnecessary: they would have spotted him anyway once they'd been told where to look. The important thing was that he was carrying my wallet with my credit cards and driver's permit. He would not lightly talk himself out of that. He would do his best, of course, but without success. The killers themselves, the men who actually did the job and who I'd seen outside the bank the day before, spoke very little English.

But they were professionals, skilled and ruthless. They would pick him off the street without a scuffle. No one would notice a thing as he was bundled into the back of the waiting car. I didn't know where they would take him, but everything would have been planned in advance. They would put a bullet in his head – that much was tradition. Then the body would be disposed of with equal permanence. They would use a lime pit, or possibly a deep hole in the foundations of some construction site, into which he would be thrown, after which rubble and concrete would be added.

That this would happen I knew with certainty. I knew it because I knew that Skeeter had betrayed me. I had suspected for some time that I could no longer trust him, and seeing those men yesterday had confirmed it. I knew that anything I told him would be relayed directly to the people who wanted me dead. He thought I had played into his hands, whereas in reality he had played into mine. I owed this reversal of fortune to pure chance. I had been in deep, deep trouble, and only the accident – coincidence if you prefer – of meeting George had saved my life. That was extraordinary, I grant you. Quite extraordinary.

A month earlier, such a coincidence would have been amusing at best, perhaps simply irritating, and certainly irrelevant. But it has always amazed me how quickly things can change. A month earlier I'd been on top of the world. I was taking risks, but then I always had, and so far I'd always got away with them. Perhaps I'd started taking my luck too much for granted. Was that my fatal mistake?

I'd used the music business as my cover for many years. When I felt myself burning out on the creative side, which had happened after a very short time, I started arranging introductions, for a fee, between people in the business and others who could provide certain services and substances

much in demand in the music world. This had led to an
increasing involvement in the financial side of things, until
a federal money-laundering inquiry had curtailed my
activities. Charges had been dropped owing to lack of
evidence, more particularly lack of witnesses owing to a
couple of unfortunate accidents.

It had been a setback, nonetheless. The people I worked
for had stood by me, but chiefly out of self-interest. Now I
was a liability, and found myself being rapidly sidelined. I
decided to take one last shot at a big pay day while I still
had the chance. I could have done it a hundred times in the
past, but never had. I'd imagined doing it and knew how it
would work, but it was just a mental exercise, neither a
plan nor an intention.

But now?

I did not see how this venture I had my eye on could go
wrong. Whichever way you looked at it, it was a cinch, a
cert, a shoo-in.

What actually went wrong was something I could not
have foreseen even as the remotest of downside
possibilities. A guy in a key position had a heart attack at
the wrong time, unravelling the whole operation.

When that happened, the guy with the heart attack
wasn't the only dead man. The next one was me – or would
have been.

Thank you, George, for being there to take care of that
problem.

My stroke of genius, if that doesn't sound too immodest,
came next. Since George was carrying my wallet, I was
carrying his. That had been something I'd made sure of as
part of our costume change. I opened it and found a couple
of hundred dollars. Desperate though my need for cash was
just then, I knew I had to give it away. There would, after
all, be plenty more where that came from. I stopped the cab,
got out, and within a few blocks had pressed notes into the

grubby hand of every addict and panhandler I could find.

The next thing I did was lose the credit cards. First of all I cracked and tore them into the smallest fragments I could, then I dropped them down a grating into the sewers of the city.

That done, I began looking for the proper setting in which to stage the next part of my little drama. Within a few minutes I had found an alley running all along the back of several shops and restaurants. It was dark and narrow and exactly what I needed. Frankly, it wasn't the kind of place through which a timorous soul like George would have chosen to take a short cut, but when it later became known that he'd been hurrying to keep an appointment with his agent, for which he was obviously late, his uncharacteristic boldness would make sense.

I slipped into the shadows, carefully picking my way past garbage pails and bulging black plastic bags. When I was certain that I was unobserved, I threw away George's wallet, which would later be found minus cash and credit cards.

The next part was the hardest. The first thing I had to do was make a mess of my clothes, tearing and dirtying them up to look like I'd been in a fight, rolling on the floor getting kicked and beaten. The next thing – and this was the bit which I say with no false modesty took the balls – was kneeling down and smashing my head on the stones until I was streaming blood and, frankly, suffering a good deal of pain. Once I'd taken as much as I could without risking a real concussion and marginal brain damage, I began crawling slowly and painfully towards the light at the far end of the alley.

True to form, the good citizens of New York stepped around and over me without a second glance for several minutes, assuming I was just another drunk and best ignored. I don't know which self-appointed Samaritan first noticed that my clothes were too good for a bum, and that the injuries to my head needed attention. By the time the cops and ambulance arrived I was, to be honest, only half conscious. I was lifted on to a stretcher and rushed with siren blaring through the city. After that I remember being wheeled beneath a long, long ceiling with strip lighting and heating pipes that seemed to wiggle as they flashed by. I was taken into what I supposed must be an emergency treatment room, where I was injected, stitched up, and finally put to bed. After that I enjoyed the finest sleep of my life.

When I awoke, bright morning sunlight filled the ward I was in. There must have been twenty or thirty beds, all occupied. I found I was bandaged and hooked up to some kind of IV drip. At least I was relieved to discover that the battering I'd given myself hadn't landed me in intensive care.

A nurse entered. She was very young and had a sweet, rather hesitant smile.

'How are you feeling?' she asked. 'You should have quite a headache.'

'Yes, I do,' I said, sounding feebler than I actually felt, 'a bad one.'

'We'll give you something in a while. The doctor wants to see you first.'

I looked about me as though only just becoming aware of my surroundings, and called to mind a scene that my old man had played in a corny fifties movie called *Spring In Piccadilly*. But I'd liked this scene when I saw it on TV one time.

'Where am I?' I said, just the way he had. 'What happened? What am I doing here?'

'You're in the city hospital,' she said. 'The police said you were attacked and robbed. The first thing we need to know is your name.'

That was perfect. Almost exactly like the movie. I let a few seconds elapse, maintaining the expression of someone about to answer willingly, then replacing it with one of growing alarm as I realized the truth of my predicament.

'I don't know,' I said. 'I can't remember.'

CHAPTER 16

I had read up on the subject and knew that psychological trauma was the whiplash of neurology: it was practically impossible, in the absence of actual brain damage, either to prove or disprove the psychological effects of injuries to the head.

Once or twice I detected a hint of suspicion behind some of the questions asked by my doctors as the days went by. 'Well, it *is* rather unusual, Mr Daly, for memory loss to persist so long after such relatively superficial injuries, but I'm sure we shall see an improvement soon.'

As for 'superficial', let *him* try doing what I had. Certainly for most people the stitches and bruising were enough. Nobody questioned my sporadic attacks of amnesia.

In fact there *was* an improvement in my condition: the more I learned of George's life, the more my memory 'returned'. But all gaps and even outright blunders could still be covered by a sudden relapse. I developed a technique of using it almost as a stutter, as though not my tongue became tied but my brain, and I found myself suddenly on the brink of a gaping hole in my train of thought. More often than not I could use it as a prompt for somebody to fill in whatever was missing.

One of the first things I had to master when I was allowed home after two days was George's handwriting. I checked through his papers, in particular his notebooks, which were all handwritten. Amazingly, the difference between his script and my own was virtually nil. But then, I reflected, perhaps it wasn't so surprising that identical twins should have similar styles. At least it was one less thing to worry about.

The trickiest part of the whole deception, I had anticipated, would be the marriage. I had mapped out a strategy to tease out of his wife, the habits, preferences and protocols of their most intimate life together, especially their sexual relationship.

But this marriage, I quickly discovered, was not all it seemed to the outside world.

I raised no objection when I found, on my return from the hospital after the weekend, that Sara had moved me into one of the guest rooms. As I was still convalescing, I chose to see it as considerate on her part. But after a couple of days, as my strength returned and I suggested a return to the marital bed, I sensed an evasiveness. When eventually I got right to the point and tried to make love to her, she became upset.

'No, George,' she said, 'please don't. Please.'

'What's wrong?'

She looked at me with a pained expression. 'How can you ask that?'

'I can ask it,' I said, letting her see that I was starting to get annoyed, 'because I would like an answer.'

'George, we discussed it all. We agreed.'

'When?'

'Last week, before I left for Philadelphia.'

I must have looked blank. I had my amnesia as an excuse, of course, but her reply had still caught me off guard.

'Are you telling me,' she asked, reading my expression, 'that you really don't remember?'

'Yes. I mean no, I don't remember.'

She turned away and cupped her hands over her face. After a while she said, very quietly, 'It doesn't matter. It doesn't make any difference.'

'Perhaps I'll be the judge of that.'

'Yes, of course, you're right. I'm sorry.' She turned to look at me again, almost pleadingly this time. 'But not now. Please, George, just not now.'

There was a kind of exhaustion in her face, as though the prospect of talking yet again about whatever problems – sexual or otherwise – afflicted her and George's marriage had completely drained her of all energy.

I reflected for a moment, and realized this was something I could make play in my favour. Allowing this distance, whatever its cause, to remain between us meant one less chance of making a bad mistake. Of course, there was always the possibility that she would get over whatever was bothering her in the next day or two and 'come around', which meant I must keep my amnesia symptoms ticking over to cover whatever holes still remained. But by then I should have a far better sense of the overall landscape of George's life than I had at that moment. So I shrugged.

'OK,' I said. 'Whatever you want. We'll talk when you're ready.'

Meeting George's friends and social acquaintances was easier than I'd anticipated. There was widespread sympathy for me as the victim of a brutal attack. My wallet had been found, as I hoped it would, minus cash and credit cards, painting the picture exactly as I'd wanted it.

Fitting into the role that people expected of me socially

was helped by that fact that they largely defined it for me through their own attitudes and manners. It was easy to see that dear old George had not been a dominant personality. Mostly all I had to do was coast along and smile from time to time.

Sara and I attended a couple of social occasions that week. There were always photographers around and I began to worry about the risk of getting my picture in the social columns, which hardly seemed like a smart move for a man who was trying to disappear. Then I reminded myself that as far as the people who had wanted me dead were concerned, I *had* disappeared. In the unlikely event of their picking up some glossy publication and seeing a photograph of the Manhattan socialite and art dealer Sara Daly with her writer husband, George, all they would see was a coincidental resemblance to the man they had murdered. The most cursory of checks would establish that George Daly had been George Daly all his life. I felt so confident of this that, even if I'd had to face people who claimed that I was Larry Hart, I knew I could have pulled off the bluff. After all, everybody knows that coincidences happen. And many people believe that everybody has a double somewhere in the world.

As soon as I felt I could do so without arousing suspicion, I began casually taking stock of 'my' overall financial situation. I was canny enough about money to be able to piece together the details I found among George's personal papers, of which there were relatively few. His earnings from writing, I discovered, were far from enough to live on in the style he had enjoyed. He had some investments, a few government bonds and some gilt-edged stock, but not amounting to anything substantial.

I saw that a modest sum was paid each month into a personal account from a source which it took me a couple of days to track down. It turned out to be a trust fund set up by his evidently very wealthy wife. The income was

apparently enough to provide for George's modest needs –
but not by a long way for mine.

Worse, I came across a copy of a prenuptial agreement
drawn up by her lawyers before their marriage. It appeared
that George had committed himself, in the event of divorce
– 'for whatever reason', I noted – to making no claims either
on her inherited wealth or on the thriving gallery she had
created. Should we divorce 'for whatever reason', my
settlement was pre-arranged at a level that might
conceivably have kept George from starvation for the rest of
his life, but would have barely covered my expenses for a
year.

I couldn't make out whether George's willingness to
accept a marriage on such terms was proof of a man so
besotted by love that he was blind to any shred of self-
interest, or of a man so defeated by life as to be grateful for
whatever crumb of security his rich wife might throw him.

The last will and testament, however, turned out to be
another matter. I found copies of both his and hers at the
back of his filing cabinet. George's was a straightforward
affair mentioning a sister in Boston and two nieces, none of
whom were going to get rich on the worldly goods he had
to bestow – unless, I discovered, looking at Sara's will, she
died first. The picture here was very different from the one
enshrined in that wretched prenuptial agreement. In the
event of her death, I inherited the apartment in Manhattan,
though not the estate in the Berkshires which I had yet to
see, and which was entailed to her family. However, I
received everything else that was not specifically willed
elsewhere. I went down the list of bequests, which were
substantial, but I calculated that I stood to inherit an
investment portfolio worth many millions of dollars.

What I needed to know now was whether this was the
current will, or whether it had been superseded by a more
recent version. A couple of codicils in it concerning one of
her cousins' children and someone who worked in the

gallery were dated only six months earlier, so there was every reason to believe that this was still the one in force.

It gave me food for thought.

I got a call from George's agent, Lou, and he took me to lunch at some dreary place in Little Italy. I had to ask him to remind me of the address owing to my temporary amnesia. I caught him looking at me oddly once or twice in the course of lunch, but then his glance went to the still visible scars on my head where the stitches had just been removed. He found my state of mind curious, I concluded, but understandable.

'What about the book?' he said. 'When d'you think you'll finish?'

George had told me, of course, about his 'synchronicity' project, and before meeting with Lou I had glanced through his notes in longhand and on his computer. They struck me as nothing but a collection of loose ends and half-baked theories that I had no idea what to do with. Besides, I'd seen how little money his books earned. I'd even gone into a couple of shops and tried to buy one; they'd never heard of him. I suspected that George's life as a writer was on the same level as his role as a husband-cum-household pet. Lou, and behind him the publisher whom I never even bothered to meet and who showed absolutely no interest in meeting me, were obviously carrying him. I could only believe that their reasons for this were the financial and social clout of George's – and now my – wife, Sara. The only question that left me with was: What the hell she was doing with a man like George?

'So how's it going?'

I realized that I hadn't answered Lou's question about the book. I shifted in my chair and leant back from the table, partly to give myself a moment to think, partly to escape the foul stench of the cigar he had just lit up.

'Well, Lou, I'd like to be able to tell you it's going better than it is. In fact I'd like to be able to tell you it's going at all.'

'What's the problem?'

I shrugged. 'I'm not sure I'll be able to persuade anybody to believe a damn word I'm saying. I'm not even sure I can persuade myself.'

He raised an eyebrow almost imperceptibly, but didn't seem troubled by the announcement. 'I'm sorry to hear that. I'm sure if there's a solution to the problem, you'll find it.'

'I'm working on it,' I said. 'If I solve it, you'll be the first to know.'

'Take your time,' he said. 'You're not tied to a deadline, there's no contract. Listen, if this doesn't work out, maybe you'll think of something else.'

And that was the end of it: clear confirmation that George's career as a writer was of no interest to anyone, least of all his agent or his publisher. We had another grappa and parted company amiably on the sidewalk.

It was a crisp late fall day with a clear blue sky. To be honest, I don't usually notice things like the weather, unless of course I have a particular reason to, for example if I'm supposed to play golf or go hunting or something. That day I had no particular reason to give a damn about the weather, but I noticed it all the same, and I felt like walking for a while. As I did so, I reflected on where I was, how I'd come to this point, and where I went from here. I felt strangely disconnected from reality – a 'pod person', that old standby about aliens who take over the lives of human beings. It was interesting, if odd, to share the perspective of the alien.

I needed something more real. On an impulse I suddenly felt I'd been putting off for too long, I made a call to Nadia Shelley.

CHAPTER 17

Nadia said she could do lunch in a couple of days. Until we sat down and raised a glass together, I let her labour under the impression that the purpose of this meeting was to talk further business of some kind. When, shortly afterwards, I confessed there was a more personal aspect to the invitation, I got the impression she had expected it but hadn't been sure. She made all the right noises of protest and reservation, everything that convention required of a respectable young woman. When I proposed dinner at the weekend (when Sara would be away again) Nadia said she would let me know. I told her to call my mobile number, which she did the following day to say she could make Saturday evening.

It was another week before we went to bed together. 'Look,' I said on the afternoon we did, at her apartment, 'if there are regrets, let's just agree to have them. But they're not obligatory.'

She had thrown her head back and laughed, that

wonderful mouth framing pearl-white teeth. Then she asked me if I loved my wife. I told her how we'd drifted apart, with neither of us making much effort to reverse the process.

'You know what I think?' she said. 'I think your wife is seeing somebody. Why else would she leave you alone as often as she does? She's almost inviting you to get involved with somebody. Doesn't she ever ask you what you do with your time?'

I shook my head slowly, staring at the ceiling.

'Never.'

'Then it's obvious.'

The thought that Sara was involved with somebody had of course crossed my mind, along with the recollection of that clause in the prenuptial agreement about divorce 'on whatever grounds'. She had nothing to lose: I everything.

'Why don't you just leave her,' she asked, 'if the marriage is as dead as you say it is?'

I sighed and wondered about telling her the truth. There was something about Nadia that made me feel I could be open with her. We had made love with all the excitement of newness and novelty; at the same time there was something more between us that felt right, as though we belonged together.

But I held back. I was in bed with her, yet in truth I hardly knew her – any more, for that matter, than she knew me. It was too soon for trust. All I knew about Nadia was that she had something of the quality of a cat: the only thing she understood was pleasure. Sheer sensuous, and sensual, pleasure. And, like all cats, she knew that the only way to get it was to go right where it was and take it.

I turned over on my side, bringing our faces close together. 'The thing is,' I said, tracing a finger softly down the curve of her cheek, 'I haven't met anyone till now that made my marriage matter all that much.'

Our mouths touched, and our bodies began to reentangle yet again. The passion that we both thought we had exhausted, at least for the moment, swept over us again with undiminished force. I was harder even than I'd been before, and she whimpered her desire as the thrill of sexual excitement engulfed us both once more.

Sara was adamant. 'We'll talk at the weekend. At Eastways.'

'Why not now?'

'Because I have to be somewhere.'

'You mean some damn art charity committee is more important than—'

'George, I'm not talking to you about *anything* while you're like this.'

'Like what? What am I like? What is your problem?'

'This memory-loss thing. I think you're doing it on purpose.'

'I got hit on the head, for God's sake!'

'Your doctor said those injuries could have been self-inflicted. They even found scratches on your hands as though you'd been kneeling down to bang your head on the pavement.'

'That is the most ridiculous thing I've ever heard!'

'You need help, George – please. You're not well. You're not yourself.'

I had been trying to get out of her some clearer statement of our situation. She refused to believe that I wasn't just making trouble, going back on 'my' word of the previous week. My amnesia bluff had been called, but I still clung on to it like a drowning man hanging on to the last thing afloat. The biggest mistake I could make now would be to admit she was right and that I'd been pretending. There was no easy way out of this. The only solution was to face up to things and adopt a reasonable manner.

'All right,' I said, as though weary of argument and sorry to have put her through it, 'maybe you're right and I'm nuts and I cracked my skull open so I could *pretend* to lose my memory. Whatever! All I know is I *did* lose it, period. So yes, I do need help – and I would like it to come from you.'

'The weekend, George. I have to go.'

I closed my eyes as though in pain and listened to her footsteps recede, followed by the sound of the apartment door closing behind her. Then I flopped on to the long white sofa behind me and stared at the ceiling.

Eastways was the house up in the Berkshires. I had suggested going up there on my own, telling Sara I needed a few of days of peace and quiet in order to think. More importantly, it gave me a chance to snoop around and generally find out what I could about the man I was supposed to be. The moment I'd spoken about going up there, Sara said she would join me at the weekend. She would come up on Friday night, then we'd have all the time we needed to do whatever talking we had to do. She seemed to think it would be easier up there.

I took the train on Thursday morning, having arranged that the man who worked for 'us' would meet me on arrival. I had of course no idea what he looked like, but he knew me and hurried up to me as soon as I emerged from the station into the pale afternoon light.

It was only a twenty-minute drive to the house. I'd found a couple of photographs of the place in George's desk, but wasn't quite prepared for the sweep of the grounds and the magnificent lake view. The house itself was standard neo-Tudor, but large and pleasantly rambling.

A rotund and motherly woman bustled from the front door when she heard the car drive up. Her name, I knew, was Martha. She and her husband Joe, who had driven me from the station, lived in a house on the estate and looked after the place. I knew they had been with the family – Sara's family – for many years, so they had known George throughout his marriage to Sara.

Martha fussed around and settled me in and asked about my health. She said she understood that I'd been suffering headaches and blackouts since I was attacked. I said it was really just occasional memory lapses now, and they were getting better, but I hoped she and Joe would bear with me when I seemed lost or even stupid for a moment. The appeal touched the mother in her, and I knew I was going to have no problems with either of them.

Despite missing Nadia, I resisted the urge to call her. We had agreed that absolute discretion was essential.

That night I ate alone and watched a movie on television. Martha had fixed me some kind of chicken with a French-sounding name, and I found to my satisfaction that the house had a fine wine cellar. It was an altogether agreeable evening, after which I enjoyed a long, dreamless sleep. I decided that I liked that house; something about it agreed with me. My only regret was that, according to Sara's will, there was no way I would ever inherit it.

No word had been spoken between Nadia and myself about getting rid of Sara. We had talked only of my leaving her. I had implied it was a question of timing, legal niceties, financial settlements. If there happened to be an accident in the meantime, it would be just that – an accident. Nadia wouldn't know enough to betray me without making herself an accomplice. So she hadn't – and wouldn't – ask questions. I was very sure about Nadia on that level. She knew what she wanted and was single-minded about getting it.

I had killed before. I had killed George, admittedly not with my own hands, but I had delivered him without a qualm to those who would do the deed. I knew beyond doubt that killing did not trouble me in any moral way. All that concerned me was whether I could get away with it – the eternal eleventh commandment, the only one that mattered. I knew that Sara's murder would be harder than George's, but I would find a way. My biggest problem was time. Her life had to end before the marriage did, and although I didn't know the details it was obvious to me that this was a badly ailing marriage.

Next morning I went through the house – drawers, files and closets – in search of anything that might come in useful. Not as a weapon so much as an angle, a way of going about things that might deflect suspicion away from myself and towards . . . who could say? Perhaps the man Sara was involved with was married and I – that is George – had been a convenient beard to keep things from his wife. Or was it a woman she was involved with? Why not? Such things happen, and often.

Another thought suddenly crossed my mind so unexpectedly that it made me jump. Was George gay? Had he been the beard for his wife's affair, or affairs, while at the same time discreetly going his own way? It was a scenario I could not dismiss and which I would have to handle very carefully if it turned out to be true. But I found nothing, no evidence of entanglements of any kind on either side. In short, nothing that I didn't already know, which was precious little. It was frustrating.

After lunch I went for a walk through the woods and down to the lake. About an hour later, on my return from a different direction than that on which I had set out, I found myself stopping to look up at a clock tower on a side of the house I hadn't so far seen. Scaffolding had been erected around two sides of it.

As I stood there, Joe came up to say that he'd given instructions for the maintenance work to be suspended while I was there in order to avoid disturbing me. I thanked him for his thoughtfulness.

The top of the tower was crenellated, and I wondered if there was a terrace. A few minutes later I found the interior stairs that led up to it. I emerged into a space that would be nice for having drinks with friends on a summer evening. The parapet on one side, I could now see, had been demolished in preparation for whatever work had to be done. The scaffolding beyond it created a temporary balcony allowing work to be done from that side. I stepped out cautiously and peered over the low protective barrier. The drop was precipitous. I imagined the sound of a human skull hitting the flagstones below, and pulled back with a shiver.

But a plan had formed in my mind. It was going to be simple now. I knew exactly what I had to do.

Half an hour later I was sitting in front of a log fire in the library, nursing a whisky and soda. Waiting for the evening, when Sara would arrive.

SARA

CHAPTER 18

I had finally told George the truth the night before I left for Philadelphia. It was the most difficult thing I've ever had to do. In fact, I really had no right to do it at all. Steve and I had agreed to keep our relationship secret so long as he had one major hurdle to get over – the party vote that would confirm his selection as candidate for the state senate. It was due to take place in just over a week's time. After that his position would be more secure, though by no means unassailable. There was over a year till the election, and a lot could happen in that time – including divorce and remarriage. But a 'scandal' now, of the 'Candidate abandons family for another other man's wife' kind, would finish him before he'd even got started.

But suddenly I couldn't go on like that any longer. I was sure that George suspected something, and I simply didn't have it in me to continue deceiving him. He didn't deserve to be treated so shabbily. For too many nights we had been lying together – in more ways than one – he trying not to disturb me as he watched me in the dark, while I pretended to be asleep. Finally, that night, I knew I had to face him. There was no other way.

I opened my eyes and looked up at him, meeting his gaze.

'It's Steve, isn't it?' he said.

'Yes,' I answered simply, unable to attempt any kind of lie or evasion.

As I say, I had no right to do it. I was putting Steve at risk. Yet it didn't seem possible do anything else.

Nor did it seem possible to undo so much with one word.

George nodded his head slowly, absorbing this confirmation of his fears. 'What d'you want to do?' His mouth was dry. I saw him make an effort to swallow.

I began to say, 'I'm truly sorry, George,' but he cut me off.

'Don't. Please don't apologize. That makes it worse. Let's just be practical. What shall we *do*?'

'Separate, I suppose,' I said. 'We can't go on living like this, can we?'

'I'll move out,' he said. 'While you're away, I'll arrange it. I'll find somewhere.'

'All right,' I whispered, 'perhaps that's best.'

It seemed unreal to be disposing of our futures as simply as that. Even if he didn't want me to apologize I felt I had to explain. I wanted him at least to understand my reasons for deceiving him for so long; I wanted him to know that I had done it reluctantly. He listened calmly, not looking at me, then nodded his head once.

'You needn't worry about a scandal. I won't make any.'

I didn't say anything, just acknowledged his words in silence, knowing that I would feel like a hypocrite if I thanked him for them.

It was his idea that he move into one of the guest rooms that night. I didn't demur – it was obviously the only thing to do short of one of us going to a hotel. Not surprisingly I didn't sleep for the rest of the night; I shouldn't think George did either. I lay there thinking about how things which seem so simple to begin with can lead to such complications and become the cause of so much pain.

We went back a long way, Steve and I – to when I was fresh out of college and working as assistant to the deputy features editor of an art magazine. He was an idealistic young lawyer working for the public defender's office. Back then he had no thought of going into politics. He was brilliant, funny and handsome, so how could I avoid falling in love with him? We were together more than two years, which is a long time when you're young. It means you start asking yourself where this relationship is going.

Maybe I put pressure on him. Did I? I hadn't meant to. I think the fact that I had money created a certain barrier between us. It was always at the back of his mind, and he didn't like it. It made him fear for his independence, his self-image as a free man: his manhood, I suppose. I half respected him for that, and half wanted to knock his brains out.

Anyway, there's little point after all this time in over-analysing why it happened: the outcome's the same. We broke up for a 'trial period', which grew longer and longer, and during which he eventually met someone else.

We stayed friends. I was invited to the wedding, and I was nice to Linda, his wife, though I never liked or trusted her. Ironically, she was exactly the kind of woman he was afraid that all rich girls were beneath the surface: selfish, vain and socially ambitious. Linda was all of those things – except she wasn't rich. However, she had every confidence in Steve's ability to rectify that little problem in short order.

I suppose I married George on the rebound – at least partly. That makes me sound like a fool, which I don't think I am, and it's unfair on him. He was different from Steve, less ambitious to change the world, more curious to understand it. He'd taught at a small university, written a couple of novels, and was actually very interesting to talk to. What I liked was that he always seemed full of ideas and different ways of looking at things. I thought life with him would be civilized and companionable.

Well, it was both those things. And if eventually I came to feel it wasn't enough, then, with hindsight, I suppose I had only myself to blame. But the fact is that all the plans and ambitions that George was full of when we met failed to materialize over the years. He'd said he wanted to write more novels but never did, although he started three. He tried writing stories, but abandoned that too. In the end he began compiling anthologies, mostly about science – which was surprising in that he wasn't a scientist. He'd been teaching law when I met him, though he said he'd never been remotely interested in the subject. His main regret was that he hadn't been taught mathematics better as a child, because if he had been he could have become a scientist – a theoretical physicist, ideally. He read everything he could on the subject, struggling for hours to absorb complex ideas such as (I remember him saying once) eleven-dimensional space. Then he would regurgitate in his books what he'd understood, but in simpler language and with the addition of, as he put it, a few speculations of his own.

The problem was that his books weren't sophisticated enough for the experts or clear enough for the average reader. They didn't sell very well, nor were they reviewed much better – if they were reviewed at all. It was a classic case of falling between two stools – a region he described, wryly but regretfully, as his natural habitat. I did what I could, through various friends and contacts, to get his books published, even if I had to discreetly sponsor them myself from time to time. I hoped my intervention was never too obvious to George. He was a dear and generous soul, but it was an inescapable fact that he'd become dull. I knew he still loved me, but in my heart, although it hurt me to admit it, I had not been able to say the same about him for some time.

I had never lost all contact with Steve. We saw each other

socially from time to time, but never exchanged more than a few words, and almost always in the company of others. We only became lovers again by chance – though I wonder whether George would have called it chance? He was starting to research a book on coincidence and was beginning to see all kinds of hidden patterns everywhere.

Steve was still married to Linda – unhappily, despite two children he adored and a thriving law practice. It was because of a client that he'd flown to Chicago. I was there to check out a couple of young artists. I met him in the lobby of the Drake, where we were both staying. We arranged to have dinner that night.

For the rest of the day I thought about nothing else. He told me later that it had been the same for him. It was like getting to know an old friend all over again, the best kind of old friend, where you can pick up right where you left off – laughing at the punchlines of each other's jokes before you even get to them. I realized how little I'd ever been in love with George, and how I'd never stopped loving Steve.

I don't think either of us to begin with had the slightest intention of spending the night together; but by the time we left the little restaurant we'd found and took a cab back to the hotel, we both knew it was inevitable.

Then began the tawdry farce of an ongoing adulterous love affair. It was something neither of us relished or felt proud of, but we had no choice. We both knew that what we wanted ultimately was to be together. The main problem, at least for Steve, was timing.

There was little residual affection left between Steve and Linda. Theirs was a marriage in name only now. If they had sex, he told me, it was strictly duty, once a month, and with the lights out. And it was over quickly. But Linda was a woman who didn't easily let go of what she considered hers. The marriage had already brought her material comfort. Now, with Steve's nascent career in politics, it offered status. She would put up with his casual affairs (he confessed to me he'd had two brief ones over the years) and she made it clear that she would even tolerate a long-standing mistress rather than give up the chance of a life inside the magic circles of Georgetown dinner parties. Who could say how far Steve's talents might take both of them?

Quite apart from the problem of an ambitious wife, who would certainly do everything in her power to destroy him if he threatened to leave her, he had his children to think about. Whether his relationship with them would survive the kind of divorce that Linda would undoubtedly put him through was an open question. I told him that personally I had never believed that children benefited from parents who stayed in an unhappy marriage for their sake, but I had no children of my own so who was I to talk?

And who was I, I asked myself, to have had the good fortune to marry a man like George, who had behaved in the face of this betrayal as he behaved over just about everything — so well that you felt you were taking advantage of him. And probably you were.

Next morning he was up before I was, and even insisted on coming down with an umbrella to see me off in my taxi. I looked back and saw him standing there in the rain, such a lonely figure. I suddenly had the strongest feeling that I would never see him again. Panic swept over me. Was he going to do something foolish? Was he capable of suicide?

I was about to tell the cab to turn around when I realized what was happening — that I was projecting my own guilt on to him. It wasn't in his nature to harm himself. It would be a selfish act, and if there was one thing that George was not it was selfish.

CHAPTER 19

My trip to Philadelphia that weekend was on legitimate business and nothing to do with Steve, who was staying with Linda at the house of some political bigwig in the Hamptons. I was looking at pictures and talking with artists and gallery owners the whole time, until one of my asistants in New York called me just after four on the Sunday afternoon.

'Sara, listen, it's all right, it's not serious, but George is in the hospital.'

I felt my chest tighten and my heart started beating hard. 'What happened?'

'He was mugged last night. They found him somewhere off Third.'

'Last night? Why did nobody call me?'

'They didn't know where to find you. The hospital just tracked me down at home.'

'George knows where I am.'

'Sara, he's got head injuries. It's not life-threatening, but he's suffering from amnesia. They say it's almost certainly temporary, but right now he doesn't even know who he is.'

I got the first train back. They were expecting me at the hospital and there was a young doctor who was insistent about talking with me before I saw George.

'I want to emphasize,' he began, 'that your husband is in no physical danger.'

'But there's something wrong with him mentally?'

'That's what I want to talk to you about. It's one of the more unusual cases of amnesia I've come across.'

He explained to me that although George's bandaged head looked pretty dramatic, his injuries were superficial and not obviously consistent with the degree of his amnesia. He didn't actually say that such a complete memory loss was impossible, but he seemed to be suggesting that it was highly unlikely. Then he paused a moment, as though there was something else on his mind but he was unsure how to broach it.

'If there's something more you think I should know,' I said, 'I'd rather you didn't hold back.'

He frowned, adopting a more confidential tone. 'Mrs Daly, there is such a thing as a *psychological* amnesia as distinct from a physical one. It can arise when the victim *wants* to forget something, and perhaps uses an accidental though not serious blow to the head as an excuse to do so. Sometimes even *engineers* such a blow.'

'Are you saying my husband hit himself on the head?'

'I'm not saying anything of the kind. I'm just asking if he might have had any reason to seek temporary refuge in oblivion. Was there anything that happened in his life prior to this event that he might have wanted to avoid confronting?'

He was watching me carefully to see what effect his words might have on me. I had an uneasy feeling that he suspected I knew more than I was telling him. He was right, of course, which made me feel worse. Probably I should have told him the truth. Maybe he could have arranged psychological help for George. Maybe, that way, many things that happened later could have been avoided.

But I held back, mainly because I couldn't say much without the risk of bringing Steve's name into it. I know I could have simply said that I had told George I was leaving him, but if they had then confronted him with this as part of his therapy he might have blurted the whole story out – unintentionally perhaps, but resulting in exactly the kind of situation we were trying to avoid. It was only a matter of weeks before the crucial vote on Steve's candidacy. I had already risked upsetting things once by making my confession to George when I did. I'd got away with it then, but I had an odd feeling that I shouldn't push my luck – and Steve's – a second time.

So I shook my head, trying to look puzzled and distressed. 'No,' I said, 'I can't think of anything.'

The doctor was right about George's appearance being dramatic. With a huge turban of white bandage on his head and bluish-yellow bruising down the side of his face, he looked like he'd been in a train wreck. He was in an open ward but in a corner bed with curtains drawn around him, sitting up with some kind of tube in his arm. When I entered his little tent-like area, accompanied by the doctor, he turned to look at me with a kind of vacant curiosity, but not the slightest hint of recognition.

'George? George, are you all right? Don't you know me?'

Instinctively I reached out to touch him, but was inhibited by his unblinking gaze and pulled back.

'It's me, George, Sara.'

The muscles around his eyes tightened as he made an effort to concentrate. I saw a moment of panic as he realized he should know me but couldn't drag anything out of his memory that made sense of the face in front of him.

'This is your wife, Mr Daly,' the doctor said in a pro- fessionally calm and reassuring voice, 'but don't worry if

you can't remember her right now. Your memory will
return, so don't be alarmed by anything that happens now.
Everything will start to make sense very soon.'

As though the words had somehow triggered the
beginnings of a recovery, a change came over George's face.
He was like a man who hadn't seen someone in twenty
years, running into them unexpectedly in the street or at a
party, peeling off the layers of change that time had
wrought to find the old familiar features underneath.

'Sara . . . ? Oh, God, Sara . . . !'

My hand, which a moment ago I had withdrawn, still
hovered between us. Now he grasped it in both of his.

'What's happening, Sara? For God's sake, what's
happening to me?'

George came home two days later. He looked slightly
alarming, with a partially shaved head and several iodine-
stained stitches that would have to be removed later. His
memory had continued to return in a fragmented way, but
he could remember absolutely nothing of the attack,
though he did vaguely recall setting out to have a drink
with Lou. According to Lou he had said he wanted to
discuss something, but hadn't told him on the phone what
it was. Now, of course, George had absolutely no idea what
it might have been.

Something else he had no memory of was the painful
conversation we'd had the night before I left for
Philadelphia. He looked a little surprised when he found
all his things moved into the guest room. I debated whether
to tell him it had been his own idea, but that would have
meant reopening the whole issue, and I was far from sure I
wanted to do that. I'd spoken to Steve, and we agreed that
a let-sleeping-dogs-lie approach was probably the best way
to handle the situation for the time being. I made some
excuse to George about it being better for him to have his
own room while he was recuperating. He accepted this,

and I just hoped he would go on doing so until his memory returned so that we wouldn't have to go through the same awful confrontation yet again.

However, that wasn't how things turned out. After a few days he started talking about moving back in with me. When I tried to avoid the issue, he became suspicious. Finally he became physical: not violent, but insistent. One night he came into my room just after I'd gone to bed and tried to get in with me. His hands were all over me and he was quite obviously excited. I pulled away and tried to put him off with more excuses – headache, tired, etc. – but he would have none of it. He kept asking me what was wrong. Finally I knew I had to face it.

'George, we discussed it all. We agreed.'

'Discussed what? When?'

'Last week, before I left for Philadelphia.'

He looked at me blankly.

'Are you telling me,' I said, 'that you really don't remember?'

He said he had no idea what I was talking about. I wondered what to tell him, where to begin. Then I made one last appeal to his fundamentally generous, gentle nature. I don't recall precisely how I put it. I know I acknowledged that, yes, there was a problem, something we'd had to talk about and deal with. Because of what had happened to him he'd forgotten all about it. I promised him that we would go over it all again, and soon, but for the moment I begged him to be patient.

His eyes burned into mine, trying to read what lay behind them. Then suddenly he relaxed. It was as though he accepted that there were things he didn't know about and perhaps wouldn't for some time, and that all he could do for the moment was let them go. I thought back to what the doctor had said about the possibility of his amnesia being psychologically as much as physically induced. Perhaps somewhere at the back of his subconscious he knew the truth and recalled, however hazily, what had happened between us that night. I don't know. I felt only a huge sense of relief that he had chosen to behave so reasonably. From that night on he accepted the status quo, sleeping alone and asking no questions, concentrating on recovering more of his still impaired memory every day.

Rather to my surprise, he was perfectly happy, anxious even, to go out and meet people. He said it could only help all the pieces to come together. So we went to a couple of dinner parties, a reception or two, an opening at the Met – a social whirl which he seemed to be enjoying, curiously enough, more than he usually did. Despite the oddness of his appearance (it would be weeks before his hair grew back and covered the scars) he was poised and pleasant, a good listener, which had always been his greatest strength in conversation; but it was extraordinary to see how he sometimes totally failed to recognize old friends, people he'd known for years who had to reintroduce themselves all over again, tell him all about their lives and what they did and who their kids were, until a glimmer of recollection appeared in his eyes. Sometimes, as I watched him, I got the impression that he was only pretending to remember, like someone suffering from the early stages of Alzheimer's; later on he might turn to me discreetly for a potted biography of somebody he'd just been chatting with as though he knew them well. He would listen carefully to the details I filled in for him, nodding thoughtfully as he memorized everything.

It was inevitable at some point that we should run into Steve and Linda.

CHAPTER 20

I knew that Steve and Linda were going to be at this particular gathering. Steve and I had discussed it beforehand, wondering whether a casual meeting between the four of us should be avoided in case it triggered George's recollection of things which for the time being he had so conveniently forgotten. We decided it would seem strange if we tried to avoid an encounter altogether, trusting either that George would remember nothing, or that even if he did he would behave as well as he had done the last time around.

Linda gushed concern over George and the ordeal he'd been through, while Steve and I tried to avoid making eye contact. I found myself watching George with a closeness bordering on obsession, looking for any hint of recollection that the lives of these three people around him were entangled with his own in a way that rendered this scene of polite social chit-chat so monumentally absurd. But there was not even a glimmer of such awareness. I caught sight of Steve breathing a discreet sigh of relief. I did the same myself.

Next day Steve and I talked on the phone and wondered what our next move should be. We could wait till George recovered his memory fully and deal with his reaction then. Or we could take the chance of forestalling an ill-timed explosion by telling him the truth now. There was a third possibility – that he might never fully regain his memory at all. In which case we would go through the whole process of confession and facing the music at some point in the future when Steve and I were not in so much danger from discovery.

Steve's main concern was that George would get his memory back at some time when he and I were alone together and react badly, perhaps even violently. I tried to reassure him that such behaviour was simply not in George's nature, but he was unconvinced. 'In the right circumstances,' he said, 'everybody is capable of violence.'

But I wasn't worried. I knew George. Then, a week or so later, something happened which made me wonder whether I knew him as well as I thought. For no reason I could see he suddenly got a bee in his bonnet all over again about our sleeping arrangements. 'You promised when I came home that we'd talk about,' he said. 'Well, I've been patient, but now I want to talk about it.'

We were going up to Eastways at the weekend and I suggested we leave the matter till then. To be perfectly frank, my main reason for this was that the crucial vote on Steve's candidacy was to take place on the Friday, after which we would be clear of the worst of the potential storm clouds that had been hanging over us.

But George would have none of it. He insisted the whole issue be thrashed out there and then. It was early Wednesday evening. George had been out all day. He didn't say where he'd been or what he'd been doing, but he was in a foul mood. He may have been drinking, though he certainly wasn't drunk.

'Look,' I said, 'I can't talk now. I have to be somewhere.'

'You mean some damn art charity committee is more important than—'

'George, I'm not talking to you about *anything* while you're like this.'

'Like what? What am I like? What is your problem?'

Suddenly I said it. I hadn't meant to, but he'd made me angry and it just came out.

'This memory-loss thing. I think you're doing it on purpose.'

'I got hit on the head, for God's sake!'

I told him what his doctor had said, even throwing in a suggestion that the scratches on his hands and knees could be interpreted as proof that his injuries were self-inflicted. I knew that I was going dangerously far there, and for a terrible moment I thought he was going to hit me. But he got his temper under control and simply dismissed the idea with contempt.

Then I tried another approach. 'You need help, George,' I said. 'You're not well. You're not yourself.'

For some reason the suggestion of therapy made him back off altogether. He held up his hands in surrender. 'All right, maybe you're right, I'm nuts. I cracked my own skull open because I *wanted* to lose my memory. But if I *am* going to get any help, I'd like it to come from you.'

'This weekend,' I repeated. 'We'll talk at the weekend.'

He decided that he would go up to the house a couple of days early. He needed some time to himself, he said, and I encouraged him to take it. I knew he would be well looked after by Martha and Joe, who were very fond of him. And I promised that I would go up on Friday evening to join him, and we would talk about things then.

My sense of relief when Steve called to say that the vote had gone through without a hitch was indescribable. Only then did I realize quite how much I had been on tenterhooks. I said I was leaving for the Berkshires right away, but he asked me to wait; he said he would be with me in half an hour and insisted on coming along. I tried to protest, but truthfully I was glad to have him. There was still too much about George's state of mind that I didn't understand and which made me nervous.

We got up there just after seven thirty in the evening. I hadn't said anything to George about Steve being with me. We agreed that Steve would wait in the car while I went in and spoke with George alone. Once I'd broken the ice, and depending on how things were going, I might call Steve in to join us.

George's first reaction when I walked in was surprise that I had called Martha and told her not to prepare dinner. 'Are we going out?' he asked. 'With people? Who? Where?'

'George,' I began hesitantly, 'there's still something we have to talk about. You remember what you said the other night.'

'We agreed we'd talk, I know. But we've got the whole weekend. Come on, relax, let me pour you a drink.'

'No, thank you. I don't want anything. We have to talk now, George. Not later. Now.'

He looked at me, shrugged, and said, 'OK – go ahead.'

I felt rather like a teacher with a backward pupil who had forgotten everything he had ever learned. As I talked about Steve I watched him closely, waiting for some response, perhaps even a sudden recollection of everything that had until now been hidden behind the curtain of his amnesia. But I saw nothing. He listened with a blankness that was almost unnatural, and into which I read successively shock, anger, disbelief and heartbreak. In reality he showed none of those emotions. His coldness was the most shocking thing about the whole encounter. He didn't look at me apart from a swift glance as I began. After that he could have been listening closely or thinking about something else entirely; it was impossible to tell. I felt I didn't know him any longer. It was a strange and worrying sensation that made me wonder how much we'd ever really known about each other. Here was a man I'd spent seven years of my life with, and suddenly we were strangers.

When I'd finished he didn't respond at all for several moments. Then he looked at me in an odd, sidelong way.

'The night before you went to Philadelphia? That was when you claim you told me all this?'

'Yes.'

He was silent for a moment, then gave a short bark of laughter, as though there was something bitterly ironic in what I had just said.

'What?' I asked him. 'Why d'you laugh like that?'

'Because it's something of a coincidence,' he said, then gave another sharp, dry laugh. 'In fact it's quite a coincidence.'

'Why?'

'You wouldn't understand,' he said, looking at me sharply and, though he tried to hide it, with such a flash of rage that I took an involuntary step away from him.

'George, tell me,' I said. 'Why is it a coincidence?'

'Forget it.'

'Please. I want to know.'

'I said drop it, didn't I? Christ!'

He was angry suddenly, shouting. For a moment I thought he was going to hit me. Instead he picked up a vase and flung it across the room, shattering it against the wall. He had never behaved like that before. I suppose, considering the circumstances, it was no great surprise that he should choose this as the first time. All the same, it was so out of character, so strange to see that rage in his eyes, to hear him speak in that tone of voice, that a deep shiver of fear ran through me.

'George,' I started to say, stumbling over my words, 'I want you to promise me something. I want you to promise me that you'll get help. I'm going to call one of the doctors who examined you in the hospital, because he can suggest somebody you could talk—'

He cut me off by grabbing my wrist and starting to pull me across the room. 'Forget it,' he said. 'I want to show you something.'

I pulled back, but he was too strong for me and I was dragged after him, protesting.

'Let go of my wrist. George, you're hurting me – let go!'

'I'll let go when we get to where we're going.'

I struggled, but his grip tightened. He was beginning to really scare me now.

'Stop it! Stop it, George!'

He turned back to say something, then froze, looking over my shoulder. I felt his grip on my wrist slacken, and I looked back. Steve was standing in the door.

Steve was a big man and he'd been an athlete in college, and he was still in shape. George was no weakling, but he would certainly think twice before picking a fight with him.

'OK, I see – so that's how it is,' George said with a sneer in his voice, looking from one of us to the other. 'You two lovebirds are figuring on taking the master bedroom and putting me in the spare room again – right?'

Steve stayed where he was in the open door, and said simply, 'We've made other arrangements. We can meet tomorrow and decide what we're going to do.'

George had let go my wrist now. I rubbed it where it still hurt. It would be bruised.

'What were you so keen to show me?' I asked him.

He looked at me. Something was going through his mind, but I couldn't guess what. It was strange to feel myself so totally on the outside of him. In the end he shrugged and said, 'It doesn't matter now.'

Suddenly, just like the other night in the apartment, all the anger seemed to have drained out of him as though somebody had pulled the plug. He turned away and ran a hand over his face.

'I think it's best if we leave,' Steve said.

George made a vague gesture, still without turning to look at us. 'Sure, whatever, I . . . I guess I'll have to find somewhere to live . . .'

Suddenly he was once again the George I knew – quiet, vulnerable, at a loss. 'There's no hurry,' I said. 'Stay here as long as you like – till you're ready to look around.'

Finally he looked at me. 'Thanks,' he said, with the hint of a sad smile playing over his face. 'That's thoughtful of you, but I won't stay long. This place holds nothing but happy memories now – mostly of what might have been.'

He looked around the room as though taking his farewell of it, then said, 'That's an oxymoron, isn't it? "Memories of what might have been"?'

The mixture of emotions I'd been growing so accustomed to these past few weeks threatened to overwhelm me. Guilt, sorrow, regret and pity – including, I'm ashamed to admit, more than a trace of self-pity – made it hard for me to speak. I managed only, 'Goodnight, George. I'll call you in the morning.'

He didn't answer me, just nodded, looking down at his hands, fingers pressed together on his chest. Almost, I thought, like a monk in prayer.

Then I turned and followed Steve out to his waiting car.

CHAPTER 21

By the time I called next morning, George had left. Joe said he'd driven him to the station just after eight. He'd left a note saying he was going to the apartment to clear out his things. When I got back to Manhattan on Sunday evening, it was as though he'd never lived there.

It wasn't until forty-eight hours later that he called me to let me know that he'd taken a one-bedroom apartment in the East forties between Second and Third. He said he'd told his lawyer to get in touch with mine and do whatever had to be done. It was the same lawyer who'd represented him on the prenuptial agreement, so he didn't foresee any problems or delays.

I asked him if he needed anything. He said no, he was fine. I told him if there was anything I could do for him, ever, anything at all, he only had to ask. He thanked me and said he knew that.

Later, much later, when I thought back on everything that had happened, I realized that a less scrupulous man than

George, quite apart from causing trouble for Steve, might well have tried to profit financially from the situation. But it had always been at George's own insistence that our prenuptial agreement specify a relatively modest financial settlement for him in the event of divorce. At the time it was drawn up he'd said with a laugh that he wanted me to know how much he wanted the marriage to work, and how sure he wanted me to be that he'd never given a damn about my money.

I know he meant it at the time he said it, though I have to say that I'd wondered, in view of his recent behaviour, whether he still meant it. It was reassuring to see that he did, and that he had remained the same man I had married.

In a way it would have been easier for me if those glimpses I'd been having this last week or two of another very different George had turned out to be the truth, and he really had become the bitter, angry man I'd seen. That way I could have walked away from our marriage feeling like the injured party. This way, however, there was no question but that he was the one who had been badly treated. I would have to live with that.

And live with it I would. I loved Steve, and if we hadn't been too young and stupid last time around, we'd have been husband and wife for many years by now. We were only putting right our initial mistake.

Poor George. I still hoped he would need my help at some point, whether in terms of money or moral support. I wanted to be his friend, maybe not his best friend any longer, but the most solid and reliable one he could ever want.

That ambition was largely the product of guilt, of course. But of a real and deep affection, too.

As for Steve and I, we were already practised in keeping things hidden even from our closest friends. He now began to work out a timetable for his divorce from Linda.

Assuming that she was going to make things as difficult as possible, he reckoned that about six months from now would be the optimum time. By then it would be effectively too late to replace him as candidate, and there would still be time to get over whatever scandal Linda created and win the seat.

Anyway, we began secretly, dreamers that we were, to plan our marriage and even a honeymoon trip to Italy after a quiet ceremony in Manhattan.

Then the sky fell in on me.

That's the phrase I've always heard people use when they want you to understand how utterly and irreparably their world fell apart. Either that or the earth opened up beneath them.

In my case I think it was both. The sky fell in, and the earth opened up. It was total and unqualified annihilation.

I had been waiting for a call from Steve. Normally he was pretty good about calling when he said he would, but for once he was late. I tried his mobile, but it was switched off. We had an agreement that I wouldn't call him at home or his office for obvious reasons, so I had no choice but to wait till I heard from him.

As the hours went by, I grew anxious. Eventually, when I glanced at my watch and saw it was already almost seven. I switched on the evening news to occupy my mind.

The second story was about Steve. He had been arrested for murder. The victim was someone I'd never heard of.

A woman called Nadia Shelley.

CHAPTER 22

George called from London. In my state of shock I recalled only vaguely that a few days earlier he'd told me he was going on a trip. It was midnight over there, and he was watching a satellite channel that carried the US news.

If it hadn't been for his voice at that moment, obviously shocked but concerned and supportive, I don't know what I would have done. Fallen apart, I suppose; but in exactly what way and with what consequences I don't even want to think about.

I'm pretty sure that one thing I would have done was call the police, and maybe Steve's lawyer, thereby unthinkingly blowing the cover we had so painstakingly established for ourselves. I would not have stopped to think how the exposure of our relationship could hurt Steve in the struggle he would now face to prove his innocence of this crazy charge. It would not have occurred to me that a married man accused of murdering one woman would look all the guiltier to a jury if it was known that he was having an affair with yet another. I shall always be grateful to George for his steadying influence in that moment as well as its aftermath.

He insisted he would cut short his trip and take the next plane back. I protested, but I wasn't fooling anybody, least of all myself. I knew I couldn't handle what was happening on my own. And I knew George was still the one person above any other who I could totally depend on and trust. He made me promise I would do nothing till he got there next day.

It was late morning when he rang from a cab on his way into Manhattan. He'd taken Concorde – an expense for which I later offered to reimburse him, but he wouldn't hear of it.

The first thing he did when he got to the apartment was sit down with me and go over everything I knew about what had happened so far. All I could tell him was what we'd both heard on television, plus the few additional details there had been in the *New York Times* that morning – including the fact that the victim had lived in the East Village, and had worked, apparently, for a detective agency.

George suddenly became very still and the colour drained from his face. 'What is it?' I said. 'Is something wrong?'

'Did you say a detective agency?'

'Yes. Why?'

'Nothing,' he said, unconvincingly.

'Come on, George, I know you better than that. Why did you react when I said "detective agency"?'

He continued to look worried for a moment, then said, 'Don't you see? Maybe they'd been hired by Steve's wife. Maybe they know all about you and Steve.'

I did see. And I was disturbed by what I saw.

'You mean they're taking that as a motive, saying that's why he killed this woman?'

'I don't know. I don't know what anybody's saying. I suppose it's possible.'

I thought for a moment, then shook my head. 'I don't believe it. There has to be more to it than that.'

'Yes,' he said, rubbing his chin and looking out over the park, thoughtful, 'I'm sure you're right. There has to be more to it than that.'

CHAPTER 23

My Darling,

I hope this reaches you. I've arranged to have it mailed outside the prison so that it doesn't fall into the wrong hands. It's important, for reasons I'm sure you will understand, that nobody knows about us. That would only make things look worse for me, and it would complicate your life in ways you would be a whole lot better off without.

Much of what you will hear about me in the coming weeks is going to cause you pain and disappointment. It's true, I lied to you. I was involved with this woman when we met — more seriously than I wanted you to know. Looking back now, I can see I was a fool not to have told you the truth from the start, but I was trying to protect you. I wanted you and only you. Breaking up with Nadia was difficult, but it was done and it was over.

I didn't kill her. Please believe that. I would have

done anything in my power to spare you what you're going through now – except murder. I beg you to believe that I am innocent.

All the same, even if I'm acquitted, which I pray I will be, I accept that things can never be the same between us. That is what I most regret.

Please remember that I love you, and always have. But don't write to me, or make any attempt to contact me. It won't help either of us.

Steve.

The letter arrived by regular mail six days after Steve was charged. It confirmed what George had said about Steve's position only being worsened if our affair came out into the open. I accepted the logic of that now, but it took all the self-discipline I possessed to do so. I wanted to move heaven and earth to help him, but I knew it was useless. I could only wait and let things take their course.

Once again, I have to say, it was a time I could never have got through without George. He continued living in the apartment he'd found, and as far as all our friends were concerned we were separated. Nobody knew the reasons why, and nobody asked – at least not in any detail. The breakdown of a marriage nowadays is such a commonplace event that it's worse than ill-mannered to pry into the reasons: it's naive.

All the same, we put the question of divorce on the back burner for the time being. I don't think either of us had any doubt that we'd go through with it, but it was no longer a matter of urgency. There were other things on my mind as the case against Steve got under way.

Gossip was rife, which was hardly surprising given Steve's relative prominence in the community. Talk was widespread that his marriage had been a sham for many years. Nadia Shelley, I heard repeatedly, was only one of many affairs he'd had – with, most people assumed, his

wife's approval, or at least in the shadow of her indif-
ference.

There was also, I was shocked to find, a widespread
assumption that Steve was guilty of the murder with which
he was charged. This was on the 'no smoke without fire'
principle, I supposed. I had to admit, when I looked at
things from an outsider's point of view, that all the
elements fell into place with an awful persuasiveness:
spitfire mistress threatens trouble, leaving compromised
married lover with political ambitions with only one
solution – murder.

What was unnerving, and what I had not been prepared
for, was the sheer weight of the evidence against Steve
when the case eventually came to court. Not only were
there photographs and letters proving his relationship with
the Shelley woman – which Steve admitted to anyway –
but the evidence for his actually having killed her was
going to take a lot of contradicting.

His story was that he'd received a phone call from Nadia
Shelley just after six in the evening. She was hysterical, he
said, and insisted that he come over to her apartment right
away. When he refused, reminding her that everything was
over between them, he said she threatened to ruin him. At
first he laughed, not believing she had any way of doing
that. But then she began talking in a confused and excited
way about campaign finance, how he'd broken the law and
she could prove it. He didn't know what she meant, but in
the end, to calm her down, he gave in and agreed to go over.

She told him to let himself in using the key she'd given
him when they were lovers, and which I was frankly a little
surprised to learn that he'd kept, though he said in court
that he had forgotten he still had it till she mentioned it. He
entered her apartment, he said, shortly after seven thirty.
All the lights were on and there was music playing loudly
on the radio. The place had been ransacked, as though
there had been a burglary. Nadia Shelley, he said, lay in the

middle of her living-room floor. It looked like there had
been a struggle. She had a cut over one eye and her clothing
was torn, but not in a way that suggested sexual assault.
There was bruising around her neck as though she'd been
strangled, though there was no sign of what she had been
strangled with.

Steve panicked. He admitted that he should have called
the police at once, but he also realized how things would
look. So far as he knew, nobody other than Nadia Shelley
herself had been aware that he was going there. In what he
described as the worst decision of his life, certainly one
that disgraced him as a lawyer and disqualified him from
any claim to serve in a responsible position in public life,
he ran out of the building and drove off in his car.

It was another couple of hours before the police were
called – by a neighbour angered by the non-stop deafening
music thumping through the walls of Nadia Shelley's
apartment. By midnight, the murder squad had collected
enough evidence to want to interview Steve. The most
telling clue was eventually her phone records – the last call
of her life made to him. In his panic he hadn't even thought
of that. They claimed that he had ransacked the apartment
in search of anything that might tie him to his victim. There
was no way of knowing, they said, how much he had taken
away, though the few things he had missed were sufficient
to point the finger of suspicion firmly in his direction.

For example, there was a photograph at the back of one
of her drawers of the two of them together. They were on a
yacht belonging to some friends of hers, Steve told the
court. Soon after they first met. The start of their affair.

Then, caught behind some bookshelves, the police had
found the cover page of a document that the prosecution
said Steve had taken away with him and presumably
destroyed. He must have dropped this single page, they said,
in his hurry to get away. It referred to sums of money
received from questionable sources. The suggestion, subtly

planted by the prosecution and angrily rejected by Steve's defence team, was that Steve was in the pocket of organized crime, and that Nadia Shelley had in some way been his conduit to them.

I didn't believe any of it for a second. The idea of Steve being a murderer was ridiculous enough. But an associate of full-time criminals as well? I could never accept that.

All the same, as the trial progressed I fell increasingly into a numbing, almost paralysing depression. The proceedings were not carried live on TV, but there was coverage from outside the court every day. And of course the newspapers carried the story in every morbid detail. There was no way to escape it other than leaving the country; but not knowing what was going on would have been worse than having to face it daily. Maybe it would have helped if I'd been able to go along and watch the trial. But George was right, as Steve had been in his letter: it was wiser not.

In the end it was the forensic evidence that finished him. They found nylon fibres in the bruising and cuts around Nadia Shelley's neck, indicating that she had most likely been strangled by a pair of her own pantyhose after being knocked unconscious, or semi-conscious, by a blow to the head.

When they examined Steve's car, they found shreds of the same fibres caught on the edge of his front fender. They had no explanation of why he took the pantyhose with him instead of leaving them in the apartment, though they surmised that in his panic he might have decided it was safer to dispose of the 'murder weapon' elsewhere. He must have had them still in his hands when he left the building, not noticing in his haste to get away that he had snagged them on the fender.

George was with me when the verdict of guilty was announced. The whole nightmare ended, as it had begun for me, with the early evening news. I had fantasized about this moment. What would I do if he was found guilty? What would I do if he was acquitted? I had whole scenarios in my head for both possibilities.

In the event I just sat there, all emotion drained from me by the tensions of the previous months. I knew only that it was over; and somewhere, somehow, I was inarticulately grateful for that fact.

It was a shock to find how disconnected I felt from the whole thing. There would be a delayed response, I supposed. But for now I felt nothing. Just exhaustion and relief.

I felt George's hand take mine and his arm slip around me, drawing me very gently to him. It was only then, as I turned my face into his shoulder, that I felt the wetness of my own tears.

That was the first night George stayed at the apartment since our decision to separate. We slept together, though we didn't make love. Next day, however, and at my suggestion, he moved back permanently. Divorce was never mentioned again. Nor did we talk about the past. By tacit agreement we looked only to the future, to the shared life we had to rebuild together out of our two lives.

In my heart of hearts I knew now that George was the only man for me. It was the second time I had turned to him on the rebound from Steve. I had always been told that passion never lasts. I hadn't really believed it until that moment, when I realized that the only things that really last are companionship, intelligence, and kindness.

I was very lucky to have George.

LARRY

Clifford was heavier than he'd looked, a difficulty compounded by the fact that he was now a deadweight. He had started to regain consciousness before I got him to the edge, so I hit him again with the same stone, this time finishing the job.

My breath was coming in short, increasingly ragged gasps. For a moment I wasn't sure I could do this. Part of it was nerves, of course, as well as physical effort. It was only the second time I had taken a human life with my own hands, so the experience was still an unfamiliar one. I hoped, on the whole, that it would remain so.

Nonetheless, a barrier had been crossed, a taboo broken. Such a flouting of convention meant a certain new freedom gained. A demon had been at once both celebrated and defied.

The last few yards were the hardest because the land rose to a kind of lip over the howling, wind blown emptiness beneath. From far below came the sound of waves smashing against the rocks. It was a perfect place to miss one's footing in the dark – especially with the amount of alcohol they would find in his body – and die without a whisper of suspicion being raised.

I managed to line him up, feet and shoulders propped between thick clumps of coarse grass to stop him rolling back. Then, with one final effort, I pushed him over the edge. His fall made no sound, and whether his body hit the rocks or disappeared in the broiling waves I had no idea. He would be found no doubt the following day or soon after, by which time I would be back in the States, with no evidence that I had ever been away.

By 'I', of course, I meant George Daly. The man who had flown into Heathrow the previous day, and would fly out the following afternoon, was Larry Hart – the same Larry Hart who had made a brief trip back to Manhattan in the middle of George Daly's recent stay in London, a trip which had coincided with the death of Nadia Shelley and the arrest of Steve Coleman.

I picked up the stone with which I'd beaten out Cliff's brains and threw it after him: it wouldn't do to have it found up on top with traces of his blood on it. That done, I started the long hike back to the rented car I'd parked almost a mile away. I looked at my watch and saw it was just after eleven. I would be back in London by one thirty, tucked up in bed in my anonymous hotel. I would be tired and would sleep soundly.

As I walked, I couldn't suppress a smile when I thought of the irony in what had just happened. His surname had been Edge, and his parents had chosen to christen him Clifford. His name had been the first thing he'd made a joke about when I'd met him in a pub near my hotel in London's Bayswater a few weeks earlier. Still, he said, it wasn't as bad as the couple called Balls who christened their daughter Ophelia. Clifford was a fund of such jokes, acquired during a lifetime in the used-car trade. Pickings were currently a little thin, I had soon gathered from the morose, self-pitying tone his conversation took on after a few large Scotches. It came as no surprise that the offer of five thousand pounds in cash instantly commanded his total and undivided attention.

He was exactly what I needed. Unmarried, unattached, a loser. Clifford was a gift from heaven. Or wherever.

I couldn't help smiling as I thought of how he was now fated to win a certain kind of cheap immortality by being listed in one or more of those anthologies of strange coincidences that George had been so fond of:

'Cliff Edge falls to death from cliff edge'.

Neither Cliff nor Nadia before him had seen their deaths coming. It wasn't that either of them had been unusually naive or stupid – certainly Nadia wasn't – so I could only conclude that my own capacity for simulation and deception was as great as I'd always believed.

Mind you, I myself hadn't seen Nadia's death coming at first. It was something that evolved over time – a matter of weeks. That night in the Berkshires, when I'd first learnt about the affair between Steve and Sara, nothing could have been further from my mind than killing Nadia. It was Sara I'd been planning to get rid of. No doubt, if I'd succeeded, Nadia would have benefited handsomely from the proceeds, at least for a time. I had never imagined our relationship would become permanent. It was a carnal fling, a good time on both sides, but with no illusions. She would have taken her pay-off when the time came and moved on without complaint. Of that I was sure.

However, that would not be the way things turned out. Coincidence would intervene – as absurdly and improbably as anything in those notebooks of George's that I found myself occasionally dipping into. I confess that the subject was beginning to exercise a certain fascination over me. For example, although I still resisted the whole notion of significant coincidences, what is one to make of this kind of thing?

A Dublin man called Anthony Clancy was born on the seventh day of the week, in the seventh day of the month, in the seventh month of the year, in the seventh year of the century. He was the seventh child of a seventh child, and had seven brothers. Which makes seven coincidences involving the number seven.

On his twenty-seventh birthday he went to a race meeting and in the seventh race backed horse number seven, which was called Seventh Heaven. It carried a handicap of seven, the odds were seven to one. He put seven shillings on the horse. It came in seventh.

Then there was a story told, apparently, by Jung himself:

As a small boy in New Orleans, a certain M. Deschamps was once given a piece of plum pudding by a M. Fortgibu. Ten years later, in a Paris restaurant, he saw a plum pudding and ordered a slice, only to learn that the remaining piece had already been ordered – by M. Fortgibu.

Many years later, M. Deschamps was invited to a dinner party where plum pudding was served. While eating it, he told the story of the earlier coincidence involving M. Fortgibu. At that moment the door opened, and the now elderly M. Fortgibu entered – having mistaken the address to which he'd been invited and burst in there by mistake.

And then there was the woman who lost her wedding ring in a field and forty years later found it in a potato she was peeling in her kitchen sink.

What can anyone say about such things? Can you simply ignore them merely because they don't make sense?

Because I was familiar, or at least becoming increasingly familiar, with the idea of these coincidences, I was perhaps less staggered and astounded than I might have been when one such event came out of nowhere and hit me squarely between the eyes.

Actually, it didn't quite come out of nowhere. It came out of one of Nadia's kitchen drawers. I was searching around for a corkscrew one night when I came across, at the back of a jumble of matchboxes, balls of string, nail-clippers, Band-aids and aspirin, a curled and cracked polaroid that sent my mind reeling.

My first thought was of something else I'd read in George's notes – the theory that just by thinking about synchronicity you can make strange things start happening around you. George had written that he didn't believe that. Looking at the photograph in my hand, I wondered briefly if I hadn't become more of a believer than George.

I was looking at a picture of Nadia with her arms around none other than Steve Coleman – the very same Steve Coleman who, only a few days earlier, had stood in the door of 'my' house in the Berkshires and told me I was history.

In the picture they were on the deck of what looked like a luxury yacht. They wore casual clothes, and there was nothing improper in the pose – except it shouldn't have existed. They weren't supposed to know each other. This, truly, was an impossible coincidence.

Yet there it was.

I took the photograph back into the bedroom, where Nadia lay propped against a bank of pillows, one wrist hooked lazily over a raised knee.

'What have you got there?' she asked.

I showed her. She gave a dismissive little laugh.

'Where did you find that?'

'Kitchen drawer.'

'God – I thought I'd thrown everything out.'

'Tell me about him.'

She looked up at me with a hint of amusement. 'What's the matter? Jealous?'

'Maybe. Tell me.'

'His name was Steve.'

'And?'

'Why d'you want to know?'

'Just . . . interested.'

I leant across and kissed her, then climbed back into bed with her. It took a while, but little by little I got the whole story out of her. They had met eighteen months earlier and their affair had lasted a year – until, obviously, Steve had become involved with Sara again. But she knew nothing of Sara. He had told Nadia he was going back to his wife, that he was trying to save his marriage – for the sake of the children more than his political career. So far as she knew, that was what had happened. She accepted it, but I sensed a lingering sadness in her, a regret for what might have been, though she wouldn't admit it.

Nor did I tell her what my real interest was in this man. I suspected that I would in time, but as a general rule I never volunteer information spontaneously. I need to think about it first. I remembered reading something in another of George's notebooks, about the meaning of a brush with synchronicity. I looked it up later:

[It is] as if some mute power were tugging at your sleeve. It is then up to you to decipher the meaning of the inchoate message. If you ignore it, nothing at all will probably happen; but you may have missed a chance to remake your life, have passed a potential turning point without noticing it.

I wasn't going to let that happen.

CHAPTER 25

The final catalyst was when Nadia found my passport – the one in the name of Larry Hart. We were at my apartment and it fell accidentally out of my briefcase when she pushed it across the table to make room for a Chinese takeout she had ordered.

Accidentally? What a suspect word that had become in the light of everything that had been happening. Could I have unconsciously created a chain of events that had led to that 'accident' and her discovery? Or had she somehow intuited the truth and engineered this accident to confirm it? Why did she open the passport instead of just handing it back with an apology for her carelessness? Do we all automatically open one another's passports when we find them? I don't know.

But she did, and it sealed her fate, my fate, Steve's Coleman's, and my wife's. It was, in short, a turning point in which a previously uncertain future took clear shape.

She needed a moment to absorb the significance of what

she was looking at. Then her eyes connected with mine. There was a hint of suspicion and even accusation in her gaze.

'What's this? "Laurence Hart"?'

I tried to look unconcerned and merely held my hand out for the document. But she pulled back as though I would have grabbed it if I could.

'Wait a minute,' she said, frowning as she searched her memory, 'wasn't that the name of the man you were looking for when you came to the agency?'

'No, I was looking for his parents. They were friends of my parents. If you remember, it turned out they were dead, but they had a son called Larry Hart.'

'That's right, I remember now. And you didn't want us to go on looking for him.' She looked at the passport photograph again, and then at me, her head slightly to one side and her eyes narrowing. 'So what are you doing with your picture in his passport?'

'It's my passport,' I said.

'*You're* Larry Hart?'

I managed a smile, as though she was making more out of a trivial matter than it was worth.

'I've used the name Larry Hart for years as a pen name under which I write from time to time. Then, when my father died, I discovered that he and my mother used to have some friends called Hart, and I was curious about them. I'd no memory of ever hearing them mentioned, and certainly nothing about them having a son called Larry. But obviously I must have heard something in childhood, which is where the name Larry Hart surfaced from later.'

She looked unconvinced. 'Didn't anyone tell you that you can get in trouble for having a false passport?'

I shrugged. 'It comes in handy when I don't want people to know what I'm up to.'

She looked at me for a while with open, almost mocking scepticism, then held the passport out for me to take.

'Whatever you're doing, big boy, you're not lying about it very well. But it's your business. Now let's eat before this Peking duck gets cold.'

It was the way she stayed off the subject for the rest of the evening that made me realize I couldn't trust her. She had become a threat, one that I had somehow to neutralize. By the time I brought in two cups of expresso from my machine in the kitchen, I had figured out how to do it.

'There's another little matter I've been holding out on you about,' I said casually, placing a steaming cup next to her. 'Your ex-lover, Steve Coleman, is planning to marry my wife.'

I will never forget the look on her face at that moment – abject and total disbelief, mixed with the kind of this-can't-be-happening denial that the plane you're in has just lost a wing, or that the eight-wheeled truck skidding gracefully towards your car is about to turn you, three seconds from now, into a greasy smear on the surface of the road.

'What did you say?' was all she could manage.

'You heard,' I said, with the hint of a smile of apology that I hoped would soften the blow that my remark had delivered. 'He dumped you because he began an affair with my wife, Sara, six months ago.'

She stared at me with her mouth hanging open. It was the first time I'd ever seen her lose such a degree of physical control. Nadia was a very centred woman, always poised and conscious of the impression she created. Now, for a moment, she was like a puppet whose strings had been cut; she just hung there, loose, at a loss, uncoordinated. Then she made an effort to collect herself.

'And you've known this all along . . . ?'

'Only since the other night, when I found that photograph of you and him.'

'Why didn't you say something then?'

'Because I was as shocked then as you are now. I didn't know what to make of it. I needed to figure out what was going on.'

'And have you? Figured out? What's going on?'

I spread my hands in a gesture that acknowledged how little I really knew. 'All I can tell you is that the more we become conscious of the coincidences that go on around us all the time, the more of them seem to happen.'

'Oh, come on, this is more than a coincidence. It's . . . it's . . .'

'It's what?'

'It's . . .'

She gave up trying to find the word, and finally burst out with, 'It's too fucking incredible to be a coincidence!'

'So what is it? A conspiracy?'

'I don't know what it is. But things like this just don't happen.'

I leant closer to her, like someone imparting a confidence. 'Things like this happen all the time,' I said. 'I know, because I'm writing a book on the subject.'

'You are? George Daly? Or Larry Hart?'

There was a hardness in her challenge. Distrust had bitten very suddenly and deeply into her.

'I am – George Daly. Forget the Larry Hart thing. It really isn't a big deal. We've both got bigger things to think about.'

'We do?'

She still didn't take her gaze off me. She knew damn well that I was up to something. The only problem was she couldn't figure out what.

'The reason I didn't mention anything about Steve Coleman and my wife was because it took me a day or two to figure out just what fate was handing us here.'

Her gaze lost none of its hardness, but I saw a flicker of new interest as she picked up the scent of opportunity. She had a larcenous soul, little Miss Shelley, and a vindictive one. I'd always sensed it in her.

Now I was counting on it.

CHAPTER 26

The story I sold her was of how, as a man romantically and passionately in love with his wife, I had blindly signed whatever papers her lawyers had put in front of me. Only later, when the marital vows began to wear thin, did I realize what a miserly settlement I had committed myself to in the event of divorce.

Frankly, I exaggerated considerably the degree of meanness with which I – George, that is – had been treated. Even though the settlement would have sounded no more acceptable to Nadia's ears than it did to mine, it had to be said – I had said it myself already – that by the lights of a mousy academic like George, it was perfectly adequate.

Nadia bought that part of the story without a problem. What she needed, however, was proof positive of the relationship between Steve and Sara. It still seemed to her beyond the bounds of all possibility that such a coincidence could have arisen. I dispelled her doubts, however, in a single call to Sara which I had Nadia listen to on a second phone.

160   DAVID AMBROSE

'Don't be misled by my tone of voice,' I warned her beforehand. 'I've made a point of staying on good terms with Sara just for practical reasons. There's no way I can break that prenuptial agreement, and so my best bet is appealing to whatever better nature and potential generosity she may have.'

Nadia understood that well enough. Strategy and tactics were second nature to her. Life was not something simply to be lived, but a progress to be negotiated, like a complex deal, or a tricky passage through some channel where every turn of the wheel had to be executed to the precise inch if the vessel was not to founder on hidden rocks. Nadia understood the need for subterfuge and lies. The tone of brotherly affection with which I addressed my soon-to-be-ex-wife on the phone caused her no problems.

'Hi, it's me. How's everything?' I began.

'Fine. A little tired. Went to an opening last night, the new John Guare play. It turned into a late night.'

'Was Steve there?'

'No. We still avoid chance meetings if we can.'

'By the way,' I said, seeming to change the subject but catching Nadia's tight-lipped expression out of the corner of my eye, 'I signed that other stuff your lawyers sent over. I guess that's about it now.'

'I guess. You OK? Everything working out all right?'

'I'm fine. How about you? Things going as planned?'

'How d'you mean?'

'Well, Steve's got his nomination now. He's going to have to talk to Linda sometime soon, isn't he?'

'Hey, we're on the phone — remember? Talk about something else.'

There was a note of surprise more than irritation in her voice. She wasn't used to my being so indiscreet, but I think I made it sound more like a casual lapse than anything deliberate. I could see from Nadia's face that it had done the trick.

'Sorry,' I said, 'I wasn't thinking. None of my business anyway. Just so long as you're OK. Listen, there's somebody at the door, I have to go. We'll talk soon.'

I hung up. Nadia did the same, slowly and deliberately, any lingering doubt in her mind banished by what she had just heard. We looked at each other.

'OK?' I said.

She nodded. 'So tell me, what d'you have in mind?'

The starting point of my plan was something that Nadia had mentioned the other night when I'd found the photograph of her with Steve. As I knew, the agency she worked for had associates who offered various kinds of financial services which no doubt dovetailed into some of the investigations they were called upon to conduct. It didn't surprise me to learn that some of these services verged upon the shady – for example, the seeking out of investment funds from sources about which it was unwise to ask too many questions. Conversely, from time to time, sources of these unwise-to-question funds would be on the lookout for opportunities where their largesse could be profitably deposited – such as the campaign funds (and slush funds) of politicians, particularly up-and-coming ones with a long-term future in front of them. One such source of finance had targeted Steve Coleman, and Nadia had, one way or another, found herself part of the bait set to hook him.

To his credit, he hadn't bitten. At least not on the money, which he immediately smelt was suspect. But he had bitten on Nadia.

She, to her credit, had neither agreed nor been asked to perform sexual favours for the benefit of her employers and their clients. However, such an eventuality was not proscribed if she chose to volunteer those favours in a private capacity on her own behalf. Such, she had decided within an hour of meeting Steve Coleman, would be the case. Nadia was not a woman to hesitate or falter when her interest was aroused.

He had talked from the first, she told me, of leaving his wife. No direct promises, nor had she demanded any. But he made no secret of the fact that his marriage was a dreary, loveless one that he doubted could continue for very much longer. Nadia, being a free-spirited and independent individual, had extracted no undertakings and entertained no fantasies of domesticity in the event of a divorce. Indeed, when he announced that he was ending their affair in order to repair his marriage, she had accepted the decision regretfully but with good grace.

Now, however, the discovery that she had been lied to caused her to feel simple, pure outrage. Her response to my suggestion that we concoct a document which, though it would prove nothing in a court of law, would terminally smear the candidate's name and reputation, was to seize on it with gusto. She knew enough to put together a series of memos, letters, and 'notes from meetings' to suggest that Steve Coleman was in bed – metaphorically – with the kind of people whose friendship no politician could acknowledge in public.

Pay day, I persuaded her, would come when he went to my wife and told her of the mess he was in. A couple of million dollars was pocket money to Sara. I confess I painted a picture of her that was not entirely accurate: for example, that she was fiercely ambitious for her next husband's career and would do anything to protect the future that she had in mind for them both. Linda, his present wife, was a problem that could be handled in the right way at the right time. Divorce was a minor scandal that he would recover from – it was all simply a matter of timing.

But the suggestion of financial impropriety of the kind we could invent – that was something he would not easily talk his way out of. And it was something, I said, that my wife would gladly open her chequebook to protect him from.

Nadia learned and rehearsed her role, which I could see she would play to perfection. The idea was that she would call Steve out of the blue and suggest that he come over to her apartment right away. He would of course refuse, whereupon she would threaten him with a scandal involving illegal campaign funding. He would almost certainly laugh that off as being unfounded and unprovable. Whereupon she would threaten a scandal which would involve his current mistress. Naturally, he would want to know where she got her information and would probably suspect me. If he mentioned my name, she would say she had never heard of me. He would never know whether I was involved or not.

What he would do, I was quite certain, was comply reluctantly with her demand. He would, effectively, have no choice. He would go to her apartment, alone, as she demanded. Whereupon the trap would spring.

The only thing that Nadia didn't know was that she was not only the bait, but as much a victim of the trap as Steve Coleman.

CHAPTER 27

A week before the big day, I boarded a scheduled British Airways flight from JFK to Heathrow, and checked into one of the largest hotels in the Bayswater district of London. The need for anonymity was paramount in my choice. I needed to be a clearly verifiable guest, but without being too familiar a face. That was where Clifford came in. Mr Cliff Edge.

'It's very simple,' I said, as we walked through the darkened streets of Paddington after leaving the pub on the night we met. 'I give you my key and you use my hotel room for two, maybe three nights while I'm away. There'll be no problem with the front desk because you won't have to talk to them, and even if you do it's unlikely you'll speak to anyone who's actually set eyes on me for long enough to remember me.'

The story I spun him was the kind that went down well with the kind of man he was. If my wife ever made inquiries, the hotel would verify I'd been a guest throughout the period when in fact I'd been enjoying a few nights in Paris with a girl from my accountant's office. I assured him that there was little chance of my wife or anyone else trying to call me, but just in case the phone did ring he was to ignore it but pick up any messages and give them to me when I returned. For this service I would give him two and a half thousand up front, and the other half afterwards.

As a secondary precaution, I made sure that my passport in the name of George Daly remained in the hotel's main safe, along with two or three other valuables and my travellers' cheques, throughout the whole period I was away. Then, using my Larry Hart passport, I took a TWA flight back to New York.

Nadia knew all about my trip to London, but not all the details or the real reason for it. I told her I had to set up an account into which my wife would pay the money that Steve would get out of her to buy Nadia's silence. Naturally, I said, I would be back for D-Day, though I had little doubt that she could perfectly well take care of herself when Steve came over. One of the things I admired about her was that she didn't know the meaning of fear – any more than she did of guilt, shame, or moral repugnance. But I promised her I would be there – not actually in the room, of course, but somewhere in the apartment, and with a gun in case of trouble.

Steve behaved exactly as predicted when she called him at his office. She was put through right away, but he sounded guarded. She told him she had to see him urgently.

'I'm tied up right now, Nadia. Can't you tell me on the phone what this is about?'

'I think you'd rather I didn't do that, Steve.'

'What d'you mean?'

'For one thing, we don't know who could be listening in, do we?'

She shot a big wink to where I sat with an extension to
my ear and my hand over the mouthpiece. I winked back.

He gave a practised laugh, though I could detect an
underlying unease in it. 'If it's all that important, come to
the office.'

'No. You come here, to the apartment.'

'I really don't think that's a good idea.'

'Steve, I'm not arguing with you. I'm telling you what
you're going to do.'

'Nadia, what is this . . . ?'

She began subtly turning the thumbscrews with talk of
campaign funds, coupled with the use of the term
'avoidable scandal'.

His voice took on a harder edge as anger took over from
uncertainty. 'I don't know what you're talking about, Nadia
– and neither do you. Whatever your game is, I'm not
playing. If you want to see me, come to the office. I'm sorry,
but I'm going to have to hang up now.'

'How's Sara?'

A fatal pause. She waved her fist in triumph; she knew
she had him.

'Sara?'

'Not on the phone, Steve – right? Let's say seven-thirty at
the apartment. Come alone, drive yourself. You know
where you can park.'

He protested some more, but he knew he had no choice.
She managed to imply that this was a once-and-for-all deal,
some kind of compensation for the fact that he'd lied when
he left her, and that he had not in fact been planning to save
his marriage but had taken up with a new mistress. She
refused to tell him how she knew this, but hinted she might
reveal her sources once the business between them was
over.

I watched his arrival from the corner of Nadia's building
where I had a clear view of the whole street. I was satisfied
that he was alone. No other cars cruised suspiciously by or

parked at around the same time. I saw him walk towards the building, coat collar turned up and hands deep in his pockets. There was no doorman, so visitors either had to use a key or be buzzed in. Nadia had established on the phone that Steve still had the set of keys she'd given him, which made my job easier. Otherwise, I would have had to wait in the apartment to buzz him in, then leave the door on the latch and make my getaway down the back stairs before he stepped out of the elevator.

As it was, I already stood across from where he'd parked his car. In my hand I had the pair of pantyhose with which, ten minutes earlier, I had strangled Nadia. I let enough time pass, a minute maybe, until Steve would be in the elevator on his way up to her floor. Then, checking there was no casual pedestrian close enough to see what I was doing, I crossed over and carefully snagged the pantyhose on the edge of his front fender. I paused only to ensure that enough fibres were torn and caught where they would readily be found later, then continued innocently on my way, slipping the pantyhose into a plastic bag in my pocket. It was possible I might need to plant them somewhere later in order to make the case against Steve conclusive, though I thought probably not. All the same, I meant to leave as little as possible to chance.

Two hours later Larry Hart boarded his return flight to London, where Clifford was paid off. Everything had gone perfectly to plan. When the news of Steve's arrest was piped by satellite to the TV set in my hotel room, I picked up the phone and called Sara. Then I called Heathrow, upgraded my return BA flight (in the name of George Daly) to Concorde, and set off once more across the Atlantic.

On the way I thought through for the thousandth time everything that had happened, looking for the flaws that might conceivably still show up. Although I knew now that Steve had panicked and run when he had found Nadia's body, even if he'd done the decent thing and called the cops, he would still have emerged as the prime suspect. The whole back-story of his affair with her, the carefully planted clues I'd left around the apartment, the nylon fibres on his fender – all these things would have made a very hard case for him to answer. The best perception of him would have been as a man who committed murder in a moment of panic, then tried to remove all the evidence implicating himself, but crucially missed some; then finally attempted the classic trick where the killer tries to establish his innocence by calling the police and pretending to have discovered the body. It wouldn't have worked. Whether he ran or stayed put, his goose was cooked.

All the same, it wasn't over yet. So far as Sara was concerned, everything went as I'd foreseen. But I knew there would be inquiries about me by lawyers working for Steve's defence. I was as ready for them as I could be. I had calculated – rightly as it turned out – that a lawyer with political ambitions would have many potential enemies. I was far from being the only suspect. The biggest risk I ran was that somehow my relationship with Nadia would become known. If that happened, I could find myself in big trouble. Should that become a risk, then Larry Hart was poised to fly to some unextraditable territory in South America or one of several other continents that I had on my list of emergency hide-outs.

A secondary risk was that the connection between myself and the detective agency that Nadia had worked for might be discovered. It was no more than a remote risk so long as nothing about Steve's affair with Sara came out into the open. But if the liaison between Steve Coleman and Sara Daly became known, then George Daly's connection with the firm for which Nadia had worked would surely surface. However, I was as prepared as I could be for that. Sara had seen my 'shock' when I had read in the paper that Steve's victim had worked for a detective agency. I would explain that I hadn't told her about my own connection with that agency because it had struck me as yet another 'weird coincidence'. A man with something to hide would have suppressed even that little show of surprise I had so carefully put on for her to see. In retrospect, it would have tended to suggest my innocence.

Investigators called on me, of course, as I had foreseen. Not cops: men working for Steve's defence. They were polite and careful in their approach. It was clear that Steve had told them about Sara, but with the injunction that the matter was not to be brought into the open unless absolutely necessary. The fact that I could prove I'd been in London when Nadia was murdered effectively took me out of the frame of suspicion, as I had intended it should. Everything was just fine – until Clifford Edge called me.

Clifford had got my address and phone number from someone at my hotel in London – some grasping palm greased by a fifty, I imagine. His sleazy loser's instincts were perhaps sharper than I had anticipated. I wasn't clear what he suspected, but it was obviously something more than my story about a suspicious wife and a dirty weekend in Paris. Whatever I was up to, Clifford thought there should be more money in it for him than he'd been paid so far.

I acquiesced with grace, and even, I must say, proud of my presence of mind, some humour. 'Cliff,' I said, 'you're as smart as a whip and a credit to my choice of you as a partner. I think I may have a big opportunity for a man like you. I'm going to be over in a couple of days, and you and I are going to talk some serious business.'

So it was that Larry Hart made one final trip to England. Cliff and I met in a pub in Shepherd's Bush. I had rented a car and told him that I needed him to drive down with me to the coast. I hinted at import–export deals, with a knowing wink that spoke of contraband and easy money. I told him I had friends from overseas I wanted him to meet;

he would be my man in the UK. It was an offer he couldn't refuse.

I had a bottle of Scotch in the car, and it wasn't hard persuading him to drink most of it. If they autopsied him, they would find enough alcohol in his system to make a verdict of accidental death a certainty. Nobody was going to make waves about the loss of a sad case like Cliff Edge, just jokes about his name and the circumstances of his departure from this life.

As I said, another coincidence.

Once they start, for whatever reason, they come thick and fast.

CHAPTER 28

The first thing I did when I got back to New York was destroy my passport – the one in the name of Larry Hart. I also had to get rid of all the other evidence that George had unearthed of my existence, including the childhood photographs and everything connected with my adoptive parents. As long as that stuff was still around, I was potentially at risk. I burned everything in a steel waste basket, then flushed the ashes down the toilet. It was the only way. Because you can hide things, put them in safe places, forget about them – but there's always a lingering risk that ten years on somebody will tear up the cellar where you buried the body. Or you'll forget you hid a secret copy of some crucial letter in your desk – until after you've sent it to the sale room. People make dumb mistakes, and people includes yourself. That's something I never forget.

I had very nearly made a couple of seriously dumb mistakes with Sara earlier. The worst had been that night in the Berkshires when I was planning to kill her, the night when she'd arrived and told me she was in love with somebody else and was leaving me. I'd almost lost it then. I grabbed her by the wrist and began dragging her towards the stairs, and only stopped when Steve Coleman appeared in the door. It wasn't that I was afraid of him. It just made me ask myself what I thought I was doing. The plan had been to push her off the tower quietly and with no fuss, because she would be unconscious already. I would merely have to ensure that she was dead after the fall, and rectify the situation if she wasn't, then call for help. I would have said she went up to the tower alone, and since I had not been responsible for the building work up there I could hardly be accused of setting a trap for her. Which of course I hadn't. That much would be plain.

As for proving I had pushed her, there was no way. It was my word that I was downstairs the whole time against the word of anyone who chose to challenge me. Unprovable.

So what was I doing trying to drag her to her death in full view of Steve Coleman? It meant I would have to kill him too. And that would be hard to explain.

I pulled myself together and did what I could to salvage the situation. I've always suspected I had something of the actor in me, and at that moment I proved it. I went straight into humble, unselfish George mode. I'd picked up enough of what people thought about him by then. I knew how humble, unselfish, dick-brain George would have behaved. I went on behaving like that for the following days and weeks.

The performance stood me in good stead. When everything collapsed under her, I was the only person Sara could turn to. I'd been in on her secret, and I'd kept it. Good old humble, unselfish George. Loyal as a favourite dog. Trustworthiness itself. The whole thing had played like a dream.

Throughout it all – the setting up of Nadia's murder, Steve's arrest, Sara's trauma – I had continued reading

George's notebooks. I found they gave me a more useful insight into who he was than anything else could have. He had a weird kind of mind, somehow turned in on itself, forever looking for 'the still point of the turning world', as he put it – whatever he meant by that. He said he'd touched it sometimes in meditation.

Sounded more like vegetation in my opinion. Mental masturbation posing as philosophy. Still, that's who he was, so that was who I had to be – to all intents and purposes.

He was more interesting on the subject he'd been working on just before his death, though maybe I felt that because the subject of coincidence had begun to interest me for my own personal reasons. Without coincidence, in fact quite a few coincidences, I wouldn't have been where I was by then, sitting very pretty, comfortably ensconced in my new – and George's old – life.

All the same, I still couldn't bring myself to believe that a coincidence was anything more than just a coincidence, no matter how amazing. There was no more to it than that. There couldn't be. No more than met the eye.

Not to George, though. Back to his notebooks:

What is this thing 'synchronicity?' What does it *mean*? Jung tells a story that suggests an answer.

'A young woman I was treating had, at a critical moment, a dream in which she was given a golden scarab. While she was telling me this dream I sat with my back to the closed window. Suddenly I heard a noise behind me, like a gentle tapping. I turned round and saw a flying insect knocking against the window-pane from outside. I opened the window and caught the creature in the air as it flew in. It was the nearest analogy to a golden scarab that one finds in our latitudes, a scarabaeid beetle, the common rose-chafer *(Cetonia aurata)*, which, contrary to its usual habits, had evidently felt an urge to get into a dark room at this particular moment.'

Up till that time, Jung writes, the woman had refused to believe that her dreams could be important in resolving her psychological problems. She could not see the connection. Now she understood how all kinds of connections might exist, and how they would explain a great many things if they did. She recovered quickly.

But what does synchronicity itself explain? Koestler writes in *Janus*:

'An essential feature of modern physics is its increasingly *holistic* trend, based on the insight that the whole is as necessary for the understanding of its parts as the parts are necessary for understanding the whole. An early expression of this trend, dating from the turn of the century, was "Mach's Principle," endorsed by Einstein. It states that the inertial properties of terrestrial matter are determined by the total mass of the universe around us.'

Like the Chinese proverb: 'If you cut a blade of grass, you shake the universe.'

But what is this shakeable universe and the blade of grass *made* of? What is the *stuff* of reality? On the cutting edge of theoretical physics now we have *String Theory*, which suggests that the ultimate building block of everything, including space, is a kind of minute string or loop which vibrates at different speeds according to whether it's going to become part of an oxygen molecule, a rose petal, Einstein's brain – or whatever. These so far purely theoretical strings are supposed to be so small as to be not only undetectable but virtually unimaginable. I read somewhere that if you blew up a single atom to the size of the known universe, one of these superstrings that made it up would still be only the size of a tree. In the end, this sort of thing strikes me as being uncomfortably close to the farcical notion of mediaeval scholars arguing in all seriousness about how many angels could dance on the head of a pin.

The point is, every time you get 'reality' down to one thing, it has a habit of turning into something else.

Physicist F. David Peat writes: 'Science may, in the end, have to look in new directions if its understanding of nature is to continue. Already many scientists are dissatisfied by the "reductionist" nature of some branches of science and with the claim that an ultimate level of reality is shortly to be reached as a result of research on elementary particles . . . The idea that reality may unfold into a complex, and potentially endless, series of levels changes the whole meaning of reductionism . . . Any level of scientific explanation depends on, and is conditioned by, concepts and meanings that arise in other levels . . .'

Jung wrote: 'We delude ourselves with the thought that we know much more about matter than about a "metaphysical" mind or spirit, and so we overestimate material causation and believe that it alone affords us a true explanation of life. But *matter is just as inscrutable as mind*.'

In other words, mind and matter are one. Back in the twenties and thirties, when the quantum revolution was getting under way, mathematicians and cosmologists like Jeans and Eddington were saying things like 'The stuff of the world is mind stuff,' and 'The universe looks less and less like a great machine and more and more like a great thought.'

It is a fact that the deeper you look into matter, the less 'material' it becomes. Cells are made of atoms and atoms are mostly space, then down below that we're into quantum indeterminacy, 'quarks' and 'gluons' and now these damn 'strings.' Matter has no more physical substance than a thought.

How much substance has a thought?

The absence of anything – no life, no universe,

nothing – is unthinkable. Try it. You cannot imagine that nothing exists. But if, as seems increasingly likely, all that exists is a thought, whose thought is it?

And why does it seem to take two forms, matter and mind? Is that just a misperception on our part, whatever we are, and however we fit in?

Or is all this speculation simply missing the point? Is something quite different going on?

Is it all about something else?

Those were the last words George ever wrote.

I wondered if he found the answer.

CHAPTER 29

Steve Coleman's lawyers put up a great fight in his defence. I decided that if ever I had a problem, I'd want those guys in my corner. But the verdict was never in question given the weight of evidence against him, which meant that the handing down of a thirty-year sentence came to Sara not so much as a shock as a final line drawn under the whole sorry episode in her life.

It had been traumatic, but I had been there throughout to soften the blow, to hold her hand and stop her dwelling too much on what might have been. She readjusted to reality beneath my unobtrusive guidance. The night of the verdict we slept together, but didn't have sex till the next morning. Though neither of us put it into words, it was symbolic of the start of a new life – together. I was ready to play my part now. I had absorbed the role. You could not tell me from the real thing.

'Do that thing you used to do,' she said suddenly, softly, through her sighs of pleasure.

I felt a prickle of panic. Various refinements and embellishments of our current not unconventional position ran through my mind. I would have to bluff.

'What was that?' I whispered back, kissing her, hoping I was not admitting to an ignorance of some dramatic eccentricity that nothing in his notebooks or the detritus of his life had prepared me for.

I need not have worried. Gently taking my hand, she guided it, and placed the tip of my finger precisely where she wanted it.

'You know . . .'

She even began the movement at the rhythm she remembered.

I was home.

I was home.

But I didn't realize how true that was until we sat together at breakfast, facing each other across the kitchen table. Although this was a new experience for me, it felt somehow right – strangely right in a way I couldn't quite explain or, for that matter, understand.

Sara looked at me over the rim of her coffee mug with a smile in her eyes that I had never seen before. There was such a wealth of feeling in that smile, so many curious contradictions, that for a moment I felt strangely unnerved. I was used to simple emotions like fear and greed. My motives were simple and clear-cut: I wanted, so I went out and got. I had no time for uncertainty or doubt. Ambiguity of all kinds had long been banished from my life; it hindered my effectiveness. Yet there I found myself looking down into its spiral depths and feeling dizzy, afraid almost that I might fall.

Quite suddenly and impulsively, she reached across the table and placed her hand on mine. 'Thank you,' she said softly.

I did not know what to reply, yet felt I should say something. 'For what?'

'For everything. I've been very foolish, haven't I?'

Her eyes had still not left mine, and I too felt unable to look away. I shook my head. 'Foolish people never take risks,' I said. 'You do. That's good.'

I watched as she got up from her chair and came around the table to where I sat. She put her arms around my shoulders and rested her face gently on the top of my head. 'Thank you,' she said after a while. 'Thank you for loving me.'

My voice cracked oddly when I tried to speak, probably because I had no idea what to say. I was rapidly becoming lost in a complex and confusing situation. I cleared my throat and tried again, at the same time hesitantly raising my hand and letting it rest lightly on her forearm where it lay across my chest.

'That's what I'm here for,' I said.

She brought her lips down to mine and kissed me. I responded by swivelling on my chair and slipping my arms beneath the light robe she wore and feeling the smoothness of her skin. She lowered herself on to my lap and sat astride me, our mouths still locked together and our mutual desire suddenly requiring urgent satisfaction. I carried her like that back to the bedroom, from which we emerged a half hour later, flushed and perspiring, to take a shower together.

It was almost eleven by the time she was dressed and ready to go to the gallery. It was a Saturday and she wouldn't normally have gone in over the weekend, but they had an opening coming up on Tuesday and there was a lot to get ready. She kissed me goodbye at the door and reminded me that we had a party in the Village that evening. I watched her walk along the corridor to the elevator. She turned and waved as it opened, then she was gone.

Back in the apartment I found myself in a strange limbo. I knew that I was slipping into the role that I was playing as though it were my life, which it was not and never could be. Nor did I want it to be. I had about as much ambition to be George Daly as I had to work in some dry goods store in Cleveland. And yet I was beginning to feel at home in his life, and comfortable. And dangerously attracted to his wife. I had always been aware that she was a good-looking woman, but I had not expected this degree of feeling between us. For God's sake, I had planned to murder her. And that plan was still there, at the back of my mind, awaiting only the right opportunity.

And yet . . . suppose Sara were to have an accident, now, after Steve's trial? Wouldn't that risk opening up the whole can of worms? After all, Steve would have nothing to lose now by admitting his affair with Sara. If she died in even faintly questionable circumstances, and I was left, as I would be, far better off under the terms of her will than under the terms of a divorce, he might well think it his civic duty to reveal my motive by telling of their affair and the fact that I had known about it. What it had been in his interests to keep quiet during his trial might now provide grounds for an appeal, a further investigation, a re-trial even. I was in a tricky position. I had to think carefully.

Couldn't I just carry on as I was? The more I thought about it, the more I could see no reason why not. I could simply live as George Daly. It was a comfortable and easy life, and the night that I'd just spent with Sara held out the prospect of it being a very agreeable one. There was something in her sexuality that excited me in ways I did not know how to describe. Nadia had been sensual and uninhibited, but somehow obvious. What you saw was what you got, and that was pretty good. But with Sara what you got was so much more than what you saw. True, what you saw was great. But what you *got*, what *I* now got, was somehow special, exclusive, mine and mine alone. At least that was how it felt. And it was a nice feeling. The first time I'd ever had it.

So, all right, I said to myself, suppose I go on as I am, living as George Daly. Of course I had no intention of writing any books, because for one thing I saw now what an empty fraud George's writing career had been. It was not something he earned a living at, just something he was being indulged in – a kept man.

For a while I allowed myself the fantasy that my future was settled, that I had found the role I would play for the rest of my life. But then the doubts set in again. It was true that I could decide to stay with Sara, but suppose she got tired of me – of George, that is – as she had before? If it happened once, it could happen again, and surely would in time. What would I do then? I would be back at square one. Why should I wait around passively for that?

I felt the need of guidance, but I didn't know from where. It wasn't in my nature to ask people for advice. Plus the things I needed advice on weren't the kind of things you talked about.

Then I remembered something I'd read about in George's notes a while back. His 'library angel'.

Did I believe it? I decided it couldn't hurt to try. I turned my head away from the bookshelves, reached out and picked a book at random.

It was the I Ching.

I knew what it was, or was supposed to be – another of those mysterious reflections of the supposed fact that the universe is a whole. I had read George on the subject – not that it was clear he entirely believed it himself. The theory was that any single set of phenomena, however small or large, is connected to everything else. Thus, if you have the knack of it, you can read a person's future and possibly that of the whole human race from the leaves left in the bottom of a teacup. Or you can figure out from the movements of the stars whether or not you should buy that new car this week, or take a trip to Vegas. The I Ching was another variation on the reading of

omens. And, I had to admit it, an omen was what I
needed at that moment.

It only took a few minutes to learn how to use it. There
were no special skills involved. You just needed three
coins, then you followed the rules at the back and looked
up the passages cited.

I got out three coins and threw them six times. The base
line was three tails, therefore a changing line, giving first:

————— —————
————— —————
————— —————
—————————
—————————
—————————

This was 'T'ai', or 'Peace'. The judgement read:
The small departs,
The great approaches.
Good fortune. Success.

'This hexagram,' I read, 'denotes a time in nature when
heaven seems to be on earth.'

Next, I looked up the alternative hexagram that was
created by the changing base line.

————— —————
————— —————
————— —————
————— —————
————— —————
—————————

This was 'Sheng', or 'Pushing Upward'. The judgement read:

Pushing upward has supreme success.
One must see the great man.

Fear not.
Departure toward the south
Brings good fortune.

What the devil, I asked myself, was that supposed to mean?

I looked out of the window in search of inspiration. All I saw was that it had stopped raining. I felt restless and decided to take a walk in the park.

It was full of noise and movement – rollerbladers, joggers, kids screaming, ghetto-blasters competing to see which would inflict most ear damage. I walked for a while without really seeing or hearing my surroundings, lost in my thoughts. I was heading north, and after a while the crowds thinned a little and the noise grew more distant. I was dimly aware that I was taking the same walk that George had taken on that first morning I had followed him. That had been a Saturday, too. But there was nothing dramatic or significant in my retracing my steps in that way. It was a walk I had taken many times since, one of my favourite routes through the park.

I came to the bench, sheltered by rocks in a corner of a winding path, where George had been sitting when we had finally faced each other. I eased myself down – as I had by now done many times – and sat hunched forward, elbows resting on knees. Just as, when I thought about it, George had been sitting that first morning.

Not only that. Now, for the first time, I found that I was playing quite unconsciously with the three coins I'd used earlier to cast the I Ching.

I looked down at myself. I was, as it happened, wearing the same clothes George had been wearing that morning. Not entirely surprising, perhaps, as I'd inherited his wardrobe. Nonetheless it was that thought, the totality of the coincidence, that broke my concentration. I heard one of the coins I was playing with hit the ground with a metallic clink. It landed on its edge and, before I could catch it, started rolling down the path to my left.

A man was coming up. He stopped the coin with his foot, then bent down to pick it up.

He wore a soft felt hat and sunglasses.

I was looking at myself.

George.

In my clothes.

Exactly as I'd last seen him.

'Hello, Larry,' he said. 'Isn't this a coincidence!'

CHAPTER 30

It took me a moment, and a lot of self-control, but I congratulate myself that I held it together.

'What in all hell are you doing here?' I said, concealing as best I could the shock of seeing him.

'Like I said, Larry – coincidence. This morning you threw the same I Ching I did just before we met that first time, right here on this spot.'

'I did? How would you know?'

He smiled faintly and shook his head, as though I'd asked precisely the question he expected. 'I know everything you've done, so there's no point denying any of it.'

My mind was racing too fast to think. I instinctively spread my hands like a man with nothing to hide. Immediately, I was embarrassed by the gesture – not because it was a lie, but because it was such a transparent lie. I had everything to hide, and he knew it.

'You're not making sense,' I said. 'Where have you been? It's been how long – eighteen months?'

I was attempting, I think, though not very convincingly, to paint myself as the injured party here. 'What happened to you?'

He took the last few steps up the path and sat down on the bench next to me, all the time not taking his eyes off me. 'Those men who were looking for you did a very professional job.' He spoke with no trace of bitterness or rancour. 'I was surrounded by three of them and bundled into a car before I knew what was happening. I tried to tell them they were making a mistake, but they went through my pockets and found your ID, and that was when I realized what a neat trick you'd pulled.'

'Come on, what is this? What are you talking about . . . ?'

He brushed my protests aside with a wave of his hand. 'I told you, I know everything. So we may as well be open with each other.'

I gave a noncommittal grunt and avoided looking at him. He went on with his story.

'They drove me way out to some place in New Jersey, put a bullet through my head and threw me in a lime pit on a big construction site. You must have upset some very unpleasant people, Larry.'

I mumbled something about it all being a misunderstanding, but he seemed not to care either way.

'So tell me,' I said, 'if they did all that to you, how come you're sitting here now?'

'That's what I'm about to explain. I know you won't find it easy to accept, but you'll get your head around it in time, trust me.'

My mind raced with possible scenarios. He'd said that the men who were after me had killed him, but clearly they hadn't. Perhaps they had *thought* they'd killed him and left him for dead, but he'd recovered. Maybe he'd been lying in some hospital for months, injured, in a coma.

'Are you on something?' I said. 'Some medication?'

He ignored my question and continued to regard me with

a strange kind of scrutiny.

'You hold a horrible fascination for me,' he said. 'In the sense that you're so nearly me, and yet so different.'

It was a stupid question to ask, knowing the things I'd done that he could never have done, but I asked it all the same. 'Different how?'

'Just different.'

Then his gaze hardened. I got the impression that he did not like what he was looking at.

'Listen to me, Larry,' he said, speaking as though the social niceties were over and it was time to get down to business, 'that was all horseshit about you and me being long-lost twins. It's more complicated than that. And also more simple in a way.'

'That's good – that it's simple. So maybe you can explain it to me.'

He gave a faint, mirthless laugh. 'Let me just say to begin with that the whole thing was basically my fault – in so far as "fault" means anything in this context. What I've discovered is that if you start pursuing coincidence too closely, you risk unravelling the fabric of your own reality – or, more accurately, your own *un*reality.'

He gave a dry little laugh at his own joke, which I was still waiting to see the point of.

'Look,' I said, 'if you want to talk English it's all right with me. As a matter of fact it's my first language.'

He ignored the crack and continued looking at me as though wondering where to start. In the end, finding no answer to that, he sighed deeply as though suddenly weary of everything, and leaned forward with his elbows on his knees and his shoulders hunched, staring at the ground.

'Are you all right?' I asked, sensing he wasn't and looking for a way to get back on top of this situation.

He gave no sign of having heard me.

'It could all end with the flick of a switch,' he said eventually in a voice suddenly flat with resignation, 'though Dave says there's a chance of his grant being renewed for another year. Of course that's one of *their* years. There's no telling how long it might seem to us. Eternity, perhaps.'

'What are you talking about? What switch? Who's Dave?'

Again he didn't answer, but after a while he pushed himself upright, sat back, and contemplated his surroundings. 'The thing you have to understand, Larry,' he said, 'is that all this, you me – everything – is very different from what you think it is.'

'Uh-huh.' I decided for the time being I'd just go along with him, let him talk.

He looked at me again. 'Do you ever think about the Big Bang?'

'Can't say I do – at least not often. Why?'

'But you know what it means.'

'Sure – the origin of the universe. Some kind of explosion.'

'An explosion which, supposedly, came out of a "singularity", which is a point of zero volume and infinite mass – which means something inconceivably smaller than a single atom, but containing all the material needed to create the universe. Have you any idea what an extraordinary notion that is?'

'Well, I guess not till you put it like that, not really.'

He looked at me for a moment to ensure that I was paying proper attention before continuing.

'There's another theory known as the Big Crunch, which says that in time the whole universe will collapse back into that same point and, effectively, cease to exist. Now, Larry, I want you to think about that for a moment and tell me – what does it put you in mind of?'

He waited. I shrugged. 'Heck, George, I don't know. What's it supposed to put me in mind of?'

'Isn't it obvious? It's some sort of power source being turned on and off – right? Like a switch.'

'Oh. Well, yes, I guess you could look at it like that.'

'Because that is precisely what it is.' He leaned towards me as though about to impart a deep confidence. 'You and I, Larry, and everything we know, are part of a program running on a computer that exists in another world outside our own. We're just bits of information, all of us and everything. A cyber-universe.'

I just stared at him. Was he trying to be funny? Or was he expecting me to take this old science fiction chestnut seriously? If so, he was crazier than I had at first thought. And maybe dangerous.

'Uh-huh,' I said, 'right.'

'Dave, by the way, is the man in charge of the computer. You'll meet him soon.'

'Ah.'

He sat back and filled his lungs, as though relieved to have unburdened himself of all this. Then he looked at me again.

'Shall we walk a little?'

'Sure, why not,' I said, getting to my feet.

We set off at a leisurely pace. As on the previous occasion we'd walked together in the park, the hat and sunglasses which I had originally been wearing, and he now wore, provided a sufficient disguise to stop people staring at these 'identical twins'.

A group of kids were playing a game of baseball some way off. He stopped to watch them, then turned to me. 'You know something? I can prove to you that this game we're watching is an illusion.'

'For real?'

I don't know if he deliberately ignored my irony or missed it.

'The speed of light, the speed of the ball, the speed at which signals travel along the human nervous system, are all measurable – right?'

'I guess.'

'So, if you add up the time it takes for the human nervous system to relay information about the ball from the eyes to the brain, plus the time it takes the brain to react, then the time it takes the nervous system to relay a decision back to the muscles, then compare that with the speed of the ball – you'll find the ball is way past the batsman before he can possibly hit it.'

I watched ball connect with bat and soar into the air.

'Then how *does* he hit it?' I asked, beginning to feel like the straight man in this partnership.

'He doesn't, of course. We just think he does.'

'I guess that must be it,' I said cautiously, trying hard not to sound as though I was humouring him.

He looked at me, knowing that I was and apparently not caring. 'The fact is,' he said, 'in many ways there's a lot *less* going on than meets the eye. How, for example, do you *know* there are six billion people on earth?'

I blinked a couple of times to show him I was considering the question seriously. 'I guess we just have to take a lot on trust,' I said finally.

'More than you dream of.'

We walked on a while more.

'So anyway,' I said, breaking the silence we'd fallen into, 'how does all this about the Big Bang and baseball explain you and me – this twins thing?'

'We're not twins. We're a computer glitch – the same bit of program in two places.'

I didn't say anything at first, just walked on in silence keeping my eyes on the ground. 'Wow,' I said eventually, feeling that he expected some kind of response from me, 'that's pretty wild.'

'Oh, I know you don't believe it now, but you will – when you meet Dave.'

'So where is this guy?'

'He's waiting for us. This way.'

He turned on to a path leading out of the park and on to Central Park West. Unable to think of any immediate alternative, I followed him.

CHAPTER 31

As we waited for the lights to change, I saw a man watching us from the far sidewalk. He was around thirty with longish, greasy-looking hair, thinning on top and hanging dankly to his shoulders. He wore a stained white T-shirt and baggy combat trousers. He looked out of shape, with a round, soft body and a complexion that didn't see enough daylight. George gave him a cheerful wave. In response he raised a white forearm, like a flipper.

George made the introductions. I didn't catch Dave's second name; in fact I don't think either of them gave it. He didn't offer to shake hands, and neither did I.

'We need to talk,' George said, 'the three of us. Why don't we go up to the apartment?'

'I don't think that's a good idea,' I said quickly. 'Sara might be home any time, and we don't want to involve her, do we?'

In fact she would probably be out for most of the afternoon, but there was no way I intended letting those

two loony-tunes get me alone in an enclosed space. George
and Dave exchanged a glance; there was obviously some
mutual understanding between them that I was not a party
to. As though by mutual consent, George turned back to me
and proposed a compromise.

'We could get a cup of coffee somewhere.'

I agreed. We walked half a block west and found a table
in a small place filled with a Saturday morning crowd
wearing trainers and sweaters wrapped around their
shoulders. They were chatting, reading the papers,
planning their weekend. A waitress came over and took our
order. George had kept on his hat and dark glasses so that
our dramatic resemblance was not so obvious. When the
waitress had gone, George turned to his friend.

'Shall I start, Dave, or will you?'

Dave's mouth puckered into an odd little smile and he
made a bobbing motion with his head. 'Maybe you should
start,' he said. He had a tendency to swallow his words that
sometimes made them hard to hear.

George turned to me. His eyes remained invisible behind
his glasses, and he kept his voice low so it would not be
overheard at neighbouring tables.

'OK, Larry,' he began, 'here's the bottom line. I've told it
you already, but you didn't take it seriously. Let's try again.
Dave comes from another world – a world outside of this
one. With a few of his colleagues he created a computer
program that was capable of simulating life – including
consciousness. We are that conscious life form, in their
computer.'

It was, I told myself, a possibility that they had escaped
together from a secure wing in Bellevue, or some other
hospital for the mentally disturbed. I probably should have
called the cops and turned them in, and might have
contemplated doing so but for the can of worms I risked
opening when the links between George and myself began
to be probed. In the circumstances, therefore, all I could do

was play for time and go along with their game.

'If we are in a computer programmed by Dave,' I said, after deliberating over George's words for a moment, 'what's he doing in here with us? I don't see how that's possible.'

'Oh, I'm just a projection right now,' Dave said, anxious to clear this little misunderstanding out of the way. 'It makes it easier for us to talk.'

On an impulse I reached across the table and grasped the soft, thick flesh of his forearm. 'You don't *feel* like a projection,' I said.

Again Dave's round face puckered inwards with that oddly self-conscious little smile of his. 'Let's just say, for the purpose of this conversation, I'm as real as you are,' he said.

'Time and space do not exist, except in so far as consciousness creates them to store the information it receives.'

I looked at George, who had just spoken. 'Is that a fact?' I said flatly.

Our coffees arrived, along with a plate of pastries that Dave had ordered.

'Look, guys,' I said, 'I'm sorry, but this is crazy. I don't know if you're playing jokes or expecting me to take this seriously. In fact there are a lot of things I don't know. But I do know one things – which is that I'm not a bunch of ones and zeroes spinning around inside a fucking computer. So give me a break, all right?'

'It's not an ordinary computer,' Dave said, his adenoidal tones thickened further by the flaky sugar-dusted pastry in his mouth, 'it's a quantum computer.'

'Consciousness is a quantum function,' George added, as though his job was to expand and explain Dave's more gnomic pronouncements.

'Well, *I'm* conscious,' I said, 'and I *know* I'm not a program in a computer, quantum or otherwise.'

George leant towards me earnestly. 'You *don't* know that. You *can't* know it. By definition.'

'Why can't I know it?'

'Because you're *in* it. Things are unknowable from the inside. You can only know them from the outside. Gödel's law – right, Dave?'

'Pretty much,' Dave said, swallowing and taking another mouthful of pastry.

'Proof of the limitations of logic,' George rattled on. 'Self-reference is the fly in the ointment of pure logic.'

'Self-reference?'

'You know – if the barber shaves every man who doesn't shave himself, who shaves the barber?'

'What's this? A quiz?'

'Go on, answer.'

I humoured him. 'He shaves himself.'

'How can the barber shave himself if he only shaves men who don't shave themselves?'

'So – somebody else shaves him.'

'The barber shaves *all* men who do not shave themselves. Nobody else does it.'

I thought about the problem.

'There's no way around it,' George said after a while. 'It's like saying "You cannot prove that this statement is false". It backfires whichever way you try it.'

'OK, very neat,' I said, 'but so what?'

'So you can neither logically prove nor disprove what I am trying to explain to you. You can just believe it or not.'

'But I'm telling you,' I said, 'I don't believe it.'

George looked momentarily defeated by my intransigence and glanced at Dave for guidance. Dave swallowed and cleared his throat. 'I think you should tell him anyway,' he said.

'OK. In this quantum computer where we are, which is our universe' George continued, turning his attention back to me, 'the same fragments of program perform different functions in a virtually infinite number of different worlds. It is at the points where these different worlds intersect that we experience coincidence.'

'Uh-huh.'

'The coincidence of your crossing my world and running into Nadia Shelley created a very complicated situation for both of us, leading to our eventual meeting in the park. Even so, the computer did everything it could to straighten the situation out, because that's what it will always do – try to keep things singular and tidy. For example, it invented that red herring about the two of us being long-lost twins in an effort to avoid getting into an inescapable loop. I told you already, we're not twins at all in the usual sense of—'

'Wait a minute,' I said, getting drawn despite myself into the mad logic of his world, 'the fact that we're twins predates any of those coincidences that led to our meeting. How could this computer have straightened things out *before* they'd already got complicated?'

George held up a warning finger. 'Remember, there is no time. "Before" is a subjective concept.'

'Oh, yeah. Stupid of me.'

'You read my notes,' he went on, ignoring my sarcasm, 'so you know that Wolfgang Pauli worked with Jung on the meaning of synchronicity. He also won the Nobel Prize for physics for his "exclusion principle", which says that no two electrons in an atom can be at the same time in the same—'

I interrupted again. 'I thought you just said there was no time.'

'Not in an absolute sense – not as something "out there". But in here – in consciousness – we use it all the time. As I was saying, no two electrons can be at the same time in the same state or configuration. The problem is that you and I are like those two electrons, whom coincidence has brought face to face. It's an impossible situation.'

I looked from him to the bland and pasty face of Dave,

with that sickly smile hovering around the crumb-
encrusted mouth into which he popped another morsel of
pastry.

'So,' I said, attempting not so much to sum up as to draw
things to some sort of point, 'what do you suggest we do
about all this?'

There was a silence broken only by the buzz of
conversation around us and the rustle of a paper napkin as
Dave wiped his fingers clean of the buttery grease he had
just been eating.

'As I understand it,' George said thoughtfully after a few
moments, 'there's no way around a glitch like this. We have
to unpick it.'

'And how do we do that?'

'That's what Dave is here to arrange.'

Dave, who was draining his coffee, put down his cup and
wiped a hand across his mouth. 'Listen,' he said, 'I really
think we should go up to the apartment to discuss this.'

I started to say something to the effect that if those weirdos
thought they were ever getting into that apartment . . .

And I froze. Without my sensing even the faintest
movement or impression of transition, I found everything
changed. In place of sitting at the coffee shop table as we
had been, we were all three now standing in the apartment.
In the main room, to be exact. In a triangle about six feet
from each other.

'Hey! How . . . ? What . . . ? Jesus . . . ! Fuck . . . !'

I listened to myself blustering incoherently as my mind
spun out of control. What had happened was impossible. It
was a dream, and yet it wasn't. This was no dream. This
was concrete, real and immediate. I could feel the floor
beneath my feet and see the Manhattan skyline beyond the
window.

The next thing I felt was George's arms around me
holding me up. 'It's all right . . . okay . . . steady . . . I know
it's a shock,' he was saying. I realized that my legs had

buckled beneath me and I must have blacked out for a moment.

'How the fuck did you do that?' I said, my voice hoarse and shaking. 'You put something in my coffee, or what?'

George hoisted me a fraction more and made sure I was going to stay on my feet before letting go of me. 'Just try to stay calm, Larry. Just stay calm.'

'Stay calm? How d'you expect me to stay fucking calm when . . .'

I was shouting now, waving my arms, gasping for breath.

'What the fuck is going on here? What the fuck is this?'

'Jesus, Larry,' George said, sounding exasperated with me, 'you're really holding out here, aren't you? You're in denial, you know that?'

I confess I panicked. And when I panic I lash out. I lunged at George, intending to grab him by the jacket. Except my hand closed on thin air. He was still standing there in front of me, solid-looking as ever, three dimensional, alive. But my hands just went through him.

Dave next, whose fleshy arm I'd laid my hand on in the cafe. Same thing. Straight through him like smoke.

'What in the name of all—? For Christ's sakes!'

'Larry, take it easy,' George said.

'Take what easy? What is this? What the fuck is this?'

I punched a wall – and nearly broke my hand. The pain brought me back to reality. Of a kind. Pain was real. You don't dream pain, not like that. If you did you'd wake up screaming.

'It's not broken. It's OK, you've not broken anything.'

George had taken hold of my hand and was examining it. I realized I could *feel* his touch. He was solid again. I started to say something, but Dave anticipated me.

'Don't expect things to behave by the normal rules, Larry,' he said. 'Right now there are no rules – at least none you're familiar with.'

'I don't believe this is happening.'

'Larry, either this is happening,' George said, his voice calm and reasonable in contrast to my own, 'or you're crazy enough to be imagining it. Tough choice, I know. But that's how it is.'

'*I'm* not crazy. *You* guys are crazy. I'm getting out of here.'

'There's nowhere to go, Larry,' Dave said, unconcerned by the dash I made for the door. Something in the tone of his voice made me stop and look back at him. 'And by the way,' he added, 'you needn't worry about Sara showing up. If you look out the window you'll see why.'

I followed his gaze out over the park. It was like looking at a photograph or one of those models of some proposed building development. Nothing moved. People, traffic, even birds in the air and planes on the horizon were frozen in place.

'We have all the time in the world,' Dave said, with the hint of a self-congratulatory smirk on his face. I stared at him, then turned back to the still life that was Manhattan, too numbed by what had already happened to be susceptible to further shock.

'How's your hand?' he said. 'It's stopped hurting, I hope.'

I had forgotten about my hand. Now that I thought about it again, I realized that I no longer felt any pain. I nodded vaguely in reply.

'All right,' he said, 'now that you're in a more receptive state of mind, let George tell you everything from the beginning . . .'

GEORGE

CHAPTER 32

There is nothing so conducive to an open mind as having someone put a gun to your head and pull the trigger – and I don't just mean that as a joke in bad taste. I mean that if your brains get blown out but you find yourself still fully conscious and watching the scene as a detached observer, though obviously unseen by everybody else, then whatever happens next is unlikely to take your breath away too sharply.

The thugs who grabbed me off the street in mistake for Larry had driven me out to Jersey, and, ignoring all my protestations, dragged me across a deserted night-time building site until I teetered on the edge of what I suspected was a lime pit. My hands were already tied behind me and I was gagged, so my screams and struggles counted for very little as I was held there, helpless, waiting in abject terror for the end. I felt the cold circle of the gun barrel at my temple, and closed my eyes.

By the way, in case you've ever wondered – yes, you hear

the bang, sort of; though it's more a kind of whooshing
sound from where you are, on the receiving end.

But then, quite abruptly, I found myself somewhere
outside and apart from the grim little scene, watching it as
though it was a piece of theatre. It was, I remember telling
myself, a classic out-of-body experience of the kind I had
often read about or heard described. It even struck me at the
time as a surprisingly obvious and even banal
psychological device to avoid confronting the full horror of
my situation. There I was, facing 'the bourn from which no
traveller returns', and the best response I could whistle up
was nothing more than a memory of some popular piece of
folklore about what was supposed to happen to people in
situations of this kind. I felt oddly disappointed with
myself.

I continued to watch, however, as my body fell, head
blown almost off, into the lime pit. The strangest part of it
was that I couldn't quite make out where I was watching it
all from. It seemed as though I was seeing the same thing
from several different angles simultaneously -- multiple
views of the same incident, like looking at a cubist
painting. But where was the singular 'I' who was doing this
multiple observing? That was a question that crossed my
mind, but which I had neither time nor inclination to
explore at that moment.

The scene began to fade as I watched. The last thing I saw
was my own body sinking gently into the corrosive
whiteness that would soon absorb every last trace of its
existence.

Yet what, not only where, was this 'I' that watched?
Instinctively I looked down to where my body should have
been – and found it there. In one piece. I was myself again.
I could see my hands, my feet, and I noticed I was still
wearing the clothes I'd had on just now when I was thrown
into the lime pit. All quite impossible, of course, but that's
what I saw.

At the same time I became aware that the scene I'd been watching, the scene of my own death, had started to fade into a kind of darkness that was closing in around it. Now another area began to lighten somewhat, enough to show me that I was in some kind of tunnel. I was moving through it, with no effort on my part, towards a light at the far end.

Pretty standard fare, I thought. Tunnels with light at the end were familiar images from all the descriptions of near-death experiences I'd ever read, though I still had no doubt that what I was going through was a real and not any kind of 'near' experience of death.

Interestingly, that knowledge provoked neither fear nor anxiety in me. It left me feeling as though I'd been given one of those shots you get before local surgery, when you are perfectly aware that something very peculiar is being done to some part of your anatomy, but it doesn't worry you in the slightest. I found myself casting a curious glance over the walls of the tunnel I was travelling through. At first I had thought they were of stone, but now they seemed to be of a softer, almost fleshy substance. The notion flashed into my mind that I was travelling through one of my own arteries, though I knew that the more likely explanation was that I was remembering the trauma of birth. That, so far as I had always understood it, was where the tunnel motif in death came from, neatly wrapping up our human life span at both ends.

Quite suddenly, but without any jolt or sense of dislocation, and well before I had reached what appeared to be the end of the tunnel, I found myself out of it and standing in what looked like a vast medieval hall or perhaps ante-room to an even greater hall. The floor and walls were of stone – real stone this time – and the ceiling was high and vaulted. Tall windows threw diagonal slabs of light across the scene, illuminating a scattering of different figures, all in period costume, mostly alone, some conferring. On the far side of the room one of them turned in my direction and made a gracious gesture inviting me to approach a door beside which he was standing. I started towards him, finding myself walking quite normally. Nobody paid me the slightest attention despite the oddness of my dress in these surroundings. The man bowed as I approached and held open the door for me to go through.

I stepped out into what I at first supposed was a garden, but quickly realized was something more. The gentle rolling landscape was made not of earth and grass but of a soft cloud-like substance. In some strange way it seemed to crystallize here and there to form the shape of a tree, or some delicately woven gazebo-like structure, while in the distance it dissolved into an impressionistic rainbow-hued landscape of indescribable beauty. Above it all hung a great dome of porcelain-blue sky, patterned here and there by clouds of pure whiteness.

Scattered throughout the scene were figures walking or conferring in groups of twos or threes, much as they had been in the room I had just left, except that here they all wore white garments that hung in casually elegant folds. I turned around, taking it all in, and to my amazement found that the door I had just stepped through was no longer there. Nor was there a wall or any other sign of the building that might have housed the great room I had just left. It was as if I had materialized out of nowhere on that spot.

I looked down at my feet, which I now saw were bare; and I was wearing the same kind of white smock or robe that everyone else had on. But it was not the suddenness of the change nor the unseen sleight of hand by which it was effected that took my breath away. The thing that did that was the sight of what I was standing on – or, rather, not standing on.

When I looked down, I saw only space beneath my feet. Space that turned a darker shade of blue as it receded, until it formed a deep and distant cobalt, with a darkness at the centre that was more than black: it was the absence of even the possibility of light.

It was then I realized that, to all intents and purposes, I was in every child's, and for that matter every cartoonist's, notion of Heaven. Which meant I had to be mad. Or hallucinating. Or something. But for the moment all I could do was throw back my head and roar with laughter.

'It's all right, don't be alarmed. We're talking you down.'

I couldn't tell where the voice had come from. There was nobody anywhere near me, and yet it seemed so close it could almost have been in my head. Which is perhaps where it was. Which would make it just another aspect of the whole crazy episode of madness I was going through.

'George, look up – to your right.'

I did so. That was when hysteria took over. I found myself looking up at a massive figure sitting on a huge throne. If you've ever looked up at the Lincoln Memorial in Washington DC, you'll know what I'm talking about. Except that, unlike Abe Lincoln, this figure wore long white robes and had a white beard, and bore an open book on his head, balanced, face down, as though he'd just put it there to protect himself from a sudden rain shower. It was this that was the cause of my mirth, because I remembered, as a small child, how this had been my first conception of God.

So that's how it was: your whole life really did flash before you. Though I had to admit it seemed less like a flash than a leisurely procession in my case. That was my first real taste of the fact that time had lost its meaning.

'Just let yourself fall back on everything you've ever been, George. You don't have to remember all the details, not all at once. You'll be able to recall any part of it when you need. Your life hasn't gone away. It's just going to be different, for a while.'

'For a while . . . ?'

I had spoken the words aloud, and the sound of my own voice made me jump. I looked around for whoever it was I had been speaking to. It wasn't 'God', because He had vanished.

Which should probably be pronounced vani-*shed*, I thought, and giggled – once again aloud.

'It's OK, George, everything's fine. Why don't you just come over here?'

Turning in the direction which 'over here' for some reason suggested to me, though I could not think why, I saw a small rectangle of silvery light in the midst of a vast grey-blue nothingness. Once again all concrete reality had faded, and I was in some womb-like space created from a kind of wispily intangible ectoplasm. When I walked towards the bidden rectangle of light, I experienced the physical sensation of crossing a floor, feeling a hard surface beneath my feet, though in relation to my surroundings I had no sense of movement at all. Yet I saw, after only a few steps, that the rectangle had grown larger and therefore by implication closer. Suddenly, though again without any sense of shock or loss of equilibrium, my surroundings underwent another instantaneous transformation.

I found myself this time in a bare, functional office. It had one window over which a blind was pulled, a door, and no furniture other than a chair and a table on which sat a computer. The computer screen, I now realized, was the silvery rectangle I had been moving towards. On it I now saw the image of someone – a man – looking out at me.

'Hi,' he said. 'My name's Dave. We need to talk.'

CHAPTER 33

I don't know how long I sat in front of that screen. As I had already observed, time seemed to have lost its sense of urgency.

Dave explained the situation with admirable clarity. I was not dead. I was caught up in what he called 'a loop'. He told me about the quantum computer which had generated my world, and how it worked on the principle of the 'many worlds' theory, with reality splitting off into endless variations of itself at every quantum branch – parallel universes, as they were generally called. Coincidences were the points at which these different universes touched. They were usually unimportant, though sometimes dramatic for the people involved. But if you began to pay unusually close attention to them, thereby introducing your own consciousness into these quantum events, as I had done, then strange things tended to happen.

'You can wind up unpicking the fabric of your own reality,' he said, giving me the line which I later embellished and used on Larry.

He went on to explain how Larry and I were two characters made out of the same bit of program but kept safely apart in our different worlds – until I started playing with synchronicity.

'Let me just be sure I've got the logic of this,' I said. '*I* drew Larry into *my* world, not myself into his.'

'That is correct.'

'And he took my place in my world.'

'Right.'

'So what's happening in *his* world right now? Is there just a hole where he should be?'

'In his world he's dead. Killed by the guys who blew your head off. In his world it was *his* head, and *his* body that was dumped in the lime pit.'

'I'm getting a little confused,' I said. 'Was *he* murdered in his world, or was it me?'

'He was murdered in his world.'

'But I was murdered in my world, in his place.'

'Correct.'

'So what am I doing here? Why aren't I dead?'

My view of Dave on the screen was basically just his head and chest, but as I watched he shifted his position and reached behind him to scratch the buttock on which his weight had previously been resting.

'That's a little tricky. It's to do with formal logic, which still applies on one level even in a quantum computer . . .'

As he droned on, I nodded thoughtfully from time to time to signal some kind of understanding, however abstract, of his words. There was what looked like a fibre-optic camera at the top of the screen on which I assumed he was watching me from wherever he was. To be honest, everything he said made perfect sense, and yet was meaningless. Because I had nothing to test it by. I was in limbo.

The one thing he'd said that had stayed in my mind as

some kind of beacon of sanity was his original remark about 'talking me down'. This, I told myself, is just the way you would talk down someone like me – talk them down from the staggering discovery that life continues on unbroken after death. This is the sort of way you would choose, in the circumstances, to talk down a sceptical science writer – sceptical about everything, including 'official' science's blanket dismissal of all methods and philosophies that fell outside its limited perspective. This was the way you would talk down such a person after death: by the use of these metaphors. I had little doubt that was the proper way to regard them – as metaphors. I remember thinking that everybody probably got their own individual metaphors for the purpose – whichever were appropriate, given their personal interests and preoccupations.

'So what now?' I asked. 'You've described how this has happened. What are we going to do about it? Are we going to do anything? Or is this just the status quo from now on?'

'No, it's not the status quo. We have to take care of the problem that brought you here.'

'My being murdered?'

'The loop. Your character is looped with Larry's. You're going to go on running around one another indefinitely, with whatever minor variations the computer can throw in each time. But nothing will really change. You'll never break out. You're locked in.'

'And what will that mean – being locked in?'

'In a sense it means you'll go mad. Only it's worse than mad, because there's no time, which means you can't ever die. The most you can hope for is that our funding runs out and my supervisor pulls the plug on the whole program.'

This brought me up sharply.

'You're have funding problems?' I asked, immediately wondering why I was so surprised by the idea. It was the last thing I'd expected to hear, yet when I thought about it in the context of everything else he'd been saying it made sense – of a kind.

Dave's image on the screen looked flustered for a second, as though he'd said more than he should. 'Don't worry about it. I'm pretty sure we're going to get renewed for another year – and a year in our time hasn't got anything to do with a year in your time. And even if they pull the plugs you won't feel anything. You'll just never have existed. But what I'm saying is, as long as you do exist, we have to iron out this glitch. OK?'

'OK,' I said, 'I guess. So what happens? Do *I* get to kill *him* next time around?'

He looked faintly disapproving at this suggestion, as though I wasn't taking the situation seriously enough. 'It doesn't work like that,' he said.

'How does it work?'

He thought a moment, as though searching for the best way to express whatever he was trying to say. It didn't look easy.

'Listen,' I said, in an effort to be helpful though still unsure quite what my role was, 'is this the only way we can communicate? Through this screen? Is there no way we can talk, face to face?'

'Sure there is. I just figured we should take things kind of gradually. But if that's what you want, why don't you step through that door in front of you?'

'OK.'

I got to my feet, moved around the table and across to the door that I had noticed when I came in – or, more accurately, when I had materialized there. As I turned the handle, I already knew from experience that it wasn't going to be like going from one room to another, or stepping out of a building into the fresh air. I would be going from one state of being to another. This time I was ready for it.

In fact it was not a very dramatic change. I found myself in the middle of a relatively modern campus. It made me think of Pepperdine in California, or Berkeley, though it wasn't entirely either. Dave was waiting for me, leaning against the low wall surrounding an ornamental fountain. He held out his hand, and I took it a little hesitantly, not knowing what to expect. It felt absolutely real.

'George, it's a pleasure,' he said, 'a real pleasure.'

'Thanks,' I said lamely, not knowing what else to say. 'Where are we?' I asked, looking around at the open spaces and the long, fluid buildings beyond them.

'Oh, just some place,' Dave shrugged. 'Nowhere special.'

I looked at the students coming and going in all directions, some hurrying purposefully, others with all the time in the world, just like on any campus I'd ever been on.

'Can these kids see me?' I asked as a group walked right by us, talking and laughing among themselves.

'You don't get it yet, do you, George? There's nobody here. There's not even me, or you. There's no "here". There are no colours, tastes, smells or sounds. It's all just information. Part of the program.'

I looked at him. 'But there is a *real* you somewhere, isn't there?'

He thought a moment before saying, almost reluctantly, 'Yes, sort of.'

'What d'you mean sort of?'

'Well, to be absolutely frank with you, we're not even sure that we ourselves aren't part of a computer program in somebody else's world, the same way you are in ours. All the same signs are there. Nobody's ever gotten to the bottom of this question, and probably never will. Maybe it just goes on for ever, like Chinese boxes or Russian dolls. And in the end it doesn't matter much. You are where you are, and that's all you've got. And it's the same for us.'

It wasn't a view I found either appealing or encouraging. As I thought about it I glanced down, and noticed that once again I was wearing the same clothes, Larry's clothes, that I'd had on when I was kidnapped and killed. By now I was getting so used to these surreal quick changes that I didn't even react.

'OK,' I said, 'so where do we go from here?'

'We go back and we unpick this thing.'

'You mean back to where Larry and I met this morning?'

He shook his head. 'I was trying to tell you – it doesn't work that way. I know it feels to you like no time has passed, but quite a lot of time has passed in the world you left.'

'How come?'

He screwed up his face as though searching once again for a way to explain an unusually complex matter. 'There are factors governing these things that we can do nothing about.'

'Like what?'

He gave a shrug that lengthened out into a squirm of deep unease. Either he didn't know the answer to that question, or the answer was impossible to put into terms that I would understand. 'It's to do with probability,' he said eventually. 'Certain things have got to happen before we can go back. They will. They must. But we have to let them.'

'Certain what?' I asked, then hazarded a guess. 'Coincidences?'

'Yeah, basically.' He looked at me as though mildly surprised by my perspicacity.

'Hey,' I said, 'not a tough call, given the circumstances.'

'You're right,' he said, and chuckled softly. Then he frowned, serious again. 'Why don't we take a walk,' he said. 'There's some stuff you need to know about before we do anything else. I have to warn you, you may not like it.'

As we strolled, he told me everything that had happened in my absence.

I felt sick.

LARRY

CHAPTER 34

For some moments after George had finished, the only sound I could hear was my own breathing. The two of them, George and his mysterious friend Dave, just stood there, waiting for me to say something. There was no sense of impatience or urgency about them. It was as though they had all the time in the world – which apparently they had, as I could still see from the window where the rest of the world remained frozen. Yet they had obviously come here with specific things to accomplish, and as soon as I was ready we would move on to them.

'Are you all right, Larry?' George asked.

'He's fine,' Dave said. 'I think we can wrap this thing up. What I propose is that the two of you go sit over there, and then we can do what we have to to get this situation resolved.'

He indicated two soft leather armchairs placed at an angle to each other before a vast abstract painting by one of Sara's artists. George started obediently for one. I, with my mind spinning and a sense of having alarmingly little fight left in me, headed for the other.

'And George,' Dave added, 'you can take your glasses and the hat off now.'

'Oh – yeah, sure.'

He did so, and we both sat there looking up at Dave, waiting.

'Before we get started,' he said, 'I have kind of a confession to make. I already indicated to you, George, that we've had some funding problems on this project lately. Which has meant we've had to cut a few corners here and there. The fact is, and I haven't wanted to mention this so far for reasons I'm sure you'll understand, we're going to have to cut another one now. Normally in a case like this – they happen inevitably from time to time – we'd have to go through a lengthy process which would involve starting up Larry's program over again and introducing him back into it. Unfortunately, in this instance we aren't going to be able to do that.'

George was listening with polite, reasonably untroubled interest. I shifted in my chair, wondering uneasily where this 'confession' of Dave's was going.

'So the thing is,' Dave continued, looking down at his feet as he took a few steps across the thick cushion of carpet, 'we're not going to be able to unpick this situation in the way we normally would. In fact we're not going to be able to unpick it at all. We're simply going to have to cut, as it were, the Gordian knot.'

He stopped pacing and looked at both of us.

'The fact is,' he said, and paused a moment to make sure we were both still paying close attention, 'that for all practical purposes, Larry's world has come to an end, so there's no way he can go back to it. As a result, the two of you are now in this world – George's world – which has created a logically impossible situation. You're not twins and you're not clones. You're two blueprints living one life. The only solution is that one of you is going to have to be eliminated.'

'Wait a second here, Dave, I'm not sure I understand . . .'

The interruption had come from George, his brow furrowing with a crease of sudden concern.

'When you say eliminate, in what sense are you meaning that?'

'In the usual sense, I guess,' Dave said.

George continued to look puzzled. 'But d'you mean . . . are you saying that one of us will have to . . . to cease to be?'

I said nothing. Something in my gut told me I already knew the answer to that question only too well. So did George: he just wasn't ready to face it yet.

Dave, I have to say, for the first time had the grace to look a little embarrassed, even shifty.

'That's about it, I'm afraid,' he answered, avoiding George's gaze. 'Strictly speaking, what we're about to do is illegal, and I could get into a lot of trouble for it. But then I have to balance that against the project, and the importance of keeping it going. We can't afford to have it brought to a halt by mishaps like this. Frankly, this research is too important.'

'But, Dave,' George persisted, in the reasonable tones of a man unable to acknowledge that his argument was already lost, 'you assured me that this whole problem could be ironed out – unpicked, you said – and everything put back to square one. That's what you told me, isn't it?'

'That's what I told you. That's how I would have liked it to be. That's how it would be in an ideal world. Unfortunately, we're not in one.'

'So what exactly *are* you saying, Dave? And why have you chosen to wait until now?'

The question came from George, but Dave directed his reply to me.

'For technical reasons, you're going to have to settle this between you. One of you has to displace the other – face to face and without any help or interference from outside. Nobody else can do it for you. Not me, not my supervisor, not even the head of the department responsible for this computer.'

'For God's sake, what you're talking about sounds like—'

Dave ignored George's whiny-voiced interruption and ploughed on, addressing both of us now.

'The problem is that because you're a conscious entity you have a very significant element of free will, which by definition only you – these two versions of yourself – can use. And you're going to have to use it now.'

'This is getting a little out of hand, and it's certainly a long way from—'

George started to push himself up off his chair as he spoke, but fell back as though held by some invisible restraint.

'What the—? Why can't I—? What is this—?'

Dave shook his head, and his voice reflected genuine regret. 'I'm sorry, but you can't get out of those chairs, either of you, until this is over.'

I tried. What Dave said was true. It wasn't a feeling of being strapped down, no straining of muscle and sinew against confinement. My body just wouldn't do what I wanted. I felt disconnected from it.

'I'm not pretending I like this,' Dave was saying, 'but I don't have any choice, given the circumstances.'

Then I realized that I had no sense of smell. Not that there was ever much to smell in that room, just the hazy, agreeable odours of comfortable living. But now I could smell nothing at all. I could hear and I could see, but I was aware suddenly that I wasn't breathing. Not holding my breath, just not needing to breathe. I was still in my body, but disembodied.

'I repeat,' Dave said, 'that the only way we're going to resolve this situation is by having one of you eliminate the other.'

George started blustering as panic took hold of him. 'This

is outrageous! Barbaric! I never agreed to anything like this . . .'

Dave simply carried blithely on like a game-show host explaining the rules to a couple of fresh contestants.

'If you'll both look down at the right arm of your respective chairs, you'll find that a button has been fixed near to where your hand is.'

I dropped my gaze. Sure enough, a disc of stainless steel had been embedded in the leather, with a central plunger raised almost an inch. I couldn't imagine how I hadn't noticed it when I sat down, though I was so accustomed to a general and pervading sense of dislocation by now that little could surprise me any longer.

'Whichever of you hits that button first will eliminate the other,' Dave said, and stood looking down at both of us, as if his role were over and from now on it was up to us.

'This is against every notion of decent civilized . . .'

I noticed George appeared to be physically struggling as he blustered and protested, not simply detached from physicality in the way I was. Perhaps it was a subjective thing; it was impossible to know.

'By the way,' Dave cut in on George's tirade, 'I forgot to mention, for the purpose of hitting this button, you will both be physically quite free, neither of you at any disadvantage with regard to the other.'

'Let me get this straight,' I said. 'Whichever of us hits this button first eliminates the other – as in "dead"?'

'Complete non-existence.'

'And the other?'

'Will live on – as George Daly, from the point where you meet in the park.'

'That first time, or this morning?'

'Oh, this morning, I'm afraid. It's too complicated to go back and unpick everything that's happened since the first time.'

'No,' George shouted. 'This is a scandal and a travesty.

Larry, listen to me, we have to stay together on this and play no part in any such—'

He ranted on, but I had ceased to listen. Whatever the rights and wrongs of the situation, they were irrelevant. In real life things happen too fast to be sure you're doing the 'right' thing. Life and death decisions are made on gut instinct. George was a jerk if he didn't understand that. But then I already knew that George was a jerk, period. He didn't deserve his life.

Fuck it, I thought.

I hit the button.

SARA

CHAPTER 35

I got back to the apartment after five. At first I didn't know if George was in. I called out, but he didn't answer. Then, when I went into the bedroom, I found him lying in his robe staring at the ceiling.

'George? Are you all right?'

He turned his head and looked at me as though he hadn't heard me come in. 'Fine,' he said.

'I called, you didn't answer.'

'I took a bath, fell asleep. I was thinking.'

I bent down to give him a gentle kiss on the forehead. 'If we're going to Rob and Charles's party,' I reminded him, 'you need to get ready. Me too.'

'Yeah, right.' He looked at his watch as he rolled off the bed and got to his feet, running his hands through his hair to shake off his drowsiness. He went into his bathroom, I into mine.

I showered, thinking yet again what a relief it was to have my hair so short that I could leave it to look after itself. It was just after Steve was convicted that I'd first cut it. I never knew if there was any connection between the two things, and even less what it might be. I read once that in France after the Second World War they shaved the heads of women who had consorted with the enemy. Was I trying to persuade myself that Steve had become some sort of enemy?

My image gazed back at me impassively from my dressing-room mirror. Why is it we can never look natural in a mirror? Because the person in it is staring at you, I suppose, and nobody ever looks entirely natural when they're staring at you. Did I ever, I wondered, look natural any more?

I hesitated between a St Laurent (long, dark and formal), and a Ralph Lauren trouser suit (also dark and formal). What was it with me these days? My dark and formal period? In mourning for my life?

Stop it. It would end one day, I told myself for the millionth time. I would stop thinking about myself and what I'd lost. I would once again be as grateful as I used to be for what I'd had in the past and for what I had now. Poor George: my unhappiness was an insult to him. It was unfair.

Why is it so hard to love nice people?

Why is 'nice' such an anaemic word?

Did I ever think Steve was 'nice'? Not really. Stubborn, independent, ambitious. A bit of a rogue. Warm, funny, unpredictable.

Mine.

These were thoughts I didn't need. Couldn't afford. That part of my life was over. It had been a mistake, I must let it go, pretend it never happened. It wasn't my fault. The fact that I had loved a murderer simply meant that the man I loved had committed a murder.

Did I still love him?

Why did I have to ask that?

I couldn't forgive him for what he did. Nobody had the right to forgive somebody else's death. Especially not me; I had been part of the cause. It was Nadia Shelley's jealousy when Steve dropped her for me that made her a threat to him. But he killed her to save his career, not because he loved me. If he'd loved me enough he'd have said to hell with his career, and we'd just have been together. But he wanted his career as well as me. That's where people always get into trouble – wanting everything.

In the end I chose a Nicole Farhi ensemble – light, knee-length, and younger than I felt. But my mirror reassured me. From the outside I looked fine. My reflection almost smiled at me approvingly.

George was on the terrace, leaning on the wall and looking out over the park, nursing a drink. He must have heard the click of my heels as I approached but he didn't turned around.

'It's time to go,' I said, 'or we'll be late.'

He seemed almost surprised by my arrival, just as he had been when I got back earlier.

'You're still lost in thought,' I said. 'Have you been working?'

'Not really.' He looked down into his drink, twirled the ice in it, then tossed it down his throat in a single gulp.

On the way down in the elevator he continued to look strangely preoccupied, staring into space, unblinking.

'George, what is it?' I said after a while. 'Is something wrong?'

His turned towards me, and his eyes seemed to take a moment to focus – as though he was on drugs, but I didn't believe that he was. As far as I knew he'd never used them.

'I'm sorry,' he said, 'I was miles away. What did you say?'

'I asked if there was something wrong.'

'No. Nothing at all. Just,' he gave a little shrug, 'some ideas I'm playing with.'

We got into the car and rode without talking any further.

'What did you do today?' I asked eventually, beginning to find our silence oppressive. 'Did you go out?'

'I took a walk, that's all. In the park.'

'Did you see anyone?'

'Like who?'

'Anyone you knew.'

He seemed to need some time to think about this. Then he said, as though it had been a difficult conclusion to come to, 'Not really.'

CHAPTER 36

I was preoccupied over the next few days with an opening
we had at the gallery on the Tuesday – a young Brazilian
painter whose first New York show this was. But I couldn't
help noticing that George remained in a distinctly strange
mood. He was restless and nervous and slept badly. Two
nights that week I woke in the small hours to find him gone
from our bed. Once he was in his study, reading; another
time he was in a guest room watching television. When we
were together he seemed somehow distracted and yet
obsessively watchful at the same time. Several times I
caught him staring at me when he thought I wasn't looking.
When I asked him why, he denied doing it.

At other times he would spend hours pacing in his study.
Twice I came across him staring out of the window in a
kind of trancelike state. It took him some time to respond
to my presence and realize I was speaking to him, then he
turned with a vacant expression as though he'd just woken
up and wasn't sure where he was. But whenever I asked

him if anything was wrong, he insisted – sometimes even snapped – that he was fine. Whatever it was, he clearly couldn't bring himself to talk about it.

The opening went well; by Thursday we had picked up enough reviews to know we had a success on our hands. The whole collection had sold out in days, and I was generally credited with having discovered another promising talent, which was gratifying. For the first time in several weeks, I began to relax.

It was George's idea that we should go up to the Berkshires the following weekend. We had stopped using the house as much as we used to; the memory of that night when I had confronted George with Steve was awkward for both of us. But George still loved Eastways as much as he always had. Again, it was an unspoken understanding that we wouldn't talk about the past, just let bygones be bygones.

Everything always unspoken. Was it simply that we had nothing to say? When we first met, I remember, we talked all the time. Like most couples, I suppose. In between talking we made love all the time, or most of it. It was nice.

'Nice' again.

It was still nice when we made love. But it was an occasional thing. As rare as really talking.

I wonder if life with Steve would have gone the same way? It showed no sign of doing so during those first two years together. The sex was still great even when he started to worry about losing control of his life through marrying a 'spoilt' rich girl.

What a fool he was to have thought like that. What a fool I was to let him. The fact that we were young is our only excuse.

Later, when we met up again, Steve and I, the sex was still great. Even better. It was like rediscovering something we both thought had gone for ever. Well, I'd thought it had gone from my life for ever. Not Steve, perhaps. He'd had mistresses.

Like Nadia Shelley.

Who had meant more to him than he'd wanted me to know.

On the Saturday we had dinner with a few friends at Tom and Cecily Winters' house; they lived only a couple of miles from Eastways. Tom was an investment banker and Cecily wrote books about gardening, which she had all the time in the world for now after bringing up three kids. They had been my parents' friends and were closer to their age than ours, as was most of the crowd they knew.

Evenings there never ran on late; we were back home before eleven. George said he would have a nightcap in the library and watch the news. I bit back an impulse to suggest he'd already had enough. I had noticed he was drinking more than usual during dinner. He'd lost his train of thought a few times when he was talking, then interrupted other people because he wanted to go back to something they'd said fifteen minutes ago. Nobody minded terribly: everybody has the right to have a couple of drinks too many from time to time. All the same it was surprising, and there was obviously some sort of hidden reason for it.

He had the good sense not even to suggest driving home. The moment he got into the car he put his head back and fell asleep. Or pretended to. Maybe he just didn't want to talk because he was afraid I might ask him yet again what was on his mind, and he would get defensive and say I was imagining it, and quite possibly we'd have an argument. This way made it simpler. I didn't disturb him, and he woke up the moment we came to a stop in our drive.

I went upstairs to undress while he had his nightcap in front of the television in the library. I flipped on the set in the bedroom to see what was happening in the world. I'd missed the headlines, but I'd catch up with them later. My hands were behind my neck unfastening the top of my dress when film of Steve came on screen. It was cut together from his election campaigns and court appearances, both as a lawyer and a man accused or murder. I watched unblinking, holding my breath, as the newscaster intoned:

'Steven Coleman, former lawyer and rising politician, who was convicted last year of murdering his ex-mistress, was seriously injured today in a knifing incident in Ballard Penitentiary, where he is serving a life sentence. The motive for the attack remains unclear, but Coleman is undergoing emergency surgery at City Hospital, where a spokesperson confirmed that his injuries are life-threatening.'

The next item continued at the same volume, but I heard nothing of it. I turned away from the screen, surprised by my inability to know how I felt about the news. It was something I hadn't been ready for. I knew there were dangers in prison for men like Steve. Others would see him as a symbol of the world that had made losers out of them, and they would hit back. I had read that he was going into a protected wing in a special part of the prison. After that I'd tried not to think about the risks. But now . . .

I felt closed in suddenly. Trapped. I needed air, but I didn't want to go downstairs to get out to the garden. I didn't want to see George. At least not just then. Almost certainly he would have seen the same item on the news and I didn't know what I would say to him. I didn't want to have to talk about it, not to him or anybody else.

There was a door from the old nursery which led to a corridor off which there was another door. Since there were no children in the house these days, it was locked only from the inside. It opened on to winding steps which led in one direction down to the ground floor of the house, and in another up to the terrace on top of the clock tower. I started to climb. I hadn't been up there for the best part of a year. We'd been having some work done, but it was all finished now. I stepped out under a clear but moonless night sky and took a deep breath of cool fresh air.

As I stood there looking out over the darkened garden, I tried to analyse how much of me wanted to rush to the hospital to be at Steve's side, and how much of me knew it was an absurd fantasy which I should let drop at once. For one thing, what made me think they would even let me see him? After all, I had no claims, no legal rights – certainly fewer than his ex-wife or his children, or any of his family. What was I to him? Or he to me? Officially?

I wondered whether she would even go to the hospital? Linda. Would she even call up to find out how he was? I doubted it. Her bitterness at what he'd done to her was total. If she had been handed the knife that had injured him she would probably have plunged it in herself.

Could she, I suddenly thought, have been behind the attack? But that was unlikely. Linda would never do anything to endanger herself, however indirectly; and being exposed as the vindictive wife behind a prison 'hit' would be far too risky. It had to be something that just happened. An incident. A prison incident.

I wondered what was happening to him at that moment. Was he unconscious or awake? In pain? Alone or with someone – a nurse, a doctor, a guard? Was he even alive or dead? I was making such an effort to conjure up his image that I realized I was trying in a desperate way to reach out and touch him somehow.

Stupid. That was enough. I had to stop. I was all right now. I must go back inside, back to George. He would be looking for me, anxious to see if I'd heard the news. I could talk about it now. I was over the worst. Under control.

I turned to start down the steps, and gasped as something moved in the shadows. It was George. I hadn't heard him follow me up, now he stood facing me, very still, like a statue.

'You startled me,' I said – unnecessarily, with my hand clutched over my heart.

He didn't say anything for what seemed like a long time.

Then he took a step closer. For some reason I took a step back. Then he said, 'You want to go to him, don't you?'

'No,' I said.

'There's no point in lying about it. I know.'

I tried to find his eyes in the darkness, but I couldn't. Then he took another step towards me. I saw his eyes now. There was something strange in them, something deep and unfathomable; or maybe he was simply so drunk he was finding it hard to focus. At any rate he was gazing at me with an intensity I hadn't seen before. It frightened me in a way I didn't understand. It was as though he had suddenly become someone I didn't know.

'George, I'm not lying . . .'

The unsteadiness in my voice betrayed the unease I felt, the sense that something was very wrong between us, though I couldn't work out what. All I wanted was to get away from that place, to be back inside, in the warmth and the light.

'Let's go down,' I said. 'We can't talk here. Let's go inside.'

He didn't move right away. When he did, it was to take another step towards me. I tried to take another step back, away from him, but found I couldn't. I was already up against the crenellated wall around the tower.

I sensed as much as saw his arms coming up in the darkness, and I leaned back, shocked by the depth of my sudden and inexplicable fear of him.

'George . . . What are you doing?. . . Please stop . . .'

I held up a hand to ward him off, at the same time stumbling against the low wall. I lost my balance and felt myself tipping over into space. With a stark horror that refused to accept that this could be happening, I realized I was falling . . .

GEORGE

CHAPTER 37

I had seen Larry's hand start to move out of the corner of my eye. I realized at once what a fool I was, sitting there protesting the morality of our situation when his only concern was to profit by it. My reflexes kicked in and I tried to beat him to the punch, but it was too late. I knew it, and he knew it. Our eyes met, and there was a glint of triumph in his look as his open palm crashed down on the button while my own was still a clear foot away.

His body continued the same fluid forward movement that had started with his hand and arm. He slumped forward in his chair, hung for a moment as though still held by the invisible restraints that hampered us both, then fell back, his head lolling to one side, his mouth open and his eyes staring. It was an expression somewhere between astonishment and vacancy. He was, unless I was very much mistaken, dead.

Dave stood over the body, nodding with satisfaction, as though this was precisely the outcome he had anticipated.

It took me a while to find my voice. Then all I managed
to say was, 'What happened?'

Dave looked over in my direction. 'Pretty much what I
thought would happen,' he said.

'Is he dead?'

'Oh, yes, he's dead.'

'But . . . he struck first.'

'Right.'

I realized that I was standing, looking down at the inert
form across from me. The restraints, whatever they were,
that had kept me in my chair had been lifted, and without
being aware of it I had got to my feet.

'Surely you knew he would,' I said.

'It seemed likely.'

I stared at him, incredulous. 'You mean you rigged it?'

Dave gave that oddly inscrutable little smile of his that I
had grown accustomed to. 'You could say that, I suppose,
though I wouldn't necessarily agree. What I did was design
a strategy to find out what I want to know.'

'And what is it that you want to know?'

He continued to look at me. There was a stillness about
him now that made his gaze oddly penetrating.

'I want to know what you'll do now,' he said.

I looked at him, perplexed. 'Why?'

His eyes didn't flicker as he continued smiling, watching
me. 'Figure it out,' he said. 'I told you this was a research
project.'

It took a moment for it to sink in. Then, as I finally
understood the enormity of what had just been done to me,
I felt as though a lead weight had been dropped into the pit
of my stomach, knocking the breath and indeed the very
life out of me.

'You shit!' was all I managed to say.

I must have looked away for a second, because when I
turned back he was gone. So was Larry's body. Nor, when I

looked at the two chairs we had both been held down in, was there any sign of those strange buttons on the arms. I searched quickly from room to room. I was the only person in the apartment.

Then I realized that the world outside was back to normal. Everything was moving again. I looked at my watch: it was a few minutes after three, but the information told me nothing. All I knew was that I was George Daly, and something had just happened to me that no one would ever believe. That was my first thought: I could never tell anybody about this. There was no imaginable way that any sane and normal person would take such a claim seriously. I would immediately be classified as clinically deluded, or at the very least a harmless crank.

Then they would discover that I was far from harmless. In the few hours I claimed I'd spent talking with the man in charge of the computer in which – allegedly – our cyberworld existed, a whole eighteen months had passed back here in everybody else's world. In that period someone had murdered Nadia Shelley and Clifford Edge. Edge's death remained unsolved, but Steve was serving life for Nadia's murder, of which I knew he was innocent. I knew that the real killer was someone whose existence I could not prove, but who had been living my life for the past eighteen months.

Or was there a way to prove it? At least a place to start? Hardly more than an hour ago I had sat with Larry and Dave in a cafe just around the corner. Surely someone there, our waitress at least, would remember us. A few minutes later I walked in the door of the place. All the tables were taken, but I saw the waitress I was looking for across the room and went over to her. I had to wait till she finished taking someone's order, then I asked her if she remembered me from an hour or so back with two other men. I described Dave and Larry in detail and pointed out the table we'd been at.

She looked unsure and a little startled by the urgency of my question. I repeated it, insisting she couldn't possibly not remember us. She kept saying she was sorry, but there were so many people through there all the time that she couldn't remember everybody. I told her I wasn't asking about everybody; I was asking about myself and two other men, and for Christ's sakes it was only an hour ago!

A man in a white apron came over from behind the counter. He was young, built like a football player, probably working his way through college. He asked if there was any problem in a way that made it sound like a warning. I told him what the problem was, and he said if Sharon didn't remember me, then that was that. Now perhaps I wouldn't mind if she got on with her work.

She hurried off towards the kitchen as though glad to get away from me. I became aware that conversations had stopped and people were looking at us. I took advantage of that to ask the whole room if any of them had been there an hour ago and remembered seeing me with two other men. No one replied.

I realized the football player had his hand on my upper arm and was steering me towards the door. When I tried to protest and pull free he tightened his grip painfully. 'OK,' he said, 'you've asked your question and gotten your answer. Now I'm asking you to leave. We don't want any trouble.'

Followed by every eye in the place I was steered out to the sidewalk, where I finally shook myself free and walked away, feeling humiliated. I walked back to our building, where I had another idea.

As I entered the lobby I saw one of our doormen, Joe, at his desk as he had been a few minutes earlier when I left. He'd also been on duty when I set out for my walk in the park before noon. I kicked myself for not having thought of this before.

'Joe,' I said, going up to him, 'you saw me go out of here just now, didn't you?'

He looked a little puzzled but answered politely. 'Sure I did, Mr Daly. Ten, fifteen minutes ago.'

'And do you remember what time I went out this morning? You did see me, I know, because we spoke.'

He frowned, thinking about this, but only to establish the time. 'Must've been around noon. Maybe a little before.'

'And you've been here ever since then?'

'Haven't left this desk.'

'Perfect. So tell me, Joe, between seeing me go out around noon and go out again fifteen minutes ago, did you see me come back at all?'

He frowned again, but seemed a little more uncertain this time. 'I believe I did, Mr Daly, but, you know, sometimes you can't be sure. People come and go and I don't keep a list or nothing . . .'

I looked up at the security camera on the wall behind his desk. 'But that,' I said, pointing at it triumphantly, 'sees everything – right?'

'Well, I guess it does, Mr Daly. That's what it's there for.' He continued to look at me uncertainly, curious about what I was driving at, but I knew I could count on his cooperation.

'Listen, Joe,' I said, 'this is very important to me, but for reasons I don't want to go into. Can you play back the tape that camera recorded and show me exactly what time I came back from my walk in the park, and whether I was alone?'

His expression changed from puzzled to concerned now. 'That's kind of difficult, Mr Daly. I'm not supposed to touch that stuff, except maybe in an emergency, and even then I'm supposed to call the security company that installed it.'

'But you'd know how to do it if you had to, wouldn't you? You'd know how to look at the tape?'

'Oh, I'd know how. Sure I'd know.'

I watched his eyes as they followed the movement of my hand to my back pocket and pulled out my wallet. 'Joe,' I said, 'I'm not going to get you into any trouble, but I really want you to do this for me. Will you play me that tape showing me when I came in between going out at midday and going out again fifteen minutes ago?'

'Well, I guess I could, Mr Daly, but. . .'

I placed a fifty-dollar bill on his desk and pushed it towards him. He looked at it with interest but made no effort to take it.

'. . . thing is, you see, I'd have to make it all right with this guy I know at the security firm, so no one'll know I stopped the tape. I could lose my job for this.'

Whether or not he was telling the truth, another fifty did the trick. He disappeared into a back room. While he was gone a senator's widow who had a pied-a-terre on the third floor went out, and a dog walker returned with two poodles belonging to an Italian couple we'd had drinks with one time. When Joe returned he resumed his seat and told me to watch one of the four monitors in front of him. He fast-forwarded till I recognized the caricatural flash of my own outline crossing the floor. I asked him to rewind.

An image reappeared, walking backwards, then froze just beyond the door and started in again. A readout in one corner gave that day's date, and recorded the exact time as 13:05.17.

The figure was unmistakably myself.

Alone.

CHAPTER 38

I went through every drawer and closet in the apartment, desperate to find one detail, however tiny, that might offer some proof of Larry Hart's existence. There was nothing, but that didn't exactly surprise me. I knew that Larry himself, after getting back from that last trip to England when he'd murdered Clifford, had destroyed every shred of evidence that he'd ever lived. I knew that because Dave had told me.

There was something else Dave had told me, something about how the program operated, something which I had later explained to Larry: how it would always do everything possible to rationalize and straighten out any loops and glitches that might arise, even by retroactive action if necessary. Could it be that I was looking for something that had once existed, but which now, because the past had been redrafted, never had? In which case I, because I and I alone could recall this deleted past, was the anomaly?

I pondered this elusive notion for a few moments,
turning in circles but always returning to the same point,
the point I realized now that I was trying to avoid: that
there was another and far more reasonable explanation to
what was going on. I had to face the fact of how alarmingly
well everything fitted into the scenario of a jealous
husband suffering some psychotic break, a fugue –
whatever the clinical term for it might be – and committing
two murders about which he recollected everything, aside
from the fact that he had committed them himself. Larry
and Dave and the whole crazy thing about a computer
universe were, by any rational analysis, more likely to be
fictions than fact – fictions I had invented in order to hide
from myself the terrible truth that I was a killer, and insane.

That explanation was supported by the security tape I had
seen downstairs – myself walking into the building alone at
the time when, in my subjective memory, I had somehow
made a magical transition with Dave and Larry from the cafe
to the apartment. Obviously it didn't happen like that,
except in my head.

Unless – that thought again – the computer was busily
ironing things out to make them appear 'normal'.

But could anyone in their right minds take such a
proposition seriously? That it was 'all just a computer'?
Could anybody accept such a notion as sufficient
explanation for the existence of the Parthenon, the works of
Shakespeare, Leonardo, Beethoven – et cetera? The list was
arbitrary and endless. The idea was cheap, cynical, and
frankly stupid.

Furthermore, when I thought about it, I realized that I
had learnt nothing from Dave that I hadn't already known
or at least speculated about in the past. I knew, for example,
that the physicist John Wheeler, who coined the term
'black hole', had said, 'There is no space and no time. There
is no *out there* out there.' I hadn't heard it first from Dave.

That was the biggest weakness of my whole story, the

most clear-cut proof that I had imagined it all.

On the other hand, of course, it was possible that Dave was more than just a caricature of some computer nerd invented by my sick and befuddled imagination. It was conceivable – certainly not impossible, not something I could totally rule out – that he was actually God, or some emissary thereof. If that was the case, then all bets were off. He could present himself in any form He chose and describe reality in terms of any paradigm He wished, including ones that were familiar to me. So the fact of my not having learnt anything totally new from Him was not inevitably and necessarily damning.

But why would God do this? To test me? Like some character in the Old Testament? To that extent, God's motives were indistinguishable from those which Dave had claimed for himself: that he wanted to find out how his programmed creation (me) would play the hand I'd been, however unjustly, dealt. That's what he'd said: 'I want to know what you'll do now.'

The questions were infinite and unanswerable. The more I thought about them, the more I began to spin in dizzying circles. Eventually I found myself thinking about something I'd written only that morning. At least it seemed to me that it had been that morning. According to the calendar I must have written it eighteen months ago. All the same, when I went into my study I found the notebook where I remembered leaving it. I opened it at the last page that bore my handwriting, and read:

Or is all this speculation simply missing the point? Is something quite different going on?
Is it all about something else?

I took a long bath and stared at the ceiling. Sara would be back soon. What would I say? What would I do? I felt myself suffused with a strange lightness of being. I checked and rechecked aspects of my mind – memories, senses, sensibilities – like a crash survivor realizing he's come through alive but needing to be reassured that his body is still in one piece and his limbs are in working order. So far as I could see, I was still functioning more or less as usual.

By the time she let herself into the apartment I was stretched out on the bed in my robe. I pretended not to hear her when she called out to see if I was home because I didn't know what to say. I had a moment of panic. This was the confrontation I had been dreading, yet at the same time was impatient for.

'George? Are you all right?'

She was standing in the door. I turned to look at her and said, 'Fine.'

'I called, you didn't answer.'

'I took a bath, fell asleep. I was thinking.'

She came over and bent down to kiss me on the forehead. 'If we're going to Rob and Charles's party,' she said, 'you need to get ready. Me too.'

'Yeah, right.'

I rolled off the bed looking at my watch, grateful for the chance to escape into my dressing room. The moment she had mentioned it I had known that we had to be at Rob and Charles's loft by seven. What I didn't know was how I knew. I hadn't known the last time I remembered leaving the apartment. How could I have? It was eighteen months ago.

Then again, if time and space did not exist . . .

That was the thought I had to hold on to, my lifeline to sanity. Because if time and space *did* exist, I was almost certainly both insane and a murderer.

CHAPTER 39

For a moment in the elevator, when she asked me again if
something was wrong, I hovered on the brink of coming out
with the whole story. But I realized, faced with the
prospect of putting it into words, how impossible that was.
I made some anodyne reply, but was convinced from then
on that she suspected something was seriously wrong.
More than once during the evening I caught her watching
me oddly when she thought I wasn't looking. As a result I
found myself watching her more closely than usual, and
probably feeding her suspicions even further. We were
getting caught up in a vicious circle. I had to find a way out.

The next day was a Sunday. It was a relief to me that Sara
would be spending most of it at the gallery, where they
were still preparing for their opening the following
Tuesday. I decided to make some kind of inventory of what
I knew and what I needed to find out about my situation.
Most of all I still needed to find some evidence of Larry
Hart's existence. I thought that perhaps I might return the

following morning to the agency I had originally hired to track down Jeffrey Hart and Lauren Paige. According to Larry, who had intercepted their report to me, they had come across records that proved his existence – though of course I only had Larry's word for that.

But did I dare go back to that office where Nadia Shelley used to work? Could I risk opening up that can of worms by probing into one of the last cases she was involved with? Even if Larry Hart *had* existed, the fact was that she had always known him as George Daly. To all intents and purposes it was George Daly who had murdered her and framed Steve Coleman. On balance, I decided, it would be wise to stay away from anything that might connect me with that crime.

I remembered that after coming across all that stuff in my father's trunk I'd gone to a specialist movie store to see what I could find on Jeffrey Hart and Lauren Paige. There wasn't much, but the guy there had searched the Web and given me a printout of their shabby careers. I had no idea what I'd done with those details; if Larry had come across them amongst my things he would undoubtedly have destroyed them when he destroyed all the other evidence of his existence. But he couldn't, I supposed, have wiped the Web – although, of course, the computer could. All the same, I decided to see what I could find.

Sure enough, I found that between 1953 and 1967 they had played together in a handful of small British pictures called *Spring In Piccadilly*, *Whistling Through*, *Girl Scout Patrol* and *There's A Spy In My Soup*. In 1973 Jeffrey alone played in *The Silver Spoon*. There was no mention of their son Larry, in fact no reference of any kind to their private life.

I racked my brains to think of some other avenue of enquiry I might explore. The only thing that came to mind was that secret trip back to New York – to murder Nadia – that Larry had made on his own passport while he was staying in London as George Daly. Sara and I had a friend with a travel company who made all the arrangements for her business trips as well as private travel for both of us. I was pretty sure that Larry would have used him to book his flight to London in my name, so I called him at home to see if he recalled doing so. I made some excuse about needing to check dates because of a book I was writing. He remembered perfectly well making, my, reservations for the flight as well as, my, hotel in London. (It's amazing how any question, no matter how absurd, intrusive or even offensive, becomes acceptable when you explain that you're writing a book.) Using the same excuse, I then said I had a favour to ask him.

'I'm trying to trace the movements of a man called Hart, Larry Hart,' I said. 'Full name Laurence Jeffrey Hart. He might have made a round trip between London and New York during the period I was in London. He also might have made a New York–London–New York trip a few weeks later. I've called a couple of airlines but they won't come up with the information without asking a lot of questions that I don't want to go into. Can you help?'

He said he'd get into it, sounding as though he quite relished the challenge of showing off his expertise.

'Who is this man?' he asked. 'Who is Larry Hart?'

'That's what I'm trying to find out,' I said.

I had a subscription to a couple of news services on the Web. It occurred to me that although I knew all about Steve's trial, I had neither seen anything of it at first hand nor had I watched the daily TV or press reports. At least, that was how it seemed to me. Of course if Larry Hart and I were one, then I must have read them in the persona of my murderous alter ego and forgotten. Either way, it would be interesting to read or re-read them now.

Within a few minutes I was scrolling through the reports and accompanying photographs. There was nothing new, no revelations that I hadn't been prepared for – until I came across one passage that shot through my brain like a bolt of lightning. Fibres of the pantyhose which had been used to strangle Nadia Shelley had been found on the fender of Steve's car. They matched exactly the traces of fibres found on her body, and they also carried traces of blood which had been matched to hers. This was a key part of the forensic evidence that had helped convict Steve.

But the pantyhose themselves had never been found. The presumption was that Steve had got rid of them somewhere, most likely destroyed them.

I, however, knew differently. I knew they had never been found because Larry had hung on to them in case he needed them later to incriminate Steve yet further. I knew this because I had been told it by Dave.

What I did not know, however, was what Larry had done with them. He must have hidden them somewhere, but where? And were they still where he had hidden them, or had he eventually destroyed them?

Why did I not know that?

If I was Larry, if Larry was my own insane and self-exculpatory invention, then I knew somewhere in my subconscious exactly what had happened to those pantyhose, but I was concealing that knowledge from myself.

If, on the other hand, they were hidden someplace I could not possibly have known about or had access to, then I, George Daly, could not be Larry Hart. Which meant that the whole mad metaphor of Dave and our computer universe was not a metaphor at all. It was the plain unvarnished and outrageous truth, which I had stumbled on by probing too earnestly into the mysteries of synchronicity.

But how to prove it either way? Still that warning note of Dave's lingered at the back of my mind – the notion that the program always strove to iron out contradictions and rationalise inconsistencies. Even if a 'loop' of the kind he had described had arisen, it had by now been closed. The glitch had been resolved with Larry's 'death' and things had reverted to their previous state. The past had been revised. Larry had never existed; only his crimes remained.

And they didn't commit themselves – did they?

Whichever way I looked at it, fate seemed determined not to let me off the hook. Guilt was closing in around me like a fog. But I refused to be overwhelmed by it without a fight. If there was any way out of this impossible situation, I was determined I would find it.

CHAPTER 40

That evening, Sunday, I joined Sara at the gallery around eight and we went out to eat with a couple of the people she worked with. When we got home she was tired and went straight to bed. I was lucky that she was so preoccupied over those few days; it kept questions and awkward conversations to a minimum, and left me with time to figure out where I went from there.

I slept barely at all that night and spent hours pacing the apartment, trying without success to distract myself by reading. I climbed back in bed alongside Sara and managed an hour or so of shallow sleep before her alarm went off at seven thirty. After that I slept fitfully a while longer, but was up and having breakfast by nine. Shortly afterwards my phone rang. It was my friend in the travel business with the information I'd asked him for.

'A passenger named L. J. Hart made two round trips within the periods you mentioned,' he said, and gave me the details – exactly as I had expected, and feared, I would hear them. I thanked him and promised him I'd give him the full story in time, if there ever was a full story – which of course, so far as he and perhaps everybody but me was concerned, there never would be.

What I knew now was that a man calling himself Larry Hart had actually taken those flights which coincided (coincidence again, but of a more sinister kind than had begun this story) with Nadia Shelley's and Clifford Edge's murders.

But if I had been that man and blocked out the memory, where in God's name had I got the extra passport, the one in the name of Larry Hart? I had no idea how to go about obtaining such a thing. True, I'd read *Day of the Jackal* years before and vaguely remembered how you could look around a graveyard, find the name of someone who'd been born about the same time as yourself, then apply for a copy of their birth certificate and use it to get a passport in their name. So had I found Larry Hart's grave? But how? Where? It didn't hang together.

Or maybe it did, but I just didn't want to see it. Maybe I was more determined to prove that Larry Hart had existed than to uncover and face up to the truth that he never had.

Or maybe I was still just going around in circles, asking all the wrong questions.

Maybe, as I had written once, it was all about something else.

But what?

That night I knew again I wouldn't sleep, and told Sara I would use a guest room so as not to disturb her with my restlessness the night before her opening. She asked me if I was sure I was all right and suggested I see our doctor for a check-up. I assured her it was nothing more than a little temporary insomnia, but I'd get a check-up anyway.

Around one, desperate for release from the agony of self-questioning and endless speculation, I took a sleeping pill.

It was something I so rarely did that I fell asleep within half an hour. That was the first time I had the dream.

I knew it was dream, yet it had such an extraordinary clarity that I had no doubt I would remember it when I awoke; indeed, I was convinced it was important that I should, though I had no idea why.

In the dream I was riding in the back of New York cab, heading somewhere downtown, when I observed one of those odd little coincidences that happen all the time but are usually meaningless. I, however, knew by now – even in the dream – that coincidences were never meaningless. What happened was that just as the taxi meter registered a tariff of four dollars forty-four cents (4:44) a digital clock on the dash registered a time of 4:44.

Aside from the coincidence, I knew at once that something was wrong. It was broad daylight. Manhattan was bustling with shoppers and visitors and people hurying between appointments.

'Your clock's wrong,' I said to the driver. 'Shouldn't it read sixteen forty-four?'

He shook his head briefly. 'No,' he said in a guttural Slavic accent, 'that's how it works.'

At that moment I noticed a woman on the crowded sidewalk. She was tall and beautiful in a top model sort of way – poised, cool, impeccably elegant. The dress she wore was as striking as she was herself. It was high-collared, tight-waisted and long-sleeved, patterned in broad stripes of black and white which seemed to coil around her body like a giant snake. She wore a wide-brimmed hat, also in black and white but with a single dash of red – a flower of some kind. The skirt was long but slashed up one side to the hip, revealing legs of utter perfection moving with a hypnotic and gazelle-like grace. She was an image of such unlikely theatricality on that dusty and mundane sidewalk that I was amazed she wasn't the centre of general and excited interest. Yet no one paid her the slightest attention.

She moved through them like a star through a milling crowd of extras, all of whom had been instructed not on any account to acknowledge her presence.

But of course that made perfect sense. This was, after all, a dream – in which, I reminded myself, everything was choreographed to some specific and intended point. The only question, I thought to myself as I continued dreaming, was: what point?

The strangest thing of all was that I recognized her, though I didn't know why or from where. But I knew at once and with absolute certainty that I had to get out of the cab, catch up with her and speak to her.

I pushed a five-dollar bill into the driver's hand and told him to drop me right there. Then I got out of the cab and started after the woman along the busy sidewalk. Strangely, although I was hurrying as fast as I could, even breaking into a run at times, I seemed unable to catch up with her. She strolled on at her leisurely, untroubled pace, forever the same frustrating distance ahead of me.

'It's all right,' I told myself, 'it's just a dream, that's why you can't catch her. The dream is trying to tell you something. You'll catch her if you're supposed to.'

Suddenly, as though that thought had been the key to closing the gap between us, I found myself right behind her, close enough to touch. I reached out for her shoulder, afraid she would get away again before she'd seen me.

She turned. Her face, beautiful in its surprise at first, took on an expression of horror as she recognized me. She threw up her hands and gave a piercing scream.

I awoke with a gasp, bathed in perspiration as though I really had been running along that warm Manhattan sidewalk. I looked at the digital clock beside my bed.

The time was 4:44.

CHAPTER 41

The opening party at the gallery was a great success, with an even larger turnout than usual of media celebrities, well-heeled collectors, and members of lofty museum boards. Personally I found the work on show to be trash, but you can't say that without having a degree in fine arts, preferably a doctorate, and the ability to write the kind of impenetrably meaningless prose in which art critics specialize. I smiled my way around the room, conversing on autopilot. But I was happy for Sara, who looked particularly beautiful that night and was clearly basking in her triumph.

We didn't get home till after two in the morning. I climbed into bed and gave Sara a big hug of congratulation – the first time I'd had the chance all evening. She fell asleep in my arms. After a while I gently disengaged myself and lay staring at the darkened ceiling.

It was no good. I couldn't sleep, and if I couldn't sleep I was going to scream. I slipped quietly out of bed and went to my study. I sat in the dark looking out at the lights of

Manhattan for almost an hour. Suddenly I became aware of
Sara watching me from the door. She was genuinely
concerned and made a real effort to encourage me to talk
about whatever was worrying me. I managed to reassure
her and sent her back to bed; the fact that she was
exhausted helped a great deal. I promised I would come to
bed just as soon as I'd finished working through some ideas
for my book – the usual old reliable standby of an excuse.

After that I went to the guest room as on the previous
night and took a pill. Once again I fell asleep relatively
quickly. Almost at once I found myself in the back of the
same cab with the same driver. His fare meter and the clock
on his dash both showed 4:44. He gave the same reply –
'That's how it works' – to my question about his dash clock
being wrong. I saw the woman on the sidewalk, exactly as
before. I stopped the cab and followed her, unable to catch
up at first, then, finding myself right behind her, I reached
out to touch her and she turned. As before, her look of
surprise turned to horror. She threw up her hands and gave
a piercing scream.

The time on my bedside clock when I awoke with a gasp
and bathed in perspiration was again 4:44.

There was no way I was going to get back to sleep, and
eventually I gave up trying. I decided to pull on a tracksuit
and go for a jog – not in the park, but there were plenty of
broad well-lit sidewalks where people ran throughout the
night without much risk of being mugged or bothered in
any way. I had already noticed in my dressing room that
there were a couple of jackets, some shirts and sweaters
that I didn't recognize and which must have been Larry's
purchases. Among them was a sleek grey and black
tracksuit which I had no recollection of seeing before and
which I thought I'd try on. Naturally enough it fitted me
perfectly. I found some running shoes, also new, and
pulled them on. As I knelt to tie them, I felt something in

the tracksuit pocket dig into my hip. I reached in and pulled out a plastic card. It was black, about the size of a credit card, and without marking of any kind on either side.

For some moments I just held it in the palm of my hand and looked at it. My mind raced with possibilities. The most likely thing was that it was some kind of key, to a hotel room, a security door, a locker of some kind. But why wasn't it marked? That suggested it was not meant to be identified if it fell into the wrong hands. Its function was to be known only to its rightful owner.

What, I wondered, was Larry's secret? And how could I go about finding it out?

I waited till Joe came on duty downstairs, and asked him about the firm which had installed the security system in our building and the friend he'd claimed to have who worked there. He gave me his friend's name without hesitation, and called him to say that I would be stopping by.

Just after ten I was in his shop, which was midtown off Broadway, asking what they could tell me about the black card. The answer was depressingly little. A quick test established that it was indeed a magnetic key as I had suspected, but beyond that there was nothing to suggest the location of the lock it might fit.

'It could be a security door, a private safe or safe deposit box of some kind,' said Leroy, Joe's amiable friend with an unruly mop of dreadlocks that covered half his face, 'even a luggage locker. I can have somebody go over it and tell you how good it is and therefore the *kind* of place that it might belong, but probably no more than that.'

'Try anyway,' I said, and left it with him. He said he'd get back to me by the next morning at the latest.

'For all his fascination with ghost stories, Charles Dickens liked to think of himself as free from all forms of superstition,' writes Brian Inglis in his book about coincidence, then recounts the following story in Dickens's own words. It obviously refers to the public readings he used to give of his works to enthralled audiences in England and America:

> I dreamt that I saw a lady in a red shawl with her back towards me (whom I supposed to be E). On her turning round, I found that I didn't know her and she said, 'I am Miss Napier.'
>
> All the time I was dressing next morning I thought – what a preposterous thing to have so very distinct a dream about nothing; and why Miss Napier? For I had never heard of any Miss Napier. That same Friday night, I read. After the reading, came into my retiring room Mary Boyle and her brother and *the* lady in the red shawl, whom they presented as 'Miss Napier'!

I was spending the afternoon searching through my collection of books on dreams – from Freud to the occult – trying to get some handle on the symbolism of my own.

To hard-line rationalists like Francis Crick, dreams are without meaning or significance of any kind, just the nocturnal rumblings of our mental digestive systems. But that only makes dreams that appear to predict the future all the more remarkable. For example:

> British Rail had a call from a woman who claimed to have had a vision of a fatal crash in which a freight train had been involved. So clear had it been, she said, that she not merely saw the blue diesel engine, but could read the number: 47216. Two years later, an accident of the kind she predicted occurred, all the details matching – except one: the engine's number was 47299.
>
> That would have been that, but a train spotter happened to have noticed that 47299 was not the engine's original number. It had been renumbered a

couple of years before from 47216. Diesels, the train spotter knew, were ordinarily renumbered only after major modifications, which this one had not undergone. When curiosity prompted him to ask why, he was told about the prediction. Apparently British Rail officials had been sufficiently impressed (they had checked with the local police, and found that the woman had previously given them useful information from her visions) to try to ward off fate by changing the number.

The sense of déjà vu is attributed by some people, those who are prepared to believe in such things, to a forgotten precognitive dream that stirs in the subconscious memory when the event predicted eventually happens. Rationalists, on the other hand, explain it by a process called 'priming', which is a demonstrable capacity of the brain to absorb information subliminally into the unconscious. In other words, you know something without knowing that you know it. Later, when the conscious brain sees something that reflects this unconscious knowledge, it experiences a sense of déjà vu.

I suppose that Occam's razor – the rule that says we should always accept the explanation that requires the smallest number of assumptions – would back the second view.

Doesn't guarantee it's right, though.

CHAPTER 42

Our nights were becoming a ritual by now. Yet again I went to bed with Sara, around midnight this time, and lay there until she was asleep. Then I slipped from between the covers and went to my study, where I tried to read. But concentration was impossible. After barely half an hour I abandoned the struggle and went to the guest room. Again I took a sleeping pill, but this time it did not have the same immediate effect.

I surfed through the late shows and then the late-late shows, and then I must have finally drifted into sleep, because I became aware that I was dreaming again. Once again I was in the back of the same cab with its clock and meter both reading 4:44, the same driver making the same remark, the same spectacularly attractive and dramatically attired woman on the sidewalk, the same chase, the same scream of terror when she turned and saw me.

But this time I didn't wake up. I was aware of a certain excitement as I felt the dream moving into unknown

territory. A second later I realized that the woman's scream
was not directed at me at all. I wasn't even sure she'd seen
me, though the only reason she had turned was the
pressure of my hand on her shoulder. But she was looking
past me, somewhere beyond, from where I now heard a
screech of brakes and a sickening thud. I spun around – and
saw that a car had knocked down a pedestrian, a man who
lay sprawled at an unnatural angle in the road.

'Call 911,' the woman said.

I turned back to look at her.

'911,' she repeated urgently, and pushed past me to
where people were now crowding around the injured man.

Once again I awoke with a start and found myself
breathless and perspiring. Once again I found myself
looking at the bedside clock.

Once again it read 4:44.

But this time the lights were on, and so was the
television. I was slumped awkwardly across my pillow
where I'd fallen asleep. And there was something on the
screen that almost made my heart stop. It was the woman
from my dream, dressed in that same encoiling black and
white theatrical creation with the dramatic wide-brimmed
hat. But this time she was against a totally white
background, which threw into sharper focus those
magnificent long black-stockinged legs.

'She walks in beauty,' crooned a deep male voice on the
sound track. And up came the logo for a brand of
pantyhose.

It was the brand that I knew had been used to strangle
Nadia Shelley.

Next morning Joe's friend Leroy from the security company
phoned shortly after ten to tell me what he'd found out
about the key card I'd left with him. In fact he'd found out
very little except that it carried quite a sophisticated code,
which suggested it was more than just a hotel or locker

room key. Also, he said, it probably opened more than one lock, for example an outer security door and then a safe deposit box. Beyond that he couldn't help. I asked him to messenger the card back to me. It arrived just as I was leaving to have lunch with Lou Bennett. I slipped it into my pocket and headed for the subway, which, I could see from the traffic, was going to be faster than taking a cab.

I had called Lou because, despite his age and his fondness for long three-martini (and then some) lunches, he was one of the smartest and most perceptive people I'd ever met. I knew he'd had lunch with Larry a couple of times and they'd talked on the phone now and again, and I wanted to find out if he'd noticed anything different about 'me' on those occasions. I wasn't going to tell him why I wanted to know, just ask the question. One of the things I liked about Lou was that you didn't have to explain yourself to him. He knew that life in general and people in particular were too complex to be easily understood, and he rarely even tried; he just observed.

It seemed that everybody and his cousin was heading downtown that morning. The subway car I got into was packed to the doors even though it was well past the rush hour. I couldn't help giving a slightly sour smile of amusement as I thought about the consolations offered by Dave's philosophy of life to this and other discomforts. That wasn't really someone's elbow in my back, and that fat man breathing in my face didn't really stink of half-chewed sugared peanuts, nor was the music leakage from the Walkman worn by some kid jammed against my right shoulder really setting my teeth on edge: it was all just information fed into a quantum computer, as was I myself, and any resemblance to painful physical reality was purely coincidental. The world was, as any Eastern mystic could have told me with or without Dave's scientific mumbo-jumbo, an illusion.

At that moment, almost as though his appearance had

been triggered by my thinking of him, I spotted Dave at the far end of the car. The shock made me gasp loudly. If anyone had noticed, which was unlikely, they would probably have surmised that the fat man in front of me had stepped on my foot. But all thoughts of personal discomfort were forgotten as I gazed at the mundane but unlikely figure down the car. Like me he was standing, pinned by people on all sides. He hadn't seen me, or if he had he was being careful to conceal the fact. Each time the train and its sardine-like cargo lurched briefly to the right or left I lost sight of him; but each time he came back into view he was still staring vacantly at some tall black man's leather-jacketed back about an inch from his nose.

Every imaginable way of attracting his attention ran through my head, and just as swiftly I discarded them. Fighting my way down the car to where he stood was frankly a physical impossibility. And even if I shouted his name I probably wouldn't be heard over the noise of the train; I would simply become, to the people around me, one of those New York embarrassments that you pretend you haven't noticed and try to avoid making eye contact with.

Then, as the train slowed, I saw him begin edging his way towards the doors. He was obviously getting out at the next station, and I prepared to do likewise.

The crowd on the platform was even worse than in the train. I lost sight of Dave almost at once and could only struggle inch by inch in the general direction I'd last seen him headed. Eventually things thinned out a little, and when I reached the foot of an escalator I briefly glimpsed him stepping off the top. By the time I got there he had disappeared. There were three tunnels I had a choice of going down; most people were heading for the one to the left, so I took a chance and went that way. Sure enough, pushing through the exit gate up ahead I saw the familiar white T-shirt and long greasy hair. I put on a sprint that should have had me catch up with him before he hit the street.

But when I reached the open air there was no sign of him. I looked desperately around in all directions, then took a chance and headed for a nearby intersection. My instincts had carried me in the right direction, because I glimpsed him on the far side, diagonally across from me and walking away. Defying the traffic and a good deal of angry honking and hollering, I made it across and managed to keep him in my sights. I caught up with him at the next corner. He spun around in obvious alarm when my hand descended on his shoulder – as well he might, because he was a total stranger.

'Hey, what the fuck is this? What do you want?' He squirmed out of my grasp as though I was about to sexually assault him.

'I'm sorry,' I said, 'my mistake. Did you just come out of the subway?'

'What the fuck is that to you? Get away from me, I don't know you!'

He scurried away, glancing nervously over his shoulder a couple of times to make sure I wasn't following him. I stood there, cursing silently. Could I really have been that mistaken in the subway car? It was possible. I'd only had a brief glimpse of the man I'd thought was Dave. More precisely several brief glimpses, my view of him constantly obscured by the swaying bodies between us.

Or could it really have been Dave down there, but I'd lost him somewhere in the labyrinth of stairs and tunnels, then picked up on this total stranger who coincidentally bore some resemblance to him?

I walked on despondently for a few blocks, then remembered Lou and glanced at my watch. The traffic was still solid, so I looked around for the nearest subway entrance. And as I did so I forgot all about Lou.

Because there, directly opposite me across the street, painted in small but distinct white characters, was the number 444.

CHAPTER 43

Despite an impulse to plunge into the traffic that rumbled past only inches from where I stood, I remained rooted to the sidewalk, staring as though afraid that if I blinked or looked away even for a second then what I had seen might vanish. Subliminally I registered that the lights had changed and the 'Walk' sign was green. I crossed with the crowd who'd been waiting, keeping my gaze fixed on that clear white '444'.

I could see there was some sort of engraved plaque of polished brass on the wall. As I drew closer I was able to make out the words 'Beacon Trust'.

My hand slid almost of its own accord into the pocket of my coat where it closed around the card that I had put there as I left the apartment. Had I known that I would need it? Was something taking its course regardless of anything I did or thought or wanted?

The door to 'Beacon Trust' consisted of two vertical capsules made of thick unbreakable glass. One was for entering, the other for leaving. Only one person at a time could do either. I watched as a man inserted a card like my own into the slot provided. The capsule swivelled open and he stepped in, paused a moment as it shut, then the other half opened and he entered the building.

I stepped up to the door and inserted my card as he had, praying that I wasn't going to find that the codes had changed and the card I had was out of date. It worked. The capsule slid smoothly open, I stepped in, waited, then stepped through into a polished marble lobby.

A couple of armed guards were on duty but paying no particular attention either to me or any of the other individuals in the trickle that came and went in various directions. I looked around, getting my bearings. A rather grand staircase wound up from one end of the lobby to a higher floor where, I suspected, I would find offices – which were not what I was looking for. Nearby was a bank of elevators, and next to that a recessed area from which several corridors ran off. It looked to me as if these led only to more offices. More promising were a set of wide steps, half a dozen at most, which led to a kind of lower ground floor of which I could see little from where I was. Not wanting to stand around uncertainly, thereby attracting the attention of the guards, I went decisively down these steps, and found myself facing a blank wood-panelled wall with a single door in the centre. Once again there was a slot in which a card could be inserted. Crossing my fingers that the same card would suffice, I slid it in. Sure enough there was a soft click and the door swung back on automatic hinges.

I stepped through into a large windowless area in which there was no sound except the constant hum of air conditioning and an occasional footstep on the polished marble floor. Various rooms opened up ahead of me and to each side. All contained nothing but floor-to-ceiling steel doors, each one obviously a private safe and bearing its own number. Those closest were only about the size of drawers, the furthest away looked large enough to take a pretty big suitcase.

There were, so far as I could see, no guards down there and no visible security cameras. I imagined that, on the whole, the kind of people who might want to avail themselves of such a facility would prefer not to be photographed doing so.

'Can I help you, sir?'

I jumped at the voice at my elbow, and turned to see an attractive young woman in a dark suit and white blouse looking up at me with a pleasant smile.

'If you'd like to tell me your number,' she said, 'I'll be glad to show you where it is.'

My number. A feeling of panic swept over me. I had no number. I didn't know what she was talking about. Any moment now I was going to be exposed as having entered under false pretences, and who knew what the consequences of that might be? I started to mumble something about having forgotten, but then I realized I hadn't forgotten at all. I'd been given the number, surely, in my dream.

'911,' I said impulsively, and with a conviction that I frankly didn't feel.

'That will be over here,' she said without a blink of hesitation. 'If you'll step this way, sir.'

I followed her to my left, through an opening the size of a door but with no door in it. She gestured to the wall in front of me, about halfway up. There, sure enough, I saw a drawer-sized steel door marked '911'.

'If you require privacy to deal with any business you may have, remember we have individual cubicles for that purpose.' She indicated four more doors, one in each corner of the room. 'If you need any further assistance, just call me, or press the buzzer on the wall.'

'Thank you,' I said, 'you've been very helpful. Thank you very much.'

I waited till she had gone before trying my card in the door marked '911'. I didn't want to discover at this final hurdle, and under her inscrutable gaze, that my dream had been inaccurate or incomplete. As I slipped my card into the slot provided, there was an immediate soft click. I breathed a sigh of relief mixed with apprehension as the small door sprang open, revealing a flat steel box with a handle attached. I pulled it out. The top was hinged, but I didn't open it right away. I headed for the privacy of one of the corner cubicles, knowing with a sickening and terrible certainty what I was going to find.

The only thing in the box was a clean white envelope, not even sealed. It contained a clear plastic bag in which were the remains of a pair of pantyhose. I could see a couple of dark stains which I took to be blood, and they were shredded where Larry had hooked them on Steve's fender to leave the traces that had sealed his guilt.

Instinctively I reached out to check the lock on the door of the little boxlike cubicle in which I sat. I knew I'd locked it when I entered, so the action was merely a response to the wave of panic that surged over me. For a moment I wondered if I would ever be able to leave that tiny cell-like place. Maybe I would stay there till they broke the door down and found my putrefying corpse. The impact of my discovery had been worse than I had imagined even in my darkest moments. I didn't know how to go out and face the world again. I think I had a kind of brief nervous breakdown sitting there on that plain bench before an equally plain table, hypnotized by that open box and its dreadful contents.

I tried to look at things logically. Had the chain of events that had brought me to this point been truly synchronicitous or in any other way out of the ordinary? Was I the victim of a fate over which I had no control? Or was I the perpetrator of crimes that my unconscious was making me belatedly face up to? Surely – Occam's razor again – I had to choose the latter as the most likely explanation. Being haunted in my dreams by what I'd done made a lot more sense than the idea that the whole universe was merely the plaything of Dave and his computer.

But how about that strange business of waking up twice at exactly 4:44 a.m.? What explanation was there for that? Well, I told myself, it's a known fact that some people can set themselves to wake up like an alarm clock, right on the dot. Maybe it's a faculty we all possess but just don't normally use. Furthermore, who's to say I hadn't been lying there with my eyes open waiting for 4:44 to come up, and only consciously registering the clock face when it did? Nobody could say that wasn't how it happened, including me.

Same thing with the pantyhose commercial on the TV. I'd fallen asleep but unconsciously registered it, maybe just the soundtrack, when it came up. I'd seen it before, so it had already connected – unconsciously – with the terrible secret that I was keeping hidden from myself.

I was beginning to sound in my head like a phone-in shrink, but that wasn't going to get me off the hook. Nothing was. Everything pointed to my guilt.

Except the possibility that Dave was real and had told me the truth.

So who had hidden that damning piece of shredded, bloodstained, DNA-rich nylon in this place? George Daly calling himself Larry Hart? Or Larry Hart calling himself George Daly? In either case the motive was the same – to keep the evidence safe until it had to be planted on Steve. And if that did not become necessary, the next logical step was to destroy it – wasn't it?

I wondered if that was why I was there. To destroy the evidence. Was that what I wanted?

My mobile rang with a startling loudness in that tiny space. I plucked it from my inside pocket and answered. It was Lou, waiting for me in the restaurant and wondering where the hell I was. I said I would be there in fifteen minutes, and hung up.

I remained motionless a few seconds more. I had responded to his question with total spontaneity; now I had to reflect whether I intended to do what I had said I would. I decided I did.

All I had to make up my mind about now was what I was going to do with that white envelope and its contents. Should I lock them up again? Or take them with me, and decide what to do with them later?

Another moment's hesitation. Then I stuffed the envelope into my jacket, unlocked the door, and left.

CHAPTER 44

'There's a story scientists like to tell,' I said to Lou over my
risotto al mare, 'about some great luminary, an Einstein or
a Bertrand Russell, someone like that, who's giving a
public lecture on astronomy. He explains how the earth
orbits around the sun and how the sun orbits around a vast
collection of stars in the galaxy, and so on and so forth. At
the end of the lecture a little old lady at the back of the
room gets up and says, "Everything you've told us is
rubbish. It's perfectly obvious that the world is really a flat
plate supported on the back of a giant turtle."'

'So the great scientist gives a condescending smile and
says, "Then perhaps you can tell us, madam, by what is the
turtle supported?"'

'"You're very clever, young man," says the little old lady,
"but you don't fool me. It's turtles all the way down."'

Lou chuckled merrily.

'Scientists tell that story,' I said, 'not because it's a put-
down of little old ladies and stupid superstitions, but

because it expresses their own worst fears.'

A bushy eyebrow lifted in mild surprise. 'How come?'

'We know there are limits to logic, limits to what we can prove, limits to what can be known about the quantum world because it's inherently unknowable. And yet scientists go on probing, discovering new particles, coming up with new theories, refining equations, all in pursuit of the Holy Grail of a unified theory – one theory that explains everything. One particle, one force, instead of the four we have now; one equation that describes the single basic building block of the universe.'

I scooped up another forkful of my lunch, which was probably as excellent as ever, though frankly I was in no frame of mind to appreciate such things. I leaned slightly towards Lou to make sure he was paying attention.

'But suppose,' I said, 'just suppose it's a hopeless quest. Suppose the universe isn't made up of any one thing that we can finally put our finger on and say "That's it". Suppose all that ever happens is that when we look at something closely enough, it turns into something else? Mass becomes energy; a wave becomes a particle; a particle becomes a superstring; and so on ad infinitum. In other words, reality is a stack of Russian dolls – open one and there's another one inside. All we're really doing is chasing our own tails. Sure, we're building rockets to Mars and microwave ovens, but those are by-products, not the goal. It's a scary thought that maybe there is no goal. Maybe it really is turtles all the way down – turtles or whatever. But no final answers. Because we're looking in the wrong place.'

Lou thought this over for a moment, then said, 'So where *should* we be looking?'

'Ah, if I knew that, Lou, I'd be able to write a really interesting book.'

'That would be nice.'

'All I know is that maybe it's all about something else.'

'Like what?'

I thought about it for a while, then took a shot. After all, it was only a conversation between old friends.

'Maybe it's not what we *are* that matters so much as what we *do*.'

Lou gave a grunt of surprise and mild disapproval. 'Are you getting religion or something?'

'Maybe "or something". Mystics would know what I'm talking about. They find the idea that we can ever define reality and hold it in our hand as laughable.'

'But mystics, as you pointed out, don't build rockets to the moon or invent non-stick frying pans.'

'That's not necessarily so, Lou. You don't have to spend your life on a mountaintop contemplating infinity to be a mystic. You can perfectly well be a chemist or a plumber or an engineer. The point is you know that reason and logic and the technology you build on them aren't going to give you all the answers.'

'Because it's all about something else that's got nothing to do with reason or logic?'

There was a glint of amusement in his eye. I suspected that Lou thought all speculation of this kind was a fool's game, albeit one that he enjoyed playing sometimes. Or maybe he was simply humouring me.

'Right,' I said. 'Reason and logic are not the way to truth.'

'Maybe we should just say fuck the truth.'

'Maybe,' I said, 'maybe not. Frankly, I don't know.'

I finished eating and sat back. Lou had ordered a dessert, but all the same he lit up one of his cigars while he was waiting for it. I watched him as a haze of blue smoke curled around him.

'Tell me, Lou,' I said, 'the last couple of times we had lunch together, do you remember what we talked about?'

He looked mildly surprised. 'Not specially. Why, what was it?'

'I don't recall. That's why I'm asking you.'

He shrugged. 'The same kind of stuff as usual, I guess.'

'You mean like this? Ideas, stuff I might turn into a book?'

'Yeah, like we always do. I forget the details. Why d'you ask?'

'Oh, no reason,' I said, feeling suddenly that it was futile to pursue the question; after all, what would it prove? 'It's not important.'

'One thing I remember,' he said after a while, gazing ruminatively at the glowing tip of his cigar, 'you told me you were giving up on that book you'd been planning to write about coincidence.'

'I did? Did I say why?'

He shrugged. 'You said it wasn't going anywhere. Which I thought was a pity. I always liked that idea. If you change your mind, we can still make a deal.'

I was silent for a moment, thinking over what he'd said. Then I shrugged. 'It's still not going anywhere, and I doubt if it ever will. It turned into a dead end.'

'Turtles all the way down, huh?'

I looked at him, surprised by how quickly he'd picked up on the metaphor. He looked back at me across the table with an expression of shrewd amusement, though I doubted whether he had any idea how shrewd he'd just been, or how bleakly amused he had a right to be.

'Something like that,' I said. 'Turtles all the way down.'

CHAPTER 45

According to Sara, it had been my idea to go up to Eastways that weekend. I had made some casual remark about not having been there for a while, and she had seized on it and decided we should go. She sensed the strain between us that week and felt, I suspected, that we needed to spend some time together alone.

As the week passed, I dreaded the prospect increasingly. My feelings towards Sara were becoming unbearably painful to me. Whoever had been with her over the past months, whether it was Larry assuming my identity or myself in some kind of split-personality phase, had established a very different relationship from any that I was capable of living with. The gulf between my feelings for her and her feelings for me (or whoever had been in my place and whose relationship with her I had now inherited) was deep and unbridgeable. I felt the same love for her I always had. I was still suffering from the – for me – recent bombshell of learning that she loved someone else. At the same time I was living the endgame of that story. In what was for me a period of days, I had gone from a state of unblemished happiness with a wife I loved and who I thought loved me, to heartbreak when I discovered she was leaving me for someone else, then almost at once to this strange limbo in which she had come back to me for companionship and kindness, which I now had to accept was all she had ever really wanted from me. I did not know how to play the role in which I had been cast. I did not *want* to play it.

Throughout my lunch with Lou, the envelope and its incriminating contents had remained in my inside jacket pocket. Not for one second during our whole conversation had I forgotten its existence. When I got back to the apartment I hid it carefully at the back of a drawer in my desk, buried under a stack of old notebooks and articles I had collected for research. Almost afraid that I had imagined the whole episode, I had checked three times the same evening that it was still there. Afterwards I had been forced to accept not only that it was a physical reality: it was also going to have consequences. Whatever they might be, there was no escaping them.

By ignoring or even destroying the evidence I con- demned an innocent man to rot in jail for a crime he had not committed. By producing it, I would almost certainly condemn myself to take his place. I had few illusions about how far a defence of 'it wasn't me but a doppelgänger because, you see, we all live in a computer' would, as lawyers say, fly.

For me, of course, that defence would be no more than the truth. I had no doubt about what I had experienced. The question was to what extent could our own experiences lie to us? It was a fact that the human mind could deceive itself to an extraordinary degree. In the end, both in theory and in practice, it was impossible to draw a clear line between the real thing and a hallucination. Maybe it was best just to accept that fact and stop worrying about it. Maybe the distinction between illusion and reality was unimportant.

But what about the distinction between truth and lies? Was I lying when I said I hadn't killed anybody? Was I lying even though I believed I was telling the truth but couldn't prove it?

If I was George and only George and had been all along, I had nothing to reproach myself with.

On the other hand, if I had turned into Larry and committed murder, I'd got away with it. I'd won. So why quit now? The only possible reason would be that I'd turned back into George, and as George I couldn't live with my terrible secret.

But suppose I turned back into Larry? Or suppose in some part of myself I still was Larry? Suppose the only reason my unconscious had prompted me to recover those pantyhose was so that I could destroy them and ensure my safety for ever?

The more I thought about it, turning and turning with the permutations of it all till my head spun, the more I wondered if Lou was right and we should just say fuck the truth.

Only time would tell: time, which was a subjective concept anyway. And events, which, if mind really cannot be separated from matter, are at least partly what we make them.

At any rate, something would happen. That was my only hope.

And fear.

We arrived at the house late on Friday evening. Martha had prepared something simple which we ate in the library with the television on – something we tended to do increasingly when we found ourselves alone together. I took a sleeping pill because I didn't want to find myself awake and restless again in the middle of the night. It was agreeable to wake up to brilliant sunlight at eight fifteen next morning. I pulled on a robe and found Sara already drinking coffee and reading the papers downstairs.

The day got off to an unproblematic enough start. In the morning Sara did some shopping: there were a couple of craft shops locally where she stocked up periodically on things that she could use as little gifts whenever the need arose. I tried to read, but concentration was impossible. I took a long walk, and as I returned found myself gazing up at the clock tower, remembering what Larry had planned for that night when Sara had driven up to join him. She would never know how close she had come to death that night. If she had not had Steve with her . . .

There was a message waiting for me from Sara. She'd run into a friend and wondered if I would like to join them for lunch in a restaurant nearby. I called her on her mobile and said I thought I'd stay home and get on with some work. Martha made me an omelette which I ate while watching more television.

That night we had dinner with a couple of old bores called Tom and Cecily Winters. The only people I ever met who were invariably more boring than them were their guests. It was a god-awful evening which for some reason irritated me even more than usual. They had always, I suspected, felt that Sara had married beneath herself. Who was this so-called author whose name they never saw in the *New York Times* or the *Readers' Digest*? Still, I was tolerated for Sara's sake, though that evening I sensed something new in the air. It was as though they knew that Sara and I had drifted apart and that maybe they wouldn't have to tolerate me for much longer. It was a feeling they made plain in all kinds of subtle ways: references to people, places and upcoming events were aimed, it seemed to me, deliberately over my head, as though by general consent I would not be around by then to participate. No effort was made to include me in discussions of subjects about which I knew nothing and cared less. I neither bred, raced nor rode horses, therefore was irrelevant to a discussion about Henry's new mare or the prospects of a win at wherever-the-hell. If I went to Aspen or St Moritz in the winter it was not to see my friends but Sara's, therefore my views on so-and-so and someone else were not canvassed. No one thought to ask if I would be going to Gertie Buggerheim's (or whoever's) party in Venice at Easter, only whether Sara would.

I wondered idly if having money, your own money, old money, automatically meant that you had to turn into a posturing phony, and tried to get a conversation going about Scott Fitzgerald and his observation that the rich were different. Obviously these people, I mentioned to a couple of them – non-judgementally, I thought – saw themselves as different from the common masses, but I wondered whether they could describe precisely what those differences were. Obviously it wasn't intellect: they weren't any smarter. So perhaps it was something else, something more important than intellect. I was willing to be instructed, and surprised. But I was out of luck. There was precious little instruction and absolutely no surprises to be had that night.

A couple of times I caught Sara glaring at me somewhat stonily and told myself there were going to be reproachful words between us later in the evening. At least, I told myself, reproachful words would be better than nothing, and cheerfully waved an empty decanter to indicate that another glass of Tom's fine burgundy would be welcome down at my end of the table if the butler would care to do his goddamn job.

Words were, I thought, on the cards when we got into the car to drive home. By then, however, I didn't feel like them, so I pretended to fall asleep. It worked, and neither of us said anything till we got home. Then, having drunk enough so that the only thing I felt like was drinking more, I told

Sara that I was going to have a nightcap in the library and watch the late news. She didn't say anything, just went upstairs. There would be words, I knew; but in time, not now.

Then, of course, the next thing that happened was that news item about Steve being attacked in prison. I knew at once it was the event I had predicted that would break the deadlock we were in. I had no idea when such an event would happen or what form it would take – how could I? – but I knew instinctively that it would happen, and this was it.

I wondered whether Sara had switched on the TV in our bedroom. In all likelihood she had, but I thought I ought to check; she would certainly want to know about this and it would be unfair to keep it from her. I finished my drink and went up.

The bedroom was empty, but the television was on – the same channel I had been watching. So I knew she'd seen the item. But where was she? I called her name a couple of times without getting a reply. I went through to the old nursery, which she used as an all-purpose space for storing things, sometimes for writing letters or reading on the chaise longue by the window. I saw at once that the far door was open. I went through and down the corridor with a growing certainty that I knew where I would find her. My feeling was confirmed when I found the door up to the clock tower unlocked.

I began to climb slowly, almost ponderously, as though weighed down by the knowledge that every step was taking me inexorably closer to something I had been approaching for some days. In fact it was exactly one week since I had returned to this world, my world, and met Larry, that impostor, for a second time in the park.

But Larry was dead now. As dead as if he'd never existed. Or was he?

Who was climbing those stairs at that moment? Whose

footfalls could I hear softly mounting towards what I could
only think of as some kind of appointment with destiny?

Why such troubled high-flown thoughts? What 'destiny'?
Whose? Larry's? George's? Sara's?

Mine?

I was drunk, I knew. My mind was clouded, but through
it all I saw or sensed a certain clarity, an outcome, an end
to my uncertainty and pain. Yet what it was I could not say.

She did not hear me approach. She stood with her back
to me, not far from the low wall, looking out over the
darkened garden and into, I felt sure, her own thoughts.

At that moment, with a conviction that startled me, I
knew what those thoughts were, and what I must do.

I stayed there for some moments, hardly breathing,
watching her. Then she turned, and I stepped forward.

She gasped when she saw me and her hand went to her
heart. 'You startled me,' she said.

I didn't say anything for a moment or two, just looked at
her. Then I took another step towards her.

'You want to go to him, don't you?'

She answered too fast. 'No.'

'There's no point in lying about it. I know.'

I could see her eyes flickering in the darkness, trying to
find mine. I took another step towards her, and she took
another step back. She was standing now dangerously
close to the low crenellated wall around the tower.

'George, I'm not lying . . .'

She tried to take another step back, away from me, and
stumbled against the wall.

I moved fast.

SARA

CHAPTER 46

I screamed and tried to fend him off even as I began to fall. His hand closed on my arm and he yanked me towards him with such force that I thought he must have dislocated my shoulder.

'For God's sake, Sara, what are you trying to do? Kill yourself?'

I didn't breathe – couldn't – for a long time. Then I collapsed against him. He held me as I shook with a sense of release that I hadn't known I was so in need of until then.

'It's all right,' he said, 'it's all right. You were afraid of me, I know. I was half afraid of myself. I didn't know what I was going to do until I got up here.'

I looked at him, forcing my eyes and brain to focus. 'What d'you mean you didn't know..?'

'It's a long story. Come on, let's go in. It's getting cold.'

He led me gently down the stairs and back to our bedroom. He switched off the television and sat me down, wanting to talk to me seriously.

'You can go to Steve,' he said. 'I'll arrange it. I can make it possible.'

I started to protest, 'How can you—?'

He placed a finger on my lips. I looked at him, I think, uncomprehendingly, as though I hardly knew him. All the restlessness, the suppressed anger, the barely controlled aggression that I'd felt around him like an electric charge those last few days had disappeared. He wasn't even drunk any longer. His speech, which had been slurred by the end of dinner, was precise and clear.

'I can't explain now. Tomorrow. I know what to do. All you have to do is go to sleep. Trust me.'

To my surprise, I did. To my surprise I slept more soundly than I had for days, as though some weight had been lifted from me, though I had no idea what it was. Perhaps simply the admission to myself, which George had made possible, that I was still in love with Steve, and nothing that happened or anyone said was going to change that fact.

When I awoke the next morning – Sunday – George was already downstairs. I switched on the television and surfed the news channels in search of anything more about Steve. There was an item which repeated what I'd learnt the night before, but which added that his condition was stable and he was out of danger.

I rang down to Martha and asked if she knew where George was. She said he was in the library making phone calls. I pulled on a sweater and jeans and went downstairs. He waved to me through the open door to indicate that he would join me as soon as he'd finished. Five minutes later he sat down opposite me in the conservatory where Martha brought us fresh coffee.

His mood was exactly as it had been the night before when we came down from the tower. It was as though some weight had been lifted from him too. He told me that he had heard the news that Steve was going to be all right and was clearly relieved by the fact.

'Who were you calling?' I asked.

'Frank Stewart,' he said. Frank was our lawyer.

'What about?'

'Getting you in to see Steve, among other things.'

'Gorge, why are you doing this? You're being wonderful, but I don't understand why you're—'

He held up his hand in a request that I say no more. 'I can't tell you for the moment, but I will – soon, I promise. After breakfast I have to drive back to Manhattan. It's probably as well if you come with me, but if you prefer to stay . . .'

'No, I'll come, of course. What d'you have to do that's so..?'

I stopped, seeing his look. I was asking questions again. 'All right,' I said, 'I'll wait until you can tell me.' Then I added, but I realized I was smiling, 'It had better be good.'

'Don't worry about that,' he said. 'It is.'

George called from the car as we approached the city and Frank met us at the apartment. He greeted me as always like an old friend, but there was something in his eyes that hadn't been there before. Each time he looked at me his gaze lingered fractionally longer than it normally would have. He knew something – about me and Steve, or so I assumed – and it had changed the way he thought about me.

The two of them disappeared into George's study for about twenty minutes and closed the door. I saw the phone in the living room light up a couple of times, so I knew they were making calls. Then there was a ring at the door. Frank came out before I could get there.

'I'll get this, Sara, I'm expecting somebody.'

He opened the door to a tall man in a square-cut grey suit who I had guessed was a cop even before Frank introduced him as Inspector Todd.

'Ma'am,' he said politely and inclined his head but

didn't offer to shake hands. Then his gaze travelled across the room to where George stood in the door of his study.

'Before we attend to the formalities, Inspector,' he said, 'I think I should tell my wife what's going on here.'

He came towards me and drew me aside and around a corner where we could be alone. I caught a look between Inspector Todd and Frank in which Frank seemed to be saying it was all right.

George took both my hands in his. 'I love you,' he said, 'I love you very much. I want you to know that, because it may help explain things a little, though I'm not sure any more if explanations amount to very much. At any rate,' he sighed and dropped his eyes a moment, when he looked up again I saw tears in them, 'the Inspector is here to arrest me. I've confessed to the murder of Nadia Shelley. It wasn't Steve. I killed her and framed him. And I can prove it.'

I hadn't noticed Frank approach, but suddenly he was there to catch me as the room began to spin and the floor melted beneath my feet.

CHAPTER 47

I don't remember much about the next few hours, except that Frank's wife Joan appeared so quickly on the scene that she must have been waiting downstairs. She was a sweet-natured woman, motherly and with five kids to prove it. She got me to bed and insisted I take a couple of pills she had with her. I'd never been much of a pill user, but I was glad of those that day. They didn't take away the shock, but they distanced it. I could pretend, at least in the moments when everything welled up and threatened to overwhelm me, that it all was happening to someone else; I knew that I was that someone else, but I was able to step back and view what was happening with a detachment that made it bearable.

Joan made it plain that she knew all about me and Steve; Frank had told her everything he'd learned from George. She made no judgements and offered no advice, for which I was profoundly grateful.

Our doctor came by towards the end of the afternoon,

took my blood pressure and made a few routine checks. He
said I seemed fine, but wrote out a prescription for some
more sedatives that Joan said she'd have sent over from a
twenty-four-hour place around the corner. Frank looked in
again to say that George was being held in custody
overnight, but a hearing had been set for the morning when
he would almost certainly be bailed until sentencing took
place. He didn't want to return to the apartment, so Frank
had arranged a place for him to stay.

I barely took any of it in. In fact it was a couple of days
before I was beginning even to think straight. That was the
first time I was allowed to see Steve. The law would have to
take its complicated course before his conviction was
quashed and he could be released, but until then he would
stay in the hospital recovering from his injuries. It turned
out that he had accidentally got caught up in a dispute
between two feuding prisoners, neither of whom had
anything against him personally.

It was so strange, almost unreal, seeing Steve again after
all that time. There was an IV drip in his arm and he was
wired up to monitoring machines as well as being
wrapped in bandages, so he couldn't move much. I leant
over and planted a kiss on his lips. 'I love you,' I said,
'everything's going to be all right.'

There was something in his eyes I didn't recognize at
first. Then I realized it was fear.

'What is it?' I said. 'What's wrong?'

'You know what I did,' he said. 'Now you know what I
really did.'

'I don't understand.'

'I didn't kill her, but I ran. When I found her there, all I
thought about was myself, my career, my future . . .'

He paused and corrected himself, his gaze still fixed
anxiously on mine. '*Our* future. It was our future I wanted
to protect, but I behaved like a coward and a fool.'

'Most people would have done the same.'

'Would they? I wonder. I used to think I wasn't "most people". That's me – a coward, a fool, *and* arrogant.'

'It's over now.'

'I've been lying here wondering what you'd think of me. Afraid you'd despise me.'

I felt such a tenderness and pity for him in that moment that I wept. All I could do was take his hand and shake my head mutely while the tears rolled. We sat exchanging looks, caresses, little smiles, like a couple of teenagers discovering love for the first time.

Later we talked about George: about the extraordinary lengths he'd gone to to commit and then conceal his crimes. It made no sense to either of us that he should suddenly turn around and confess like this. Steve asked if I would be talking to him; I said I assumed so.

George was granted bail as expected, and I asked Frank to arrange a meeting between us. Frank said George was against it, and he himself was unsure it was a good idea. But when I insisted they both gave way.

I wasn't allowed to know the address where George was staying – something to do with the terms of bail – so we met in an empty office at Frank's law firm. There was an unreality about the encounter that was almost tangible, as though everything in the room, including ourselves, had been coated with some special high-gloss varnish which brought us into sharper and more dramatic focus, yet somehow made us artificial – copies of our real selves.

I didn't have much to ask him, except why? Not why he had committed the crimes (he claimed to have also killed a man in England; police there were looking into it), but why confess now?

He gave a curious smile – not sad, not even resigned. Tranquil, I suppose, if I had to find a word for it. It was the kind of smile I'd seen on the faces of (it seems so strange to say this in the circumstances, but it was true) mystics,

contemplatives, philosophers: people for whom the
material mundane world held little attraction. Not that
they despised it, but they'd somehow seen beyond it, risen
above it, and were no longer hostage to its shallow charms
and trivial fortunes.

'It's something I can't explain,' he said, 'because if I did it
would sound too crazy to believe. I'm not even sure I believe
it myself. All I can say is that I know I'm doing what's right,
and for some reason that's more important than anything,
including being able to explain why. Explanations aren't
enough. In the end it's just turtles all the way down.'

I must have looked puzzled, because he smiled and told
me a story about some scientist and an old woman. I
laughed. It seemed impossible, but I actually laughed in
that dreary and rather dark little room, and he looked
pleased that I had.

'I'm not sure what all this means,' I said. 'I don't understand
all of it. But I want you to know that I'm sorry, genuinely sorry
for my part in driving you to do what you did.'

'Don't be. It wasn't you. It wasn't Steve. Maybe it wasn't
even really me. Maybe we're all driven from another place
by forces we know nothing of – like puppets of the gods,
you know? Or figures in some computer game. Maybe
we're just part of a research program being run by a socially
dysfunctional nerd in some underfunded cosmic lab.'

'God is a socially dysfunctional nerd?'

'Who the hell knows,' he said, and laughed. 'Explanations are just an art form.'

'*Just* an art form?' I said.

He continued to smile. 'Okay, delete "just". Maybe you
should organize an exhibition.'

'On the theme of "Explanations"?'

'Why not? You should do it.'

I thought for a moment.

'Maybe I will,' I said.

And that's where we left it.

Acknowledgements

Many of the coincidences quoted in this book (although none of those on which the story actually hangs) are taken from the extensive literature that exists on the subject. I would particularly like to record my thanks to and admiration of: *Synchronicity, Science and Soul-Making* by Victor Mansfield; *Synchronicity, the Bridge between Matter and Mind* by F. David Peat; *Patterns of Prophecy* and *Incredible Coincidence* by Alan Vaughan; *Jung, Sunchronicity, and Human Destiny* by Ira Progoff; and, perhaps most importantly, *The Roots of Coincidence* by Arthur Koestler.

**SIMON &
SCHUSTER**

Also by David Ambrose

A MEMORY OF DEMONS

Tom Freeman thinks his demons are behind him. He has
been sober for ten years, after a period of alcohol and drug
abuse that almost killed him. His career is back on track,
and he is happily married to Clare. They have a baby
daughter, Julia.

But when she begins to speak, why does Julia insist that
her name is Melanie? And that Tom and Clare are not
her real parents? Child psychiatrist Dr Brendan is
baffled by her case, but accepts that children are
sometimes born with memories of a previous life that
cannot be explained away.

Tom makes his own enquiries, leading to the chilling
discovery that his daughter is posssessed by the spirit of
a missing girl, presumed dead, who disappeared
exactly when and where Tom suffered his last alcohol
and drug-fuelled blackout . . .

OUT NOW IN HARDBACK

**ISBN 0 7432 3070 1
PRICE £12.99**

**POCKET
BOOKS**

THE DISCRETE CHARM
OF CHARLIE MONK

DAVID AMBROSE

*It was some moments before Charlie turned his gaze back to
Control. When he did, there were tears in his eyes.
'What have you done?'*

*'Something that evolution wouldn't have accomplished in a
million years, left to itself,' Control replied calmly. 'You're
custom-built, Charlie, a hero for our time . . .'*

Charlie Monk is the ultimate superhero. He has no fear. He
has no conscience. And he has no memory of his past.

Dr Susan Flemyng is an expert in memory. She can repair
damaged memories, or create new ones.

So why has she planted a memory of herself in Charlie's
head? What is the dangerous secret that ties their lives
together? Can they trust each other enough to find out?

David Ambrose conceives yet another mind-bending
thriller that will keep you turning pages far into the night.

ISBN 0 7434 1613 9
PRICE £6.99

**SIMON &
SCHUSTER**

This book and other **Simon & Schuster/Pocket** titles are available from your bookshop or can be ordered direct from the publisher.

☐ 0 7434 1573 6   **Coincidence**   £6.99
☐ 0 7432 3070 1   **A Memory of Demons**   £12.99
☐ 0 7434 1613 9   **The Discrete Charm of Charlie Monk**   £6.99

Please send cheque or postal order for the value of the book, free postage and packing within the UK; OVERSEAS including Republic of Ireland £1 per book.

OR: Please debit this amount from my:

VISA/ACCESS/MASTERCARD ....

CARD NO ....

EXPIRY DATE ....

AMOUNT £ ....

NAME ....

ADDRESS ....

....

SIGNATURE ....

www.simonsays.co.uk

Send orders to: SIMON & SCHUSTER CASH SALES
PO Box 29, Douglas, Isle of Man, IM99 1BQ
Tel: 01624 83600, Fax 01624 670923
www.bookpost.co.uk
Please allow 14 days for delivery.
Prices and availability subject to change without notice.